The Road to YOU

MELISSA TOPPEN

Editing by Amy Gamache @ Rose David Editing

Cover Design by Judi Perkins @ Concierge Literary Designs & Photography

Table of Contents

Copyright
One
Two
Three
Four
Five
Six
Seven
Eight
Nine
Ten
Eleven
Twelve
Thirteen
Fourteen
Fifteen
Sixteen
Seventeen
Eighteen
Nineteen
Twenty
Twenty-one
Twenty-two
Twenty-three
Twenty-four
Twenty-five
Twenty-six
Epilogue
Acknowledgments
Stalk Me

Don't find love- let love find you.
That's why it's called falling in love-
because you don't force yourself to fall,
you just fall.

-Unknown

Stolen- Dashboard Confessional
Tightrope- Ron Pope
Dress- Taylor Swift
Angel on Fire- Halsey
I'm Yours- Alessia Cara
Move Together- James Bay
Armor- Fly Upright Kite
The Rush- Dashboard Confessional
Dusk til Dawn- Zayn featuring Sia
Train Wreck- James Arthur
Mercy- Lewis Capaldi
Dusk and Summer- Dashboard Confessional
Meaning of Life- Kelly Clarkson
Theme Song— Take Me Home- Jess Glynne

Chapter One
Elara

Seven Years Ago – 15 years old

"Tell me you're kidding, butter bean. You can't actually believe this is a good idea." My friend Kam laughs nervously below me, head cocked back as he watches me climb up the massive tree stretching out over Lake Cowan.

I've been climbing this tree since I was a child – having spent nearly every summer here with my Aunt Carol since I was little.

I love everything about North Carolina. The weather, the sights, the smells, the sounds, the people, the ocean – I love it all. I keep telling my mom I'm going to move here one day but I don't think she really believes me.

"Come on, El," Kam continues to object from below.

"Don't be such a wimp," I call over my shoulder, grabbing onto another branch as I pull myself higher.

I met Kam only a couple days after arriving here this past June. His family had relocated from Nevada a couple of years ago and even though they purchased the house next door to my Aunt Carol's, surprisingly enough, that's not how we actually met. I had been riding my bike down the large hill that runs through the middle of town a little too fast when I wiped out, ripping my knee up pretty good. He was working at the local hardware store and saw the whole thing through the front window. The look on his face when he reached me was priceless. You would think the boy had never seen blood before. It was only after he insisted on walking me home that I found out he lived next door. How he had lived next door that long and I never knew is beyond me. Then again, the houses are far enough apart it's not something I would have easily known.

The rest is history. We've pretty much been inseparable since that day. Though I'm kind of surprised I haven't scared him off by now. I've always been a bit of a dare devil, pushing myself and my abilities to the absolute limits. Whereas Kam is a bit more cautious. I think that's what makes our friendship work so well. He pulls me back when I go too far and I push him forward when he needs to let loose a little.

"El, that's high enough." Kam's voice is further away than before. I turn, looking down to see him several feet below me.

"It's not that high. You should come up here and see for yourself," I holler, a wide smile on my face.

"So we can both break our necks? I'll pass," he retorts, shaking his head.

"Suit yourself." I turn, balancing myself onto a thick branch that extends out over the lake.

"Come on, Elara. You aren't seriously going to jump, are you?"

"Why else do you think I climbed all the way up here?" I respond without looking in his direction.

"I don't like this."

"You don't have to like it. You're not the one jumping."

"Come on, El. That's enough. Just come down."

12

"If you insist." I turn, smiling widely down at Kam, not entirely sure if he can see my face from this distance, before very carefully letting go of the branch above me that I've been using to keep myself steady.

Kam says something else right as I jump, but his words are lost to the wind that rushes through my ears as my body free falls through the air, hitting the water seconds later.

Pushing upward, I break the surface just moments after going under, a wide smile on my face.

"You're crazy. You know that?" Kam's standing on the edge of the dock, arms crossed over his chest, a backward baseball cap covering his messy brown hair.

"And you're a baby." I splash at him, treading water to keep myself up.

"No, I just don't have a death wish."

"Neither do I," I object, swimming toward him.

"You sure? Because it sure seems like it sometimes." He steps forward and reaches down, helping to pull me out of the water.

"It's called living, Kam. You should try it sometime." I slide onto the dock and turn, taking a seat on the edge before patting the space next to me.

"This from the girl who stripped down to her underwear and climbed a good thirty feet up a tree barefoot," he grumbles, sliding down beside me.

"Well how else would you have had me do it?" I smirk, knocking my shoulder against his.

"Um, not at all," he says like he's stating the obvious.

"You need to learn to relax every once in a while. I made it out okay, see?" I hold my arms out. "Not a scratch."

"I just don't get you sometimes."

"And yet you still love me," I challenge, batting my eyelashes dramatically at him.

He bites back a laugh and shakes his head, turning his gaze to the water.

After a long stretch of silence, he finally says, "I can't believe you're leaving tomorrow."

I know exactly how he feels. It seems strange knowing that after spending every day of the last two months practically joined at the hip that it's going to be months before I see him again.

"See, I knew you loved me," I tease, not willing to give into the sudden wave of sadness that washes over me.

"Shut up, you know I do." He chuckles. "But seriously, it's going to suck here without you."

"You survived before me," I remind him.

"Yeah, but that was before I knew you existed."

"I'll be back." I kick my feet back and forth, my toes grazing the water below.

"In nine months." He lets out a slow breath.

"And here I thought you'd be glad to get rid of me." I link my arm through his and lay my head against his shoulder – our height difference pronounced even when we're sitting.

"Maybe just a little," he smarts, laughing when I pull back and lay a hard smack to his bicep.

"Jerk," I fake offense, loving the way his crooked smile lights up his face.

"So violent." He rubs his arm, a trace of amusement still on his lips.

"You asked for it." I wag my finger at him.

"Perhaps I did." He chuckles again. "We should probably head back," he adds, abruptly standing, before turning to help me to my feet. "Kane is probably on his way home by now and my parents will kill me if I'm not there when he gets in," he says, referring to his older brother who's been in Europe all summer. "He's only here for less than a week before he leaves for Northwestern."

"You think it will be weird? Not having him here anymore?" I ask, making my way toward my clothes that are piled at the bottom of the tree.

"A little. Then again I thought having him gone this summer would be strange but I really haven't missed him that much. Maybe because I've had this crazy blonde keeping me on my toes all summer."

"I'll take that compliment." I laugh, pulling on my cut off jean shorts.

"Good, because I meant it as one." He grins; watching me get dressed like it's another day and seeing me in my underwear is nothing out of the ordinary.

Then again, it might actually not be now that I think about it. That's just the kind of person I am. I've been stick thin my entire life and don't have much of anything to cover up so why should I care anyways.

"Although, I think I've probably been pretty close to giving you a heart attack or two this summer if I remember correctly, so maybe it shouldn't be a compliment," I say, pulling my tank top over my head.

"That's probably true," he agrees, closing the distance between us as I slip on my flip flops. "Maybe I'll take it back."

"You wouldn't," I scoff, laughing when he drops an arm over my shoulder, leading me toward the field that lines the back of his and my Aunt Carol's properties.

"I really am going to miss the hell out of you, butter bean." He uses the nickname he gave me earlier this summer, that carefree grin finally finding its way back onto his handsome face.

I'd be lying if I said that smile doesn't do something to my insides. It does. But I've somewhat learned to compartmentalize the way Kam makes me feel. I can't deny that there's something there but I doubt he'd ever see me as anything more than a friend. I mean, trust me when I say he can do way better than a too skinny girl with no boobs,

15

straggly blonde hair, and a slightly unhealthy addiction to anything dangerous.

"I'm going to miss you too," I finally say after what feels like too long. "Promise you won't forget about me while I'm gone?" I tease, even though deep down that's a real fear I have.

"Like that would ever be possible." He smiles down at me and my stomach does a little flip flop.

This has been the perfect summer spent with the perfect boy. At fifteen, things don't get much better than this. But now our summer is coming to an end and I think I'm really grasping that this is it. This is our last day together. After today it will be nearly a year before I see him again and the thought weighs a lot heavier on my heart than I'd expected it to.

"You say that now," I huff, finally commenting.

"Hey." Kam stops walking, turning to face me. "Look at me, El." I look up and meet his hazel gaze, trying to commit every speckle of blue and green to my memory. "This summer has been the best. And when I say I'm going to miss you, I mean like every single day from now until June." He grins down at me.

"You're my best friend, ya know?" I say, trying not to get too emotional.

"And you're mine." He cups my face. "Butter bean and tater tot against the world." He laughs at our ridiculous nick names for each other. "Forever."

"Forever," I repeat, not realizing in that moment how short our forever would turn out to be...

****

Present Day

I watch the rain as it hits the slick dark cherry wood surface and trickles off the side. It's an endless cycle on repeat. Drops land, roll, then soak into the earth, one after the other, disappearing just as quickly as they come.

It's easier to focus on the rain, on the sound it makes as it cascades from the sky and collides with the dirt. It's easier to pretend that, like the rain, this too will pass. Only it won't. Nothing can undo what's been done. Nothing can bring him back.

Nothing...

I blink back the tears that threaten to spill. I can't fall apart. I can't give into the emotion suffocating me from the inside out. I can't. If I do I may never find the strength to pull myself back together.

I turn my face upward and close my eyes, allowing the small pellets of water to pepper my face. It reminds me of the day that Kam and I danced in the rain. Cliché I know, but that's just how Kamden was. He loved the simple, sweet things in life that only ever seem to happen in the movies. Like, well, dancing in the rain.

We were walking down the road to where his truck was parked after spending the day on the beach. It was the last summer before our senior year and Kam had spent nearly every day of that summer trying to teach me to surf. It wasn't forecasted to rain that afternoon but that didn't stop the sky from opening up and drenching us more than we already were.

I remember the way Kam laughed. How he tilted his head back and held his arms out, embracing the inevitability that there was no possible way we were going to outrun the storm. How he smiled when he turned to me and took my hand. The next thing I knew he was twirling me in the middle of the street.

I don't think I've ever laughed as hard as I did that day. A day when I thought the world was perfect. A day when everything made sense.

Now I'm afraid nothing will ever make sense again.

I can't make myself understand this. I can't rationalize it. All I keep asking myself is *how*. How do I live in a world that doesn't have Kam in it? How can I go back to my life when he was such a monumental part of it? How will anything ever feel okay again?

"It just will, butter bean." I can hear him as if he were standing right next to me. "You just have to put one foot in front of the other and push through." It's what he said to me after my mom died. In my mind I know he would say it to me again.

It was one of the hardest things I'd ever been through. For a teenage girl, losing your mom to breast cancer during your senior year is about one of the worst things that could happen. But like Kam said I would, I did get through it. Only then I had him to help me. And now…

I look down at the brace on my arm, trying to ignore the overwhelming guilt that comes with knowing what I've done. Only I can't ignore it. I can't pretend like I don't know who's to blame. I can't pretend I'm not the reason my best friend is lying in a casket just feet in front of me.

Kam is gone and it's all my fault.

"Elara."

I look up when I hear my Aunt Carol next to me. She gives me a soft smile, one that reminds me too much of my mother which only makes my stomach knot harder. Maybe if I had my mom here, maybe if I hadn't lost them both, maybe then this wouldn't be so difficult. Only I know that's not true. No one can fill the loss of Kam. No one.

I look away, not able to hold her gaze for more than a few seconds. Only then do I realize that most of those in attendance, including Kam's parents, have already made their way back to their cars. Only a handful are still standing close by, having quiet conversations. Meanwhile, I feel stuck in place with my mind a million miles away.

I blink, the fog that settled around me the day of the accident only growing thicker with each moment that has passed since. The tightness in my chest grows heavier knowing that I have to leave him here. For a brief moment I wonder if I'm suffocating. I struggle to pull in even the slightest amount of air and the ground feels unsteady below my feet.

I sway slightly, feeling like I might vomit at any second but then every molecule in my body freezes the moment my gaze lands on a pair of dark eyes. I know who they belong to without even looking at his face. I'd know those eyes anywhere.

Kane.

Our gazes lock but I can't tell if he's staring at me or through me. His eyes are darker than I remember. His mouth set in a tight line, his face expressionless. He looks as empty as I feel and that thought alone is enough to have me taking my Aunt Carol's hand in an effort to steady my too weak legs.

I don't really know Kane. He spent four years in Illinois and has travelled quite extensively since he graduated college a couple years ago. Hell, I've only met him once in the seven years Kam and I have been friends and that was at Kam's high school graduation party about four years ago. And even then he wasn't very friendly.

I remember the way his eyes seemed to follow me everywhere that night. How I felt like I was going to crawl out of my skin every time I'd catch his gaze across the yard. To say he put me on edge is putting it mildly.

Not only is he intimidating as hell, he's also one of the most attractive men I've ever seen up close. He possesses all of the same physical qualities as Kam – strong jaw, full lips, thick dark hair. Only unlike Kam who was flirtatious and fun loving, Kane is all hard lines with a deep expression that makes him look permanently put off. Which of course only adds to his intrigue.

Unfortunately his pleasantries stop at his looks. Kam wasn't lying when he told me his brother was on the serious side. I think that's giving him too much credit. Asshole might be the better term. Though I feel bad even thinking that now.

Kane's eyes bore into mine with the heat of a thousand fires and I feel like I'm going to melt right here. He knows I did this. I can see it in his eyes. He blames me for taking his brother away and he's right to blame me.

I don't know how much time passes before Kane finally breaks the connection, turning and walking away, leaving me feeling like he's taken what little air that remained in my lungs with him.

I want to go after him, tell him how sorry I am, though I doubt it would do either of us a bit of good. Nothing I can say will bring Kam back. So instead I stand here and let him walk away.

"We should go," my aunt says next to me. Even though I know she's right, I can't seem to get my feet to move.

"I don't know if I can," I choke over my words, a few tears squeaking past the concrete wall I've built behind my eyes.

"I know how much you love him, El. And I know how much you wish it was you lying there and not him, but I'm glad it's not." Her words pull my gaze to hers and I'm not entirely sure how I feel about what she just said. "I've already lost your mother," she says in way of explanation.

"I put him there," I grind out under my breath, not wanting to draw attention to our conversation.

"No you didn't, Elara. It was a tragic accident, nothing more. You know Kam would say the same thing."

"I was always pushing him too far, taking too many risks. He'd be alive if it wasn't for me."

"You don't know that," she soothes.

"Yes I do." My words catch in my throat. "This was my fault, whether you see it that way or not."

I can feel it coming, the tidal wave I've been managing to outrun is finally catching up to me and I know it's only seconds before it takes me under completely. I have to get out of here before that happens.

"El." Carol reaches out for me.

"Just don't. Okay?" I pull out of her grasp. "You can't make this better. No one can." The words have barely left my mouth before I'm spinning around and taking off through the cemetery.

It's only seconds before I've removed my heels and begun to run. I run so hard and so fast that within minutes my lungs are begging for mercy. I run until my feet are throbbing and my stomach cramps. I run until I feel like I can't run another second before I run more. I push myself as hard as I can, needing to feel something, *anything*, even if it is physical pain.

It's raining harder now – the sky opening up and pouring down on me like the heavens are sharing in my pain. When I finally collapse on the beach a good two miles from the cemetery, I'm not entirely sure how I made it all this way. Especially without shoes in the pouring rain. I cry into my hands, my tears mixing with the rain, my sobs racking me so hard my entire body shakes from their intensity.

I close my eyes and I see him; his hazel eyes, his easy smile, the boy who has owned my heart for the last seven years, the man I grew to love in ways he will never know to be true. And now he's gone.

There's so many things that I'll never get to say. So many moments we'll never get to share. Kamden Thaler wasn't just my best friend; he was the love of my life. A love so true and pure that I know to the deepest depths of my soul I will never share that kind of connection with someone again.

Kam was my beginning, my middle, and my end. Without him, I'm lost. Without him, I don't even know who I am.

And so I let myself go. I let the wind carry my cries and the rain wash away my tears. I let it all go, knowing with complete certainty that nothing will ever be the same again.

Chapter Two
Elara

Five years ago – 17 years old

"You've got to get up quicker." Kam laughs, shaking his head at yet another failed attempt for me to stand on my surf board.

"Easier said than done," I huff, laying down to paddle further out into the water.

"You're overthinking it. You've got to trust your instinct. Let the water tell you when it's time." Kam paddles next to me, matching me stride for stride.

"Do you hear yourself right now? You're talking about water like it has the ability to communicate." I stop, pushing up to straddle the board. Kam follows my lead, mirroring my actions so that we are both floating side by side.

"You don't think it does?" He cocks his head and hits me with that boyish grin of his.

"Do you really want me to answer that?" I laugh.

"For someone who pretends to be so fearless, I'm noticing you have some control issues."

"Screw you, I am fearless," I say in mock offense.

"Then prove it. Give up control. Let something else guide you for once in your life."

"Why would I want to do that?"

"Because I think you'll find it's quite freeing." He shakes his head, a thick chunk of wet dark hair falling into his face as he does.

My heart does a little pitter patter in my chest as I watch him push it out of his face —enjoying the way his muscles flex as he moves his arm, allowing myself to steal a small glance at his toned chest and stomach.

Kam Thaler really is something to look at. The perfect combination of sexy and boyish charm. There isn't one thing about him that I don't find myself completely infatuated with. He's the total package, both inside and out.

When my eyes make their way back up to Kam's face, he's looking at me with the same cocky smirk he always does when he catches me ogling him. He knows he's gorgeous and he loves nothing more than giving me shit when I'm forced to acknowledge this fact as well.

"Don't look at me like that," I snip. A full blown smile stretches across his face at my words.

"Look at you like what?" he asks innocently.

"Like that." I point in the general vicinity of his face.

"I'm not looking at you like anything."

"Oh my god you are so infuriating." I groan dramatically, looking back just in time to see a nice set of waves coming in behind us.

"This is it." Kam switches gears the moment he sees my attention has been pulled. "You got this, butter bean. Wait until I give you the signal, then paddle as hard and as fast as you can. Got it?"

"Got it." I lean forward on my board, waiting for Kam's instructions.

"Now, when you drop into the wave keep your body loose. Let the water guide you," he continues.

"Loose. Got it," I repeat. Nervous energy pings through me like an electric current.

"Paddle, El. Paddle." The words barely leave Kamden's lips before I'm off, paddling as hard and fast as I can, just as he had instructed.

I try to focus on the feel of the water beneath me, remembering everything Kam told me about trusting my instincts. When I feel the wave surge behind me I quickly pop up, able to hold my balance for the first time as I drop into the wave.

Kam hollers somewhere off in the distance but it's drowned out by the roaring of the water and my pulse thumping loudly in my ears.

This is it. The rush. The adrenaline. This is what I live for. Only it's so much more than that because as Kam said, I have no control and I am the master of controlling every situation. Yes, I do crazy things and am a bit of a daredevil but in everything I do I have complete control. Out here, I'm at the mercy of the ocean, of the waves, of the water falling around me as it closes in on me.

Just like that, the wave swallows me whole. Within seconds I'm under water, my body twirling and spinning with the current. I feel the strap around my ankle tug as my board is pulled behind me but I have no real sense of direction to push myself to the surface.

After what feels like too long, the pull subsides and I'm able to regain enough composure to kick my way to the top, breaking the surface just moments later, sputtering and gasping for air.

"Elara," Kam says as he paddles up next to me. "You okay?" he asks, concern apparent on his face.

"Okay?" I cough, hoisting myself up on my board despite how exhausted I suddenly feel. "I'm perfect." I smile, not missing the surprise that flashes in his eyes.

"Okay," he says slowly.

"That was incredible. Did you see me?"

25

"I did. You did amazing. But are you okay? You were under for a while."

"I'm more than okay."

"Did you hit your head down there or something?" He looks at me like maybe I've lost my mind a bit. Hell, maybe I have.

"You were right. I just let go and let the water have me. It was incredible."

"You really are something else. You know that?" He chuckles, finally relaxing a bit.

"Can we do it again?" I ask excitedly, ready to give it another go.

I don't even care that I got pulled under. In fact I think that's what made the whole experience that much more of a rush. Now I just want to prove that I can do even better the next time.

"If you're sure."

"Absolutely," I say, lying down on my board. "Race ya." I laugh, taking off before Kam even has a chance to settle onto his board.

"Oh hell no." He laughs behind me.

****

"Do you ever think about the future?" Kam's gaze is locked on the water as the waves roll in.

After spending the afternoon and most of the evening in the water, Kam and I walked over to Piers, a small little outdoor food stand that sits right on the beach, and got hot dogs and sodas before making our way to our favorite spot in the sand. We've been sitting here for nearly an hour, enjoying the quickly approaching sunset.

"I mean really think about it," he adds before I have a chance to say anything.

"Sometimes," I answer his question after a long beat. "Why do you ask?"

"I thought I'd be more excited, you know?" He shifts next to me, wiping a chunk of sand from his leg. "I mean, it's our last year of high school. I've been looking forward to this since elementary school. But now that it's here, I don't know. I guess I feel differently than I thought I would."

"It's scary." I admit, leaning my shoulder against his. "We're going to be closing a chapter that's practically been our whole lives up to this point."

"It's not just that though. I think I'm afraid that once it's real I'm going to end up disappointing everyone."

"What do you mean?" I stare at the side of his face, my eyes tracing the lines of his profile, my fingers resist the urge to reach out and touch him.

"I don't know. I guess I think there's no way I can live up to Kane." He lets out a slow breath, his gaze finally meeting mine.

"Why would you ever need to live up to him?"

"Because he's the shining star. The apple of my father's eye." He kicks at the sand beneath his feet. "I'll never be able to match what he's done and I'm afraid that's what my father expects."

"You're not him. From what you've told me, you and your brother are nothing alike. Do you really think your parents expect you to follow in his footsteps?" I swivel in the sand so that I'm facing his side.

"Maybe." He shrugs.

Reaching out to take his hand, I cup it between both of mine and wait until he's looking at me before continuing. "You may not be a scholar, Kamden Joseph Thaler. You may not travel abroad or earn a full scholarship to some fancy school. But you don't need to either. You are uniquely you; perfect in every sense of the word. And no matter what you choose to do, no matter how big or how small, you're going to rock the hell out of it."

"I think you're giving me a little too much credit."

"No I'm not. Because I know you and I see every day what an incredible person you are. Because unlike your brother, you're not just determined and intelligent. You're also passionate and loyal and probably the best person I've ever known in my entire life."

"Probably?" He cocks a brow.

"Okay. Most definitely." I laugh, leaning my forehead against his shoulder.

"That's more like it." He drops a kiss to the top of my head.

"In all seriousness though," I continue, lifting my face to look up at him. "You're going to do great things, Kam. No matter what that might be."

"What about you?"

"What about me?" I question.

"What are your plans after you graduate?"

"The same as they were the last time you asked. I'm still weighing my options." I smirk, knowing what he's wanting to know and purposely not saying it.

We've talked about the possibility of me moving here after graduation but I have yet to make any promises at this point. It's something I've been considering for the last couple of years, ever since our first summer together. And even though he would be the main reason I would come here, he wouldn't be the only reason.

I love North Carolina. Over the last couple of years it has come to feel more like home to me than my real home in Arkansas. As of right now, I've got my eye on Southern State, the largest community college in the area, and my aunt has already agreed to let me stay with her rent free as long as I'm in school. So everything has already been put into motion for me to move, but I have yet to tell Kam any of this because I didn't want to get too ahead of myself. We still have an entire year of high school before any of this can be a possibility anyway.

"Weighing options, huh? Care to divulge what those might be?"

"Oh you know, probably go to community college or something comparable to make my dad happy. I've been looking at a few places. Guess we'll have to wait and see."

"What places?"

"Just a few different ones." I smile.

"Are you messing with me, El?" He quirks an eyebrow at me.

"Maybe." I laugh when he lunges for me, pinning me beneath him in the sand.

"You better start talking or I'll be forced to tickle it out of you," he warns, smile firmly in place.

"You wouldn't."

"Oh I would." He lowers one hand to my side and gives it a firm squeeze.

"Kam," I scream, withering beneath him.

"Start talking." He laughs when I try to shove him off of me, squeezing my side again when I clamp my lips shut and shake my head no.

"Okay. Okay." I finally concede when he gets me in the spot right against my ribs that I absolutely cannot stand.

"Well..." He hovers above me, waiting for me to say something.

"How would you feel if we were neighbors for real?" I ask. My heart thumps wildly in my chest as his smile stretches so wide it practically takes over his whole face.

"Seriously? You're going to do it?" he asks excitedly.

"I think so."

"Oh no. No I think so here, bean. Either you are or you aren't. Don't toy with my emotions."

"Fine, I am. Happy now?"

"You have no idea." He pushes back, pulling me up with him.

Instead of reclaiming his seat, he rocks back on his knees and pulls me into his arms. I take a deep inhale of his ocean scented skin as I wrap my arms around his neck.

"Happy doesn't even begin to describe it." He pulls back, finally releasing me after several long seconds.

I slide off his lap back into the sand, pulling my legs up to my chest. Kam settles in next to me, knocking his shoulder against mine.

"We're gonna be okay, ya know? Me and you." I offer him a little additional reassurance from his earlier admission of self-doubt. "We don't have to have all the answers right now. We've got each other and our whole lives ahead of us. There isn't anything we can't do if we set our minds to it."

My words bring a smile to his lips as he reaches over and nudges my chin with his knuckle. "I envy that about you. Your ability to never accept anything less than what you want."

I want to correct him. Tell him that's not a hundred percent true, but of course I don't. Kam means too much to me now to ever risk putting that kind of pressure on our relationship. I can't lose him which means I can't have him in the way I really want.

"I don't know if I'd go that far," I object.

"You are the bravest person I've ever met."

"I'm not brave. Not really. I'm just really good at pretending."

"I don't believe that for a second," he counters.

"And here I thought you knew me so well," I tease, knocking my shoulder into his the way he did mine moments ago.

"I do. That's my point." He snags a piece of my hair caught by the wind and tucks it behind my ear, his hand lingering on my cheek. "I'd be lost without you, butter bean." He grins sweetly.

"And don't you ever forget it." I crinkle my nose.

Kam chuckles, his hand falling away before turning his attention back out toward the water.

"I love the hell out of you, Elara Menten," he says, not looking in my direction.

"I love the hell out of you, Kamden Thaler," I repeat, allowing him to take my hand as together we watch the last slivers of daylight disappear over the horizon.

****

Present Day

It's been hours. At least I think it's been hours. I have no real sense of time. No real grasp on anything happening around me. The rain stopped a while ago but left behind a dreary mist that seems to fit the theme of the day.

My aunt has tried to call me several times since I took off earlier, as has my dad, but I couldn't bring myself to answer. I don't think I have it in me to talk to anyone right now. Especially not my dad.

I just can't.

So here I sit, watching the waves roll in, the tide getting closer and closer with each minute that passes. I keep waiting for it to reach me, hoping it will eventually pull me under and I will disappear into the sea forever.

When I look hard enough at the water, it's like I can see us. Me and Kam. I can see him floating on his surf board next to me. Hear him yelling instructions as I try to push up on my board as a wave rushes toward me. Feel his laughter resonate through me when I wipe out. The deep chested laugh that he only did when he found something truly funny. I can see us out there, happy and carefree.

And then I remember that nothing will ever be that way again and the crushing heaviness settles back on my chest making it nearly impossible to breathe.

I'm so consumed by the ache, by the splitting pain in my chest and the unbearable knot in the pit of my stomach that I don't even notice a person approaching until they're taking a seat next to me.

I turn my gaze to the side, half expecting to see my Aunt Carol. Only it's not her I see. My pulse quickens instantly as I take in the faded lines and colors of Kamden's old Dodgers baseball cap before meeting the dark eyes that rest beneath it.

Kane doesn't say a word. Instead he pulls his knees up to his chest and directs his gaze out to the water. I open my mouth to say something at least ten times before finally deciding not to say anything at all.

I have no idea why he's here. I don't know if he came looking for me or if he simply stumbled here by accident the same way I did. All I know is that saying to him what I need to say seems like an impossible task and so, I choose to say nothing at all.

Waves roll in one after the other and his focus never breaks. I can't stop staring at him from the corner of my eye. Completely transfixed by how much he looks like Kamden right now and how much comfort that brings me – even though it shouldn't.

"This was my brother's favorite place," he finally says after several long minutes of silence. His voice is deep and hoarse, giving away the emotion in it.

"I know," I say, a slight shake to my words. My focus still on the water as it finally reaches my feet, covering my toes before it's sucked back again.

"Did he ever tell you why?" he asks, his gaze meeting mine for the briefest moment before turning forward again, continuing without waiting for my reply. "He almost drowned here. In that very spot." He points to somewhere off in the distance. "He was thirteen at the time and had only been surfing a couple of months. He was trying to show off for some girls that were at least three or four years older than him. He got too cocky and tried to tackle a wave he had no business being on. Ended up wiping out and got stuck in the current. He was under for a good minute or two before he finally resurfaced."

"And that's why this was his favorite place?" I question.

"Said it was the one place that reminded him of how quickly everything can be taken away. That even though we think we're in control, we never truly are."

His words hit like a hammer to my heart. It's something Kam said to me on more than one occasion – knowing how badly I crave control. Hearing it repeated by Kane only intensifies the ache in my chest.

"It was two solid years before he got on a board again after that," he continues when I make no attempt to comment.

"He never told me that story," I say, managing to push past the lump in my throat.

"Not surprising. He hated telling that story." He shakes his head, kicking at the sand below his feet.

"What made him get back on it?" I ask, wanting to keep him talking.

If I close my eyes and listen, I can almost hear Kam's voice instead of Kane's. The two are so very similar in that way. Selfishly, that's all I really want—for him to be his brother. For Kamden to still be here with me.

"You did." He picks up a handful of sand, watching it slide through his fingers.

"Me?" I question.

"The summer he met you was the summer he started surfing again. He never said it outright but I know it was because of you. You challenged him. You made it impossible for him to be afraid. He really loved you. I hope you know that."

"I really loved him." I swipe at the tear that falls down my cheek.

Twenty minutes ago I didn't think I was capable of crying more tears, yet here I am, welling up again like a still open wound that won't scab over.

"I can't believe he's gone." He says it like he still hasn't fully processed the truth neither of us wants to accept.

"Neither can I." It's all I can manage to say. There are no words, nothing that will offer him or myself even one ounce of comfort. So instead I sit in silence. I sit next to a man I do not know and selfishly take comfort in knowing that for just this one moment, I'm not alone.

He was his brother after all – someone who knew Kam his entire life, someone who grew up right alongside him. If anyone understands the loss and grief I feel it's Kane. And even though I'm responsible for that loss, I don't have it in me to deny myself the smallest sense of comfort by having him next to me.

He's not Kamden. He will never be Kamden. I know that. But for just a moment I let myself pretend he is. I look out over the horizon and envision that it's Kam next to me. I pretend that it's just another dreary summer day like ones we've seen so many times before. That nothing has changed.

I live in that moment – embracing it – because I know once it's over I'll never get it back. I'll never get Kamden back. I'll never get to see his smile or hear his laugh. I'll never get to feel the warmth of his embrace or smell the salty scent of the ocean that always clung to his skin. I'll never get to look into those hazel eyes again, the blue and green speckles I used to make a habit of trying to count are lost from me forever.

A second tear trickles down my cheek, followed by another, but I refuse to look at Kane. I refuse to acknowledge that he's not who I want him to be, who I need him to be. I keep my focus locked on the setting sun, wishing I could disappear over the horizon along with it.

Chapter Three
Kane

Four years ago

"So, she finally did it, huh?" I ask, leaning back in my chair as my gaze goes to my brother. "I have to admit, I didn't think there was a chance in hell you'd get her to move here," I say, referring to my brother's best friend Elara. AKA: the girl he's been secretly in love with for nearly three years now.

"I wish I could take the credit." Kam leans forward, placing his elbows on his knees, his favorite Dodgers hat pulled low over his eyes. "With everything that's gone down with her this year I think she needs to get away. Start fresh somewhere."

"You're kidding yourself if you think her coming here has nothing to do with you." I smirk, not quite sure how my younger brother can be so dense sometimes.

"She needs a friend right now, so yeah, maybe it has a little to do with me. But her Aunt Carol is here. And she's her mom's only sibling. I have no doubt she needs that connection to her mom right now. Shit, man, can you imagine if something like that happened to our mom? Having to stand by and watch her die a little bit more every single day. Makes me sick even thinking about it."

"Yeah, I'd rather not think about it," I admit, shaking off the thought. "Regardless, I think it's good that she's coming here. I'm sick of you moping around like a lost puppy every time she leaves."

"You're never here. How do you know if I mope?"

He leans back in the rocking chair, the porch boards creaking as he does.

"Mom," we both say in unison.

"So when do I finally get to meet this girl?"

"Elara," Kam interjects.

"Elara," I repeat the name I've heard more times than I care to admit. Elara is all Kam talks about. Ever.

"She's supposed to get here the day before my graduation party. You'll probably meet her there. And you better be nice to her."

"What the hell is that supposed to mean?" I quirk a brow at him.

"Exactly what it sounds like. Don't be an asshole."

"I'm never an asshole," I object.

"Dude, you're always an asshole." He chuckles, shaking his head at me.

"I'm trying really hard to not get offended right now but you're making that kind of difficult."

"I'm just saying to go easy on her, okay? She's important." He stands, crossing to the railing that wraps around the large front porch of our parents' house.

"You think I don't know that?" I push to a stand, stepping up next him. "So is this the year you're finally gonna make your move on her?" I nudge him with my elbow.

"It's not like that," he objects.

"You sure about that?" I question, turning to rest my lower back against the porch railing so that I'm facing the house while he's facing the yard.

"She's my best friend."

"Your best friend that you've been in love with for three years," I state matter of fact.

"I love her. I'm not in love with her. There's a difference."

"Who are you trying to convince, Kam?"

"What the hell do you know anyway? You've been living in Illinois the past three years. You come home for a quick visit and you already think you've got me all figured out?"

"Whoa, calm down." I hold my hands up in front of myself in surrender.

"Sorry." He lets out a slow breath, adjusting his hat. "I'm nervous about having her here full time," he admits after a long moment.

"Why's that?"

"It's just, I don't know." He seems to lose himself in thought for a long moment.

"You're worried that if she's here all the time you won't be able to maintain the line you two have drawn in the sand for reasons I'll never understand."

"That's not it," he objects, quickly correcting himself. "Okay, maybe it is." He sighs.

"You clearly have feelings for this girl. Why not do both of you a favor and tell her. If I had to guess I'd say she probably feels the same way."

"You don't even know her. You can't make that assumption before you've even met someone."

"Fair enough." I nod slowly. "But I know you, kid. I know that look. This girl has got you hook, line, and sinker. Might as well make your move now rather than spending the rest of your life wondering what could have been."

"What do you suggest I do? Walk up to her the minute she gets here and pronounce my love for her."

"So you are in love with her." I smirk.

"And you wonder why I called you an asshole." He pushes away from the railing, pulling open the front door just moments later.

"Kam." I chuckle when he throws me a glare over his shoulder before disappearing inside.

Man, that girl must have him even tighter than I realized. That only makes me even more curious about her. Kam has the attention span of a toddler. If she's that under his skin then she must be something special. I just hope for his sake he doesn't get hurt.

****

Present day

I don't want to look at her. Looking at her makes me think of Kam and thinking about Kam hurts too fucking much right now. And yet I can't stop myself from stealing glances at her out of the corner of my eye.

It's easy to see what Kam saw in her. She's beautiful.

Her long blonde waves are drenched, sticking to the back of her dress. Her mascara is smeared and her eyes are bloodshot, and still I think she's the most beautiful girl I've ever seen up close.

I remember the first time I met her. Kam was so nervous. A semblance of a smile plays on my lips as I recall how quickly he swept her away moments after making the introduction. I had barely recovered from the shock of laying eyes on her for the first time before he was pulling her away to meet other family members and friends, clearly worried I would be an asshole to her, as he had so bluntly put it.

Of course that didn't stop me from watching her all night. I knew she belonged to Kam. There was no question in my mind there. I could tell by the way she leaned into him every time she got the chance. By the way she looked up at him

39

like he was the only person she could see. If Kam was worried she didn't feel the same way his worry was definitely misplaced. It was clear to anyone who cared to look; those two were crazy about each other.

I still don't fully understand why they never got together. It's something I tried talking to Kam about a few times over the years but he was adamant that pursuing anything would ruin their friendship. Honestly I think he was just scared for what he felt for her. And now she'll never know.

The thought brings everything back to the forefront of my mind. I have to keep reminding myself that Kam is gone. My brother is dead. And here I am, sitting next to the girl he secretly loved for years, wishing it was me laying in that grave and not him.

Elara shifts next to me, discreetly trying to wipe a tear away without drawing attention to herself. I catch sight of the brace on her arm, remembering that not only did she lose Kam but she was there when he died.

Fuck this was a bad idea.

My chest tightens and I feel my own emotion threatening to spill to the surface. I shake my head trying to pull myself together.

"Do you want to go somewhere?" I ask without actually meaning to.

"What?" She looks at me, her brows pulling together in confusion.

"Let's get out of here."

"And do what?"

"Fuck, I don't know. Anything but this." I gesture around us. "Why don't we get a bite to eat?"

"I'm not hungry," she quickly replies, turning her gaze back out to the water.

"Look, I get that we aren't friends and that you probably don't like me and that's okay. But right now can we just pretend that we are? Because I don't know about you but I could really use a friend right now."

Her gaze slowly comes back to me as she thinks over my statement.

"Who said I didn't like you?" I can't help the small smile that hits my lips at the innocent way she asks the question.

"Considering you haven't spoken to me despite seeing me multiple times over the last few days, I think you've made that pretty clear."

"I'm sorry if I made you feel that way. I've just got some stuff going on in my head. Don't take it personally."

"So should I also not take it personally that you think I'm an asshole?" This time she pulls back a little, surprise evident on her pretty face.

"I don't think you're an asshole."

"That's not what my brother said." I poke fun at her, needing to distract myself for a minute. To feel something other than sadness that's been blanketing me like a second skin. "After he introduced us at the graduation party you told him he was right, that I did seem like an asshole."

"I can't believe he told you that." She blinks, clearly not sure how to react.

"I think he was trying to discourage me."

"From what?"

I *almost* tell her the truth. That I'd threatened Kam that if he didn't make a move on her I would. Not that I really would have, even if Kam didn't tell me exactly what the stunning Elara had thought of me after the party. I never would have done that to my brother. Of course I decide against telling her any of this.

"Nothing," I finally answer, pushing up to my feet before turning to look down at her. "So what do you say?" She looks from my face to my hands that are stretched out toward her, back to my face. "Let me buy you dinner. It will make me feel a little better," I add.

41

"I should try to eat something. I guess," she finally says, reaching her uninjured hand up to take mine, allowing me to pull her to her feet.

"Anything you're in the mood for?"

"Can we go to Zachary's?" she asks, as she attempts to wipe the caked sand from the back of her dress before leaning over to retrieve her heels.

"The old place over on Charles Street?" I ask, waiting until she steps up next to me before turning.

"It was kind of me and Kam's place. He would always take me there for pancakes." She gives me a sad smile as she walks next to me.

"Zachary's it is." I nod. "Though I think we should probably change first."

"Yeah." She agrees, looking down at herself. "That's probably a good idea."

"I can drive you over to your place," I offer, gesturing to my black Audi parked right to our left. "My stuff is at my parents' anyway," I say, knowing she lives in the apartment over her aunt's garage next door.

"I don't know if I should be riding in your car." She gestures down to her wet, sand covered dress.

"It'll be fine," I promise, laying my hand on the small of her back as I guide her toward the car. I don't miss the way she tenses the instant the contact is made.

I get her settled into the passenger seat before crossing around the car and climbing into the driver's side. It's eerily quiet as we make our way down the near vacant coastline. Elara sits completely still next to me, her eyes fixed out the window.

By the time we pull into my parents' driveway just a few short miles from the beach, I'm fully expecting her to back out. So when she exits the car, telling me she'll be right back, I'm honestly a little surprised.

I watch her as she crosses the yard, disappearing inside the detached garage that sits to the right of the main house just moments later.

Slipping inside the front door of my parents' house, I quietly make my way up to my old bedroom where I've been crashing the last few days, hoping to not draw attention to the fact that I'm here.

The last thing I want to do right now is deal with my parents. I know that sounds bad but I'm having a hard enough time dealing with this shit as it is. Having to watch my mom's tears stream down her face on constant repeat is more than I can handle right now.

Luckily the house is quiet and I'm able to sneak into my room undetected, reminding me of all the times I've tiptoed into my room before, hoping mom and dad wouldn't catch me coming home from a late night party. God that seems like a life time ago.

Quickly stripping out of my damp suit and into a pair of jeans and long sleeve shirt, I stop when I catch sight of my reflection in the mirror that hangs on the back of the door. I stand there for a long moment, realizing for the first time how much I really do look like Kam – especially wearing his hat.

"What the fuck are you doing, Thaler?" I ask out loud, pulling the Dodgers cap off my head to look at the frayed material.

This hat was Kam's favorite. He wore it almost everywhere. I thought about putting it inside his casket but at the last minute changed my mind, deciding I wanted to hang on to it.

I'm still studying the hat, wondering how Kam would react if he knew what I was doing right now, when I catch a glimpse of Elara crossing the yard through the bedroom window. Quickly sliding the cap back on my head, I make my way downstairs, taking the steps two at a time before pushing my way outside.

I swallow down the hard lump in my throat, not able to take my eyes off her as we both make our way toward the car from opposite directions.

She replaced her black dress with dark leggings and a long gray sweater that almost hangs to her knees, her long blonde hair now tied into a messy knot on top of her head. She's so damn beautiful that for a moment I forget who she is entirely and just focus on the way her hips sway as she walks. On the way she nibbles her bottom lip nervously when she reaches the car. And the way her sweet vanilla scent engulfs me the instant she climbs into the seat next to me.

"Ready?" I ask, watching as she nervously pulls the arm of her sweater over her brace.

"Ready," she answers after a moment, nodding.

Slipping on my seatbelt, I back out of the driveway, meeting Elara's gaze in the reflection of the window for the briefest moment before she quickly looks away.

"Can I ask you something?" I ask after several long moments of silence have stretched between us.

"Okay." I see her glance in my direction out of my peripheral vision but I keep my gaze locked on the road.

"You loved my brother?"

"Is that a question?" She seems confused.

"No. I mean, you loved him. I know that. And I know how much you meant to him. So why did you two never…"

"Why did we never date?" she finishes my sentence, clearly picking up on where I'm going with this.

"Yeah."

"It's complicated."

"Most things are."

"You wouldn't understand." She shrugs.

"Try me," I offer.

"Kam was my best friend. And I was in love with him," she admits, looking back out the window. "At first I

44

thought he didn't feel the same way. But as time went on I knew he did. I could tell."

"Then what was the hold up?"

"I don't know, honestly." She lets out a slow breath. "I guess I didn't want to be the one to come out and say it. I needed him to do it. It seems so stupid now. All the time we wasted." She sniffs and only then do I notice the tears that have once again welled in her eyes.

Without thinking I reach over and squeeze her hand, not missing the way she once again tenses at my touch.

"I told him I was in love with him the day of the accident," she admits, a couple tears streaking down her cheek. "I told him I loved him and then I watched him die."

In an instant, I'm yanking the car to the side of the road. After unclasping my seat belt and then hers, I have her in my arms within seconds of putting the car in park.

"Shhh," I whisper into her hair, fighting back the overwhelming urge to just let myself go right along with her.

"Be strong for her," I hear Kam say in my mind. *"Take care of my girl."*

"We missed out on so much." She turns her face into my chest, clenching the sleeve of my shirt with her good hand as the sobs rack through her. "We wasted so much time."

I don't know what to say to that. I don't know a single word that can comfort her right now. So I do the only thing I know to do. I hold onto her as tightly as I can and let her cry herself out.

I don't know how much time has passed by the time she finally pulls away. Maybe it's seconds. Maybe it's several minutes. All I know is that when she pulls back and looks up at me with swollen blood shot eyes, I nearly lose it.

"I'm so sorry." She withdraws quickly like she's only now remembering who she's with.

"Don't apologize. You have nothing to be sorry for."

"I have a lot to be sorry for," she mutters under her breath, wiping at her cheeks.

"What do you mean?" I ask.

"Nothing." She shakes her head before meeting my gaze. "I'm just sorry to dump all my stuff on you. You and your family have suffered such an unimaginable loss and here I am acting like I'm the only one affected by this."

"You're not dumping anything on me. Selfishly I want you to need me because in some weird way I think I need you."

"Why would you need me?" She seems genuinely confused by my statement.

"You were the closest person to my brother. You knew him better than anyone else. I guess being close to you makes me feel closer to him."

"You remind me a lot of him," she says, once again pulling the sleeves of her sweater over her hands. "Being near you makes me feel closer to him too."

"What do you say we skip the pancakes? I think we're in need of something a little stronger than syrup," I suggest.

"I think that sounds like a good idea." She gives me a soft smile and I swear in that instant my heart kicks back to life, finally beating inside my chest for the first time in days.

Chapter Four
Elara

"He did what?" I cover my mouth to contain the laughter that bubbles in my throat.

"You heard me." Kane chuckles, taking a long pull of beer before setting his bottle back on the small bar table that separates us. "Completely naked."

"And you let him do it?" I gawk, trying to process the story he's been telling me for the last several minutes with the heavy buzz running through my veins.

"He knew the stakes and he took the bet anyway." Kane shrugs, smile firmly in place.

"So he ran through the front yard full of people completely naked?"

He nods, laughing like he can picture it perfectly in his head. "I will never forget the look on my mother's face."

"Remind me to never play cards with you." I shake my head, trying to envision Kam as a ten year old boy streaking through his parents' yard in the middle of their Fourth of July cookout.

"Technically it was our cousin Brock who named the punishment for losing, not me."

"As if that makes it any better. You still let him do it."

"Trust me, there was no way I was talking him out of it. Kam always kept his word. If he said he was going to do something he did it. He agreed to the terms of the game. Hell, he was walking out of the garage with half his clothes off before any of us had processed that he was actually going to do it right then and there."

"Oh my god." I laugh. "Your poor parents."

"Trust me, they were pissed. But they got a good laugh out of it too. Well, after everyone had left they did."

"Kam was never like that with me. He was never the one doing the crazy things. He was the one always trying to talk me out of doing them."

"That's just because he cared so much about you. He probably didn't want to see you get hurt."

"He used to get so mad at me," I say, tracing my finger around the rim of my glass. "I told him he reminded me of my father. The way he used to scold me whenever I did something he thought was dangerous or reckless."

"Sounds like my brother." He nods knowingly. "He was always a bit of a wild card but when it came to taking real risk, he always aired on the caution. Hell, surfing was even a bit of a stretch for him. But he loved the water so much there was no keeping him out of it. His love for the sport overshadowed his fear," he stops, falling silent for a long moment.

I know what he's thinking. *How could someone who always played it safe die the way he did?* The answer is me. And as much as I want to say that, as much as I want to tell him how all of this is my fault, I can't find it in me to utter the words.

I guess selfishly I don't want him to look at me the way I know he will once he learns the truth.

"He told me about you though," he continues after what feels like forever.

"Told you what?"

"What a daredevil you are."

"I don't know that I would go that far." I shake my head, needing away from this conversation and the guilt that accompanies it. "What about you? Are you a risk taker or are you like your brother? Liking to play it safe."

"I think I'm a little bit in the middle. I don't take unnecessary risk if I don't have to, but I also love the thrill of doing something that pushes the boundaries. I'm all about the experience."

"Is that why you like to travel so much?" I ask. "Kam told me about all the travelling you do for your job and about how much you travelled before that as well," I say in way of explanation.

"I guess, yeah. It takes me out of my comfort zone and submerges me into an entirely different world. I love experiencing different cultures, meeting all different kinds of people, seeing the world in a completely different way."

"Sounds amazing."

"It is," he agrees. "What about you? You travel at all?"

"Nope." I take a drink of my cranberry and vodka, before continuing, "I've only been here, Arkansas, and Florida."

"Seriously?"

"My mom loved Clearwater. We vacationed there every year so I didn't get to see a lot of different places growing up. And then of course my Aunt Carol lives here and now so do I. Other than that." I shrug as if to say there's nothing else.

"Wow. Sounds to me like we need to get you out of here, show you a different part of the world."

"Is that so? What? You gonna fly me to Paris or something?"

"Do you want to go to Paris?" he asks, his expression void of humor.

"Not really no."

"No?" he questions, cocking his head to the side. "Paris is a beautiful city."

"I'm sure it is but if I was going to go out of the country I'd want to experience something not quite so touristy."

"Well clearly you've thought about it. Tell me, if you could go anywhere in the world where would it be?"

"Manarola Italy," I answer without hesitation.

"Well that's very specific." Kane chuckles. "Care to elaborate why that location?"

"My dad's grandparents are from Italy. Manarola is where my great grandfather and grandmother lived. I think I'd like to see where I came from more than I would some fancy tower."

"I like that."

"What?" I ask, feeling slightly squeamish under his penetrating gaze.

"That you would rather connect to your roots than visit somewhere just to visit. We should go there someday."

"*We*?" I choke around the drink I was in the middle of taking.

"What? You don't want to travel with me?" he fakes offense.

"Well, I don't really know you," I remind him.

"Yet," he states matter of fact.

"Yet?" I question playfully, taking another drink.

"Give me time, Elara. I just might grow on you."

"We'll see about that," I quip.

Kane laughs at my rebuttal, finishing off his beer before gesturing to my near empty glass. "You want another?"

"I probably shouldn't." I place my palm over the opening of my glass. "I think I've had too much as it is."

"Three is too much?" He grins. "Lightweight."

"I won't argue there. I don't drink very much and considering I've only had pretzels from the bar to eat I think I'm even more intoxicated than I normally would be," I say, realizing just how buzzed I actually am. Not to

50

the point that I feel like I can't function or anything but enough that I feel a bit unsteady on my stool.

"Perhaps food would have been a better idea before drinks," he offers, holding his hand up to signal the waitress as she walks by.

Asking for the check, he waits until she walks away before turning his attention back to me. "I guess since I got you sloshed the least I can do is feed you," he teases, his dark eyes almost black under the dim bar lighting.

"How very gentlemanly of you," I deadpan, taking the last drink of my vodka cranberry before scooting the glass off to the side of the table. "And here I thought you were an asshole."

"Oh, I am an asshole," he promises. "But only when I want to be." He stares at me intently for a long moment before a wide smile breaks across his face.

He looks so much like Kam when he smiles. Honestly, I'm not entirely sure how that makes me feel. A part of me loves how much he reminds me of Kam. Being here with him has shown me just how similar they really are. It's almost like having a piece of Kam still here on Earth.

But for all their similarities they are also very different. And in their differences I am reminded that he isn't Kam, no matter how much I wish he was.

"I'll keep that in mind," I finally respond, swallowing past the knot that has once again lodged itself in my throat.

****

"So you live in Chicago?" I ask, taking a large bite of pancakes while Kane sits back in his chair across from me sipping coffee.

"Technically yes, though I travel so much for work I don't know that I would say I actually live anywhere."

"Kam told me you do some kind of consulting?" I question, having not cared much at the time.

"Risk Management." He nods, taking another sip of coffee.

"And what does that entail exactly?"

"I'm hired by outside companies to identify threats, assess the vulnerability of critical assets, determine the risk, and identify ways to reduce those risks."

"I have no idea what you just said," I admit, a small smile on my lips.

"Yeah, exactly." He chuckles.

"So you go in and make sure that companies don't take any unnecessary risks to help protect their business?"

"Sort of." He nods. "That's an easy way to put it I guess."

"And you get to travel a lot doing that?"

"Because I'm not employed by any one company, many of the companies that hire me have offices out of the country. When working with these clients I travel to them for the length of the contract I've been hired for."

"You must see some pretty amazing places doing that."

"I have."

"Tell me your favorite place that you've been."

"That's hard." He thinks on it for a moment. "I guess I'd have to say my favorite so far is Madrid. I lived there for almost four months last year and really fell in love with it."

"Doesn't it feel weird, going somewhere for that long, getting used to the way of life, and then coming back here?"

"Sometimes. Sometimes I'm glad to be home, other times I wish I could go back. It just depends on the location and the job."

"That sounds incredible though."

"It really is," he agrees.

"Did you choose this profession because of the travel opportunities?" I ask, enjoying having a conversation that doesn't revolve around anything too heavy.

"Yes and no. I didn't set out with the goal to be a risk management consultant but it turns out I'm really good at seeing the bigger picture. The travelling is just a bonus," he says, leaning forward to place his elbows on the table. "What about you?"

"What about me?"

"What do you do for a living?"

"Oh, well right now I work as a receptionist at my aunt's salon but that's not the end goal."

"What is?"

"I'll let you know once I figure it out."

"You went to Southern State with Kam, right?"

"That's right."

"What did you major in?"

"English." I curl my nose. "In retrospect it probably wasn't the most responsible choice to get an education in something I'm not sure I'll ever use."

"Then why English?"

"Honestly I really don't know. I guess I thought maybe one day I would try my hand at writing. I've always wanted to do screenplays, on top of other things."

"Really? That's interesting."

"It's silly and something I'll likely never do. Really I just went to college to make my father happy. It didn't hurt that Kam was there with me." I let out a slow breath. "Kam on the other hand, he knew exactly what he wanted to do."

"When he said he was majoring in photography I didn't think he was actually serious," Kane admits.

"But he did it." I smile past the sadness welling in my chest. "He was always so talented. The way he saw the most ordinary things was like he was looking at them with a different type of eyes. He found beauty in everything."

"Some things are more obvious than others, I guess." The way he says it makes my skin prickle from the inside out but I shake it off, knowing I'm probably in no state of mind to assume he's talking about me.

"Anyway, I guess it doesn't matter now." I sigh, setting my fork onto my plate, suddenly feeling like there's no way I can stomach another bite.

That seems to be all it takes. One minute I feel okay, the next I feel like the walls are closing in on me. The panic slowly starts to creep back in, brought on by discussing a future Kamden will never get. A future I took from him. Feeling like I might suffocate at any moment, I stand abruptly and take off through the small restaurant.

"Elara," Kane calls after me but I'm already outside by the time his voice registers.

I cross to the side of the building and lean over, putting my hands on my knees as I take calculated breaths, willing myself not to vomit.

"Elara." Kane stands next to me, yet I hadn't heard his approach.

"Just leave me alone, Kane." I don't change my position, my eyes closed tightly.

"I don't understand. What did I do?"

"Nothing. Okay? You didn't do anything. I just need you to go."

"Elara." He says my name the way Kam used to always say it when he wasn't sure how to handle me – hesitant, like he's afraid I might snap at any moment.

"I just can't. I can't sit in there and talk about him like he's never coming back."

"He's not coming back," he says somberly.

"You think I don't know that." I stand upright, my gaze finding his in an instant. "You think I don't know he's dead. I watched him die." My voice shakes as it rises. "I watched his eyes close for the last time five days ago and now I'm sitting in the restaurant he used to always bring me to, talking to his brother who I keep trying to pretend is him. But you're not him, Kane. And I hate you for that. I hate you for not being the person I want you to be. And that's totally irrational and unfair, I know, but I can't help it."

"I get it, believe me I do."

"Only you don't, Kane. You don't understand at all. You weren't here. Your life didn't revolve around him." I swipe angrily at my tears. "I'm lost. I don't even know which way is up or down anymore. I'm so twisted up inside. I feel like I'm suffocating every second of every day and nothing makes it better. I tried pretending with you. I tried pushing it to the back of my mind and focusing on something else if even for the briefest moment but that has only served to make me feel even more guilty."

"You have no reason to feel guilty," he argues.

"Yes I do," I scream, emotion getting the better of me.

"Why?" His temper flares and for the first time I see the true pain engrained in every pore of his face. Pain he's been trying to hide all night.

"Because I lived," I choke. "I lived and he died."

"You can't do that to yourself."

"Yes I can, because it's my fault."

"It's not your fault, Elara. It was an accident."

"I don't know if I can live with this." My voice is borderline hysterical.

"You're going to have to find a way to. For Kam if nothing else. He wouldn't want this for you. This guilt you're carrying. You know he wouldn't."

"Yeah, well I'm not sure it really matters anymore."

"Of course it does." He takes a step toward me. "And I don't care how much you say you hate me, I know you don't. You need me," he says, sliding the Dodgers hat from his head and gently placing it on mine. "I know you do because I need you the same way." He forces a soft smile as he adjusts the hat on my head, stepping back to really look at me. "There. Looks much better on you."

"Kane." I reach up and run my hand along the frayed bill of the hat.

"Kam would want you to have it."

"I'm sorry for what I said." I let out a frustrated breath, finally able to get a small grasp on my emotions.

"Don't be." He reaches over and takes my hand, giving it a gentle squeeze. "Come on, I'll drive you home."

Chapter Five
Elara

Two months later...

"You sure you girls don't need my help?" My dad's voice is muffled as I balance my phone between my face and shoulder, trying to tape up the moving box in front of me.

"I think we've got it under control. I don't really have that much stuff. Besides, by the time you'd get here I'd likely be done." I straighten my posture, pushing the finished box to the side.

"I still can't believe my baby girl is finally coming home."

"Dad, I hate to break it to you but I haven't been your baby girl for a very long time." I chuckle, tossing a few shirts into one of the boxes reserved for clothing.

"You will always be my baby girl, peanut. Always. I just wish mom could be here to see what an incredible young woman you've grown into."

"Me too." I push past the sadness that settles over me, not wanting to get into this with him right now.

It's not that I don't like talking about my mom, I do. I want to remember how amazing she was. I want to honor her memory by keeping it alive for as long as I live. But it's hard when so much has happened recently and so many wounds are still so fresh.

The loss of Kam not only ripped a hole right through me, it also reopened the wound left by the loss of my mother four years ago. It's honestly hard for me to even think about at the moment. I've lost so much over the last few years.

"She'd be so proud of you, I hope you know that." My dad pulls me back into the conversation.

"I don't know about that." I sigh, taking a seat on the corner of my bed.

My gaze immediately goes to the large white two story house next door. Kam's house. I have a perfect view of it from my apartment above Carol's garage. It's one of the many reasons why I've decided it's time to leave. I can't bear to look at it knowing Kam isn't there anymore.

"I am." My dad once again pulls me from where my thoughts have drifted. "Don't sell yourself short, Elara. You're only twenty-two. You just graduated college three months ago. You've got time to figure things out. In the meantime, I will be so happy to have you home. I told you that I talked to Amy at the Freeport Journal, didn't I?" my dad asks, referring to the small town local newspaper that is pretty much obsolete at this point but somehow manages to still stay in business.

"You did."

"She called me yesterday. Said once you get settled to stop in and see her. I think she has a couple positions she's willing to consider you for. Might help get your feet wet and establish some experience. Even if it's not what you want to do long term, I think it will be a good stepping stone."

"Okay, I will make sure to stop by to see her next week if I can," I say, knowing I need to line up a job sooner rather than later.

The last thing I want to do is be one of those children that live with their parents forever. Though I'm sure my dad wouldn't complain, especially considering I'm his only child. I on the other hand, am hoping moving back to my childhood home will be very temporary.

"It's going to be so good to have you home, sweetheart. Do you know when you plan to head out yet?"

"I promised Carol we'd do dinner tomorrow evening so I'll likely leave the next morning."

"Okay. Just make sure you call me when you leave and be sure to check in along the way."

"I will."

"And don't stop off at any rest stops. Make sure to go to a populated gas station if you need to stop for any reason."

"I know, Dad." I shake my head even though he can't see me.

"I just worry about you driving that far by yourself."

"Dad, it's less than fourteen hours. I think I can handle it."

"I know. But I'm your father and it's my job to worry about you."

"I'll be fine. I promise. But I really do need to get off of here if I want any hope of being able to finish packing before tomorrow."

"Okay. Don't forget to call me when you leave," he reiterates.

"I won't, Dad."

"I love you, peanut. Tell Aunt Carol hi for me."

"I will. Love you too."

Ending the call, I drop backward onto the bed, staring up at the ceiling as I try to sort through the nervous energy that's been buzzing through me since I made the decision to move home.

A part of me is excited. I miss my dad terribly and it will be really nice to be around some of my friends again. The other part of me feels like I'm running away. I hate to look at it that way but to an extent it's true.

It's too hard being here. Everywhere I go I see Kam. Everything I do I'm reminded of him; of memories we made together before he died. The more time that passes the more I find myself avoiding all the places we used to go together. I've even started taking a different route to work every day to avoid passing Zachary's, which I haven't visited since that night with Kane.

Just the thought of Kane causes a weird stirring in my chest. His dark eyes flash through my mind and I sit up abruptly, my gaze immediately finding Kam's old Dodgers hat that's sitting on top of my dresser.

I remember the night Kane gave me that hat, how he claimed to need me as much as he thought I needed him. Turns out he didn't need me all that much considering he flew back to Illinois the next day without as much as a goodbye.

I found out from his mom a couple days later when I stupidly walked next door to see him only to find he was no longer there. I didn't expect to be as disappointed by the news or as hurt as I was for that matter.

I guess I had hoped we could be friends. Or maybe I had just naively believed that he would somehow step in and fill the void that Kamden had left behind. I've realized since then that there's not a single person on this earth that could take Kam's place – and I don't want them too either.

Standing, I cross the room and pick up Kam's hat, running my fingers along the frayed bill. Looking up into the mirror that's attached to the dresser, I slide the hat on my head, remembering all the times Kam had done it for me.

A sad smile graces my face as I take in my reflection moments before my gaze lands on the picture of me and Kam taped to the bottom left corner of the mirror. I pull it off, peeling the tape from the back before turning it upright again. Kam's smiling face is the only thing I can focus on.

I run my finger over his photograph, wishing I could shake this feeling that by moving back to Arkansas I'm betraying his memory somehow. Honestly I just didn't know what else to do.

I've spent weeks walking around like a zombie. Not able to eat. Barely able to sleep. Until one night I made the decision that the only way for me to move on was to leave this part of my life behind me. And in doing so, I'm leaving Kamden behind as well.

It's not lost on me that this is the exact thing I did when my mom died – I ran away. But leaving home feels different this time around. Back then I was running to Kam, not away from the memory of my mom. Now, I have no one left to run to.

Don't get me wrong, my dad is amazing, but he's not my mom. He's not that good at talking about feelings and anytime I try to discuss anything of real importance he has no idea what to really say. So while I'm happy to go home to my dad, I also know that I'm going to have to find a way to heal on my own this time. No one can do it for me.

Taking the hat off, I tuck the picture of me and Kam inside it and lay them at the top of one of the moving boxes. Closing the sides, I quickly tape the box up, determined to not let myself fall back into the same cycle I do every time I wallow for too long.

Kamden is gone. I've given myself two months to wrap my head around that fact and yet it still doesn't seem real most days. Regardless, it's time I stop living in the past. I'm not doing anyone any good by hiding out in this apartment all day long trying to shut out the world.

So with a renewed sense of determination, I continue packing, knowing that even if it doesn't feel like it now, this will be the best thing for me in the long run.

****

"I was hoping you'd come by and see me before you left." Mary Thaler smiles at me through the screen door before joining me on the porch. "You're all packed up then?"

"I am." I rock back on my heels. "I just wanted to come say goodbye to you and Kris before I headed out."

"Kris is at the office this morning. It's likely he won't be home until later this afternoon. He's going to be sorry he missed you."

"I should have come yesterday evening," I say, knowing I had planned to but decided against it last minute.

I knew saying goodbye to Kam's parents would be difficult so I kept pushing it off. These are two people who treated me more like a daughter than the girl who lived next door. Over the years they've become family and leaving them behind is not an easy thing to do.

"Normally he would have been here but I guess there's some accounting issue that couldn't wait until Monday morning." She swipes her hand through the air.

"That man works too much." I shake my head on a smile, knowing she whole heartedly agrees.

"Don't we both know it." She chuckles. "I think it helps him though. Gives him something to focus on."

"I understand that," I agree, not really sure what else to say.

"It's going to be strange not having you next door anymore," she redirects, her hazel eyes so much like

Kam's it's difficult to meet her gaze. "I bet your dad is excited to have you coming back home."

"He is." I nod, knotting my hands together.

Sensing my unease, Mary reaches out and takes both of my hands in hers. "You're doing the right thing, Elara. You know you are. Kam wouldn't want this life for you. He'd want you to move on, to be happy, and that's what we want for you too."

"I know." I fight back the tears that instantly well in my eyes at her words.

"We are sure going to miss you though."

"I'm going to miss you too."

"You make sure you call every now and again, okay? Let us know how you're doing."

"I will."

Mary releases my hands and instantly pulls me into a hug. It's one of those hugs that only mothers can give. The ones that make you feel safe and loved. I remember how my mother's hugs would always make me feel better, no matter what was going on.

"You take care of yourself, my sweet girl," she says before finally releasing me and taking a full step back.

"I will." I offer her one last smile before quickly turning and walking away, not able to look back in fear that I might never leave if I do.

This isn't just about leaving Mary and Kris. It's about leaving the place that holds every single memory of Kamden in it. It's about saying goodbye. To Kamden. To his parents. To the town I thought I'd live in for the rest of my life. To the girl I used to be and to the girl I am now.

Carol meets me at the car moments later, babbling hysterically about how much she's going to miss having me around. After spending the next fifteen minutes crying like we're never going to see each other again, I finally climb into my car and pull away, watching Kamden's house grow further away in the rearview mirror before it finally disappears from view.

I push back the tears that threaten to spill over, knowing I'm going to have to save them for the one last stop I need to make.

It only takes me about ten minutes to reach him. I know exactly where he is, even though I haven't been able to bring myself to come here since the day of his funeral. Pulling off the small street, I climb from the car and cross the expansive green space peppered with hundreds of head stones until I find the one I'm looking for. *Kamden Joseph Thaler* engraved across the front in thick letters. It's the first time I've actually seen it – his name etched across the front of the headstone.

"Hey, Kam." I slide down onto the ground in front of his grave, reaching out to run my hand along the cool stone. "Sorry I haven't come to see you sooner. I'm sure you understand why," I say as if he's sitting right in front of me.

"So, I'm moving back to Arkansas today. I've got my car packed up and ready to go but I needed to come see you first." I blink away the tears that are already threatening to spill over. I've cried more times than I care to admit over the last couple of days. I never dreamed that saying goodbye would be quite so hard.

"Dad's thrilled of course." I clear my throat and continue, "Aunt Carol not so much. And me, well I don't know that I'm really sure how I feel right now. A part of me knows it's for the best. But the other part of me feels guilty leaving you behind."

I pull at a few long pieces of grass that have sprouted in front of his head stone.

"I know you understand and I know you want me to be happy. But happiness is in short supply these days. Has been ever since you left. But I'm trying, Kam. I promise I am. It's just really, really hard." Tears trickle down my cheeks but I don't bother to wipe them away. It's just me and Kam right now.

"Anyway, I have your old Dodgers hat. Kane gave it to me. I hope you don't mind that I'm taking it home with me. I know how much you loved that old raggedy thing. I also have your camera. You left it at my house the last time you were there, remember? I haven't been able to bring myself to look at the pictures saved on there but one day I think I will. Hopefully there's not too many embarrassing ones of me. Then again, I think I might like it if there are. Because you always did love catching me at the worst possible moments." I laugh through my tears.

"I miss you so much, Kam." A tidal wave of emotion hits me and it takes me several long moments to pull myself from the weight of it enough to speak again.

"I meant what I said that day when I told you I love you. It wasn't just because you kissed me either. I think I fell in love with you the first day I met you and that love only continued to grow over the years. At first I was angry, angry that we never got our chance. But then I realized that we did. We may not have shared certain things but in all the ways that count, I was yours and you were mine. I think in a way I'll always be yours." I pause, thinking over my next words.

"I need to tell you I'm sorry. I know you think I don't have a reason to be sorry but we both know you're wrong. I'm the reason you're here, even if you don't want to admit it. You always let me off so easy. Anytime I would ever do anything wrong you were always making excuses for me, trying to justify my bad choices. I guess it was your way of protecting me but you can't protect me from this, Kam. You know that as much as I do."

I stop, letting the memory of his voice wash over me. If I really concentrate, I can hear him like he's sitting right next to me.

"I can't change what happened, I know that. And I'm trying to find a way to be okay with it. Some days are harder

65

than others but I'm trying to be the strong person you always said I was. I don't know if I've ever truly been strong or if maybe you just brought something out in me that I didn't see myself, but I'm trying."

I close my eyes and lift my head toward the sky, focusing on the light breeze that dances across my face – on the sound it makes as it rustles through the trees. I picture Kam sitting right next to me, holding my hand, telling me that everything is going to be okay. And then in the silence of that moment I finally find the strength to let him go.

"I guess I should go," I finally say, slowly climbing to my feet. "I'll miss you every day of forever." I lean forward and press my lips to the top of his headstone before softly whispering, "Goodbye, tater tot."

Chapter Six
Elara

I turn away from Kam's grave, an odd sensation of relief washing over me. Like this was what I needed all along – to talk to him.

I look up, prepared to walk away holding onto that feeling when the ground beneath my feet seems to shift slightly and for a brief moment I let my mind convince itself that Kamden is standing right in front of me.

His hair is a little longer, a little darker, but it's his nose, his mouth, his firm jaw, and staggering good looks. It's only when I reach his eyes that reality seems to snap back into place. In that moment, I'm overwhelmed with both disappointment and excitement, the latter not an emotion I expected to feel realizing that the man I'm looking at isn't Kam.

"Kane." His name falls from my mouth unintentionally and I quickly wipe my cheeks with the back of my hands, knowing I probably look like a mess right now. "What... what are you doing here?" I stutter, suddenly very aware of the intimate conversation I just shared with Kam and wondering if he overheard.

"Thought I'd stop by and have a chat with my little brother." He nods toward Kam's headstone behind me. "You?"

"Same." I shrug.

"How have you been?" he asks, scuffing his foot against the ground.

"I'm hanging in there. You?"

"Same." He looks at me for a long moment, seeming like he wants to say more but refusing to.

"Well, he's all yours." I force a small smile, nodding before quickly stepping past him and making my way back through the cemetery.

I can't handle dealing with Kane right now. Not when I'm so close to getting the hell out of here in one piece. I wish I didn't feel that way. I wish things between us could be different, but they aren't. There's no sense in pretending like we care about how the other is doing. He made his feelings on that matter very clear when he left without a word.

Now if only that were my truth… Unfortunately I think I care a little too much, but I'm not going to let him know that when he clearly has no regard for me.

I'm not sure why I feel like he owed me a goodbye, but I do. After the evening we shared, the bond we formed around our mutual love for Kam, I guess I thought that maybe we'd be able to help each other. Then again, him leaving might have actually helped me in the long run. There's something about him that I can't quite put my finger on. Something that tells me I should steer clear.

"Did I hear you say you were leaving?" His words wash over me just moments before I reach the car and my entire body freezes.

I turn slowly to find him standing just feet from me. "You were listening to my conversation?" I grind out, embarrassment and anger boiling to the surface.

"I didn't mean to. I didn't know you were here until I heard you talking. By then it was already too late."

"So you just kept listening?"

"It wasn't like I meant to overhear you."

"Somehow I doubt that," I snip, my emotions all over the place. "That conversation was between me and Kam. You had no right to listen."

"I'm sorry." He lets out a slow breath, running a hand through his dark hair. "I just saw you sitting there and I guess I kind of froze." He waits to make sure I'm not going to respond before asking the question again. "So are you leaving?"

"Not that it's any of your business, but yes, I am."

"You're running away." It's a statement not a question and I pull back like he's physically slapped me right across the face.

"Excuse me?"

"Just an observation." He holds his hands up in front of himself in surrender.

"More like an opinion and you'd do well to keep it to yourself."

"Are you mad at me for some reason?" He drops his hands, studying me curiously.

"Why would I be mad at you?" I cross my arms over my chest.

"I should have said goodbye." His features soften and he lets out another slow breath like he's just now realizing why I would be upset.

"Yeah well, it's not like we're friends or anything." I make a move to turn. "I have to go." Before I can get even one full step in, his fingers are wrapped around my forearm pulling me to a stop.

I turn my face to the side, instantly dizzy by how close he is. Sucking in a hard breath, I hold it, wishing that I knew him well enough to anticipate his next move.

"I want to be your friend, Elara." His voice is like velvet in my ear and goose bumps immediately erupt across my neck. "I just... I needed some time." He releases my arm, allowing me to take a step back and put a little distance between us.

"No, I get it." I brush it off like I couldn't care less.

"It doesn't seem like you do."

"You don't know me well enough to assume you have any idea what I think or feel." I stand my ground, convinced that pushing him away is the right thing.

He's already proven that he can bounce in and out of my life with little regard for how that makes me feel. And even though the rational side of me knows that he was going through his own grieving process, the other part of me is pissed for reasons I don't fully understand.

"Fair enough." He rocks back on his heels.

"I really should go. It was good seeing you again, Kane." This time I manage to get a couple of steps in before his voice has me coming to an abrupt stop.

"It's difficult for me to be near you."

I don't turn around to look at him. I can't.

"Why?" I ask, my back still to him.

"Because my brother loved you and every time I look at you all I see is the life he'll never have," he admits, defeat clear in his voice. "Because you make me feel things I don't have any right to feel. Because when I'm with you..." he trails off, not finishing his sentence. "The night of the funeral you pulled me out of a very dark place. You smiled at me and suddenly everything felt different. I couldn't handle the guilt that left me with. I'm sorry for leaving the way I did but I panicked."

"I guess I know the feeling," I admit, slowly turning back toward Kane. I couldn't help but wish he didn't look

70

so much like Kam, yet at the same time wishing he looked a little more like him.

"I *do* want to be your friend, Elara. You were the person my brother loved most in the world. I feel like I owe it to him to make sure you're taken care of. I just couldn't do that before now."

"I don't need someone to take care of me," I interject. "I just needed a friend."

"I know that. And I'm sorry I couldn't be that for you. But I can now. I came back for you."

"For me?" I question, confusion clear on my face.

"I regretted leaving the way I did the moment I left. But I had an assignment in L.A. and it gave me some much needed time to process a few things. It took me a while but I'm here now."

"Well, I'm sorry you wasted the trip back because I'm leaving. Like right now," I say, gesturing to the car sitting a couple of feet behind me.

I hate how dismissive I sound. I hate that I feel like I have to push away the only person that has been able to bring me even a semblance of peace since Kam died. But I hate how he left even more. No matter how irrational or unfair that may seem, I can't pretend like him leaving the way he did – when I needed him the most – didn't have some effect on me, because it did.

"Just like that?" he questions.

"Just like that," I confirm. "Look, we don't have to make that night more than it was. We were both sick with grief and for a brief moment we were able to give each other a little reprieve. That's all it was. We weren't friends when Kamden was alive and we don't have to be now. So whatever you're thinking – don't."

"Do you always do that?" A slow smile spreads across his face. It's the same smile Kam used to give me when I would nervously ramble.

"Do what?" I swallow hard.

"Assume you know exactly what someone else is thinking?"

"That's not what I'm doing," I object.

"Isn't it?" he questions. "Did you ever consider that maybe *I* like you, Elara? That maybe *I* enjoy being around you? That maybe that one night with you was the only time I've felt alive since Kam died?"

"But you left," I say, having trouble finding my words.

"And I told you why. I just needed some time."

"Well I'm sorry but now I need time," I say, my hands knotting together the way they always do when I'm anxious. "Because you're not the only one that felt a certain way that night. In a weird way being near you was like having a piece of Kamden back and that's not fair to you or to him."

"I'm not my brother."

"I know," I interrupt.

"Let me finish." He takes a step toward me. "I'm not my brother," he repeats. "But that doesn't mean *we* can't be friends."

"Why do you want to be my friend so badly?" I hate how the question sounds.

"Because you are the only person on this earth that understands what I've lost and maybe because I like how I feel when I'm around you."

"How do you feel?" I ask, nervous energy exploding in my stomach.

"Like I can breathe."

His admission leaves me feeling slightly weak in the knees and I immediately move to refocus.

"Kane."

"I know it's unfair of me to ask you but I'm going to anyway."

"I'm leaving," I interrupt before he can finish.

"Stay, Elara." He doesn't let me deter him.

"What?" I question.

72

"Stay," he repeats.

"I can't stay. I've already left. All of my things are in my car and my dad is expecting me first thing tomorrow."

"So call him. Tell him you've changed your mind."

"Why? So you can leave again in a couple of days? Why would I stay here for someone who isn't staying here themselves?"

"Then just stay today," he suggests, taking another step toward me, closing the gap between us. "You can leave tomorrow."

"I can't. I have to do this and I have to do it now. Otherwise I might never leave."

"Why do you want to leave so badly?"

"Because I feel like I'm suffocating here. Everywhere I look, everything I do, I see him everywhere. He's everywhere." I sigh, not able to hold my guard up any longer.

Like Kam, Kane seems to have a way of knowing how to push me just right to get me to open up. It's both unnerving and a little refreshing. It feels good sometimes to just say what I'm feeling. It's something I don't do often enough.

"Now you know why I left," he says after a long moment.

"Then don't ask me to stay."

"Come with me then."

"Come with you where?"

"Italy," he states like it's no big thing to invite someone to Italy. "Come with me," he repeats.

"To Italy?" I blurt, confusion clear in my voice.

"Why not? You said if given the chance it would be the one place you would choose to visit. Well here you go. I've got a contract that starts in Milan next week. It's a short three hour trip to Manarola, exactly the place you want to go."

I don't comment on how surprised I am that he remembered exactly where I wanted to visit and instead focus on the absurdity of his proposal.

"Do you hear yourself right now? You barely know me yet you want me to pick up and go to Italy with you?"

I'm convinced he's messing with me and yet the look on his face says he's completely serious.

"Best way to get to know a person." He shrugs like what he's asking isn't totally insane. "Besides, I'll be working a lot of the time so you'll be free to do whatever it is you want to do. Tell me this doesn't sound exactly like what you need."

"You must be out of your mind if you think I'd consider going to Italy with you."

"What are you afraid of, Elara?"

"I'm not afraid of anything."

"Doesn't seem that way to me. I'm offering you a chance to escape; the very thing you claim you want to do. Yet you're looking at me like I've suggested we run off and elope." He chuckles, clearly finding humor in my reaction.

"Okay, I'm done having this conversation." I shake my head, a trace of a smile on my lips.

"It's so easy to see why he loved you so much." His words catch me way off guard and it takes me several seconds to recover enough to actually say something.

"I should go," I blurt, heat flooding my cheeks.

"So you keep saying." He steps forward and reaches out his hand. "Give me your phone."

"Why?"

"Just give me your phone, Elara." He waits patiently as I reach into my back pocket and retrieve my phone, dropping it into his outstretched palm moments later.

"What are you doing?" I ask, watching him type something across the touch screen but not able to see what exactly he's typing.

"Programming my number into your phone," he says like it should be obvious. "That way if you change your mind, you can reach me." His phone sounds just seconds later. "And now I have your number as well." He grins, handing me my phone back.

"I'm not going to change my mind," I insist.

"Even if you don't..." he starts.

"I won't," I immediately interject.

"Even if you don't," he continues, "at least this way I have the means to call you."

"And you expect me to believe you're actually going to?" I give him an apprehensive look before shoving the device back into my pocket.

"Guess you'll have to wait and find out." He smiles innocently and I swear my heart picks up speed a little.

Get it together, Elara. I scold myself. It's hard not to get caught up in a man like Kane. I remember the first time I met him, how attractive I thought he was. Though his good looks were easier to ignore back then because I thought he was a conceited asshole. Now, well, now I know there's a lot more to Kane than I originally thought and when he looks at me the way he's looking at me right now it's nearly impossible to ignore the way my entire body reacts to him.

Trying to shake off the thought, I refocus.

"Guess so," I say, hesitating longer than I should. For some reason I'm suddenly not wanting to leave.

"Have a safe trip." He steps closer, pulling me against his hard chest before I have a second to react, his arms closing around me.

I find myself relaxing into his embrace almost immediately. A weird sense of belonging the most prominent thing I feel. Being in Kane's arms feels oddly familiar and yet entirely new at the same time.

I take a deep inhale, half expecting to smell the familiar scent of the ocean on his skin as I always did on Kam's. But instead my senses are overwhelmed by something completely different. Faint cologne mixed with what I can only assume is his laundry detergent. He smells incredible and yet I'm disappointed at the same time. Even still, I find myself holding onto his scent longer than I should.

I wish I could understand why Kane makes me feel so off balance but truth be told I have yet to really sort through why this man makes me feel the way he does. I don't think I've spent enough time with him to fully understand it.

At first I thought it was his connection to Kam. The similarities between the two of them and how much he reminds me of his younger brother. Now, I'm realizing that Kane has a hold of me all on his own that is completely separate from Kamden.

I figured it out the day I found out he left with how disappointed I felt. I blamed it on my grief over Kam but deep down even then I knew there was more to it. Not that I really understand what that more is, only that there definitely is more with Kane.

Finally managing to pull out of his embrace, I peer up at his face for a long moment, resisting the urge to reach up and touch him the way I always did with his brother.

"I'll see you around, Kane." I offer a small smile as I step back.

"Yeah, you will." He nods, his dark eyes not leaving mine.

"See ya." I spin around, not sure what else to say or do.

"Bye, Elara," Kane says before he turns and heads back through the cemetery toward Kam's grave.

I stand next to the car and watch him for a long moment wishing things were different. Wishing Kam was still here. Wishing leaving his brother wasn't proving to be so difficult that I have to physically force myself into the driver's seat, and even then it takes me a good five minutes to finally convince myself to pull away.

Leaving Kam is hard enough on its own. Leaving both Kamden and Kane, well that's proving to be harder than I ever imagined it would be.

Turns out Kam wasn't the only Thaler brother that knew how to get under my skin. I'm just not quite sure how I feel about that yet.

Chapter Seven
Elara

Kane: *Have you changed your mind yet?*

It's the same message I've gotten from Kane every single day since I arrived home three days ago. In fact, it's the only message I've gotten from him.

I stare at the screen of my phone for a long time, wondering if I *have* changed my mind. Am I actually considering this as a possibility? I mean, *Italy*. Never mind anything else. Wouldn't it be idiotic to turn something like this down?

I have the ability to go. I don't technically have a job yet and thanks to Kam I already have my passport and all the things required to travel outside of the country. We had been talking about going somewhere exotic to celebrate college graduation during the weeks leading up to the ceremony. Kam had his heart set on Mexico whereas I just wanted to be with him. It didn't matter where we ended up. And since that trip never happened, maybe this is my chance to get away…

Don't be stupid, Elara. I scold myself.

Yes, the offer is tempting. And I'd be lying if I said I haven't laid in bed imagining what a trip like that could be like the last couple of nights. To be able to just disappear for a while. Exist in a completely different place where there are no memories, no ghosts, no past following me around. A place where I can let all of that go and focus on me for a while.

I could go see where my family comes from. I could try new foods and sight see. I could meet new people and experience a different way of life.

Am I talking myself into this?

I wish I could say that going to Italy is the only thing weighing on my mind but that wouldn't be the truth. I've also thought about Kane, a lot. I've thought about what it would be like to go away with him. About what he's really like when he lets someone in. I've imagined us walking the streets of Italy, eating dinner together, stopping in little local shops so I can buy things for my Dad and Aunt Carol.

It's picture perfect and yet it just doesn't quite fit. Maybe it's because Kane isn't Kamden. Maybe it's because after everything I don't feel like I deserve something like this. Or maybe it's because deep down I know how insane it would be to pick up and fly half way across the world with a man I don't really know.

Then again, I've always been known to push the boundaries. Why stop now?

Remember what happened the last time you got a crazy idea, El. Kamden's voice is clear in my mind, almost like he's sitting right next to me… Like I need the reminder.

I shake off the thought, dropping my phone face down on the table in front of me.

"Everything okay?" my dad asks, pulling my attention to where he's sitting directly across from me, slicing his steak with a knife that appears to be too dull. "You were staring at your phone pretty intensely there." He points his fork in the direction of the device.

79

"Yeah, fine." I shrug, poking at my baked potato.

"You know, you're as bad of a liar as your mother was." He chuckles, waiting until I meet his gaze before continuing, "She could never make eye contact when she was lying. Gave her away every time. So tell me, peanut, what's on that phone that has you looking so conflicted."

"You'd think I was crazy if I told you."

"Try me." He smiles, the wrinkles around his deep brown eyes seeming to have multiplied overnight. Not that they haven't been there for a long time but I just now seem to be noticing how much my father has aged.

"Does it have to do with a boy?" he asks when I still haven't said anything. His inquiry makes me feel like I'm sixteen years old all over again.

"It's complicated," I admit, setting my fork next to my plate.

"A boy you like?" he pushes, giving me that knowing dad smirk.

"That's a hard question to answer," I admit. "It's not really like that."

"Then what's it like?"

"It's Kamden's older brother, Kane." I sigh. "He made me an offer and while I think it would be insane to accept it, I'm having a hard time justifying why I shouldn't. Does that make sense?"

"Depends on the offer." My dad gives me an encouraging smile.

"He asked me to go to Italy with him," I blurt, the statement sounding even more absurd out loud.

"Oh." He straightens his posture. "I didn't realize you two were that close."

"We're not. That's the problem."

"I'm confused." He scratches his chin like he's not really sure what to say.

"Trust me, so am I." I laugh, taking a drink of my tea before setting the glass back down.

"So a boy you don't know…"

"He's hardly a boy, Dad," I interrupt.

"Excuse me." He clears his throat. "So a *man* you don't really know has offered to take you to Italy and you're unsure of whether or not you should go?" he asks it like a question.

"Well it wouldn't be like you're thinking. I would simply go with him but I wouldn't necessarily be there with him. If that makes sense."

"I really should be better at speaking female at this point but, honey, I really have no idea what that means." He chuckles.

"He's going there for business. I would be tagging along and get to do my own thing while we're there. He will be working and I will be doing, well whatever I want to do. And before you say it again, no, I don't know him well. But I do know him well enough to know I'd be safe with him."

"How long would you be gone?" he asks, catching me a bit off guard. I expected him to slam his fist down on the table and forbid me from going anywhere, not that that's my dad's style.

He's always been the rational, laid back one. It was my mom that was the unpredictable spit fire. Wonder where I get it from…

"I'm not really sure. I didn't really ask any details," I answer. "I shot him down pretty quickly and up until now haven't really entertained the idea as a real possibility."

"Then what's changed?"

"I'm not sure," I admit.

"Maybe getting away wouldn't be such a bad thing." My dad gives me a soft smile. "You've been through a lot, Elara. Maybe some time away will be exactly what you need."

"What I need is to get a job and start living my life as an adult."

"You don't need to start living your life, Elara, you're already living it. And if you're not careful it will pass you right on by. Trust me, I know. Opportunities like this don't come around every day. If you like this man and you trust him, then I say go for it."

"Seriously?" I look at my father like he's sprouted five more heads.

"Seriously." He drops his napkin on the table and stands. "Stay here for a second," he says moments before disappearing from the dining room.

I'm still trying to process his words when he reappears holding a huge photo album. Crossing around the table, he takes a seat next to me, sliding my plate out of the way as he opens the album between us.

"What's this?" I ask, leaning over to look at the multiple pictures that line the page in front of me.

"This is the trip your mother and I took to Italy three months after we met." He smiles, running his finger across a picture of him and my mother standing on a hill, backed by the bluest water I think I've ever seen.

"Wait, I thought you went to Italy on your honeymoon."

"We did. We also went when we first started dating," he says, his gaze locked on a very young looking version of my mother.

She looks so happy. So beautiful. So free.

"She thought I was crazy when I asked her too."

"But you guys were a couple. This is completely different. I hardly know Kane."

"Dating worked a little different back then. In reality, your mother and I didn't really know each other all that well either. Your grandfather was very strict and even though your mother was eighteen when we met, the first few weeks of our relationship was spent under his watchful eye. I think maybe that's why I came up with the idea to get away in the first place. My grandparents still had property there so I only had to rustle up enough money for two plane tickets and for us to eat for a few days." He smiles, losing himself to the memory.

"Your mother thought I had lost my marbles. She flat out refused to go with me. But, after a couple of days I was able to convince her."

"How'd you do that?"

"I told her I loved her."

"And she just couldn't resist." I smile, loving listening to my dad talk about my mom, a woman he loved more than anything on the face of this earth.

"No one can resist the Menten charm, peanut." He winks, turning his gaze back down to the photo album. "I know the circumstances are different but those two weeks in Italy were some of the best your mother had. This isn't about anything but you. Honey, if you're given the opportunity to do something like this, you have to take it. Otherwise you'll end up regretting all the things you never did. Wouldn't you rather know?"

"You make it all sound so easy."

"Take it from an old man, some things really are that easy. We just tend to overcomplicate everything."

"You're hardly old, Dad." I knock my shoulder against his, earning me a wide smile. "Look, hardly any gray." I point to his thick head of dark hair teasingly.

"You are so your mother's daughter." He chuckles before falling serious again. "You've been through a lot recently, El. And in reality, so has Kane. You lost your best friend but he lost his brother. Maybe this will be somewhat of a healing experience for both of you."

"But I just got home. What about the job at the newspaper? I'm supposed to be an adult now. You know; job, house, all the things adults are supposed to have."

"You've got your whole life to be an adult, Elara. All of those things will be here when you get back."

"You really think I should do this?" I can't believe the turn this conversation has taken. Here I expected my father to talk me out of even considering it. Instead he's practically pushing me into it face first.

"I do." He stands, sliding the photo album directly in front of me. "If you don't believe me, ask your mother," he says, gesturing to a picture of her smiling on the steps leading up to a tall, mustard yellow house.

Leaning over he lays a soft kiss to my head before grabbing our plates and disappearing into the kitchen.

I spend the next several minutes looking through the contents of a photo album I didn't even know existed. There are tons of pictures of my mom. In each one she's smiling, the action so easy and natural that her happiness radiates from all around her.

I always thought my mom was beautiful; tall and thin with long blonde hair and blue eyes that matched the sky, but seeing her like this, as a woman and not just my mother, I'm starting to see her in an entirely different light.

I imagine what it would be like to see all the places she saw, touch the things she touched, and stand in the very place she stood all those years ago. And the more I think about it the more my answer becomes clearer.

Without putting anymore thought into it, I pick up my phone and unlock it, Kane's message still pulled up on the screen. I type out a quick response, my thumb hovering over the send button for several long moments.

Do I or don't I? Am I really going to go to Italy? And if so do I really want to go with Kane? I could always book my own trip – though lord knows I certainly can't afford something like that right now. Who knows if I ever will be able to.

My dad's right. I get one chance. I've never been afraid to take a chance before and I'm certainly not going to start now. I need to feel like Elara again instead of this hollow skin I've been walking around in since losing Kam. And that means I need to *act* like Elara again.

I pull in a deep breath and push send, watching my own message appear on the screen below Kane's just seconds later.

Me: I'm in.

His response comes almost instantly.

Kane: Are you messing with me?

Me: I said I'm in, didn't I? Unless you've changed your mind.

My stomach swirls with doubt. Maybe this wasn't such a good idea. Maybe he really did ask me never expecting I'd say yes.

Kane: Not a chance.

His response calms the nervous energy buzzing through me slightly but it's not enough to get rid of it completely.

Me: How long will we be gone?

Kane: About four weeks. Give or take a few days.

Me: Four weeks?

Holy shit. Four weeks in Italy with Kane Thaler? What the hell did I just agree to?

Kane: You can't back out now. I've already bought your ticket.

Me: That quickly?

Kane: I purchased it two days ago.

Me: Why would you do that?

Kane: Because I knew you'd come.

Me: There's no way you could have known that.

Kane: Okay, so maybe I just hoped you would.

Me: I can't believe I just agreed to this.

I take a deep breath, typing out another quick message before he can respond.

Me: When do we leave?

Kane: Sunday night. I'll meet you at Arkansas International Airport on Saturday and we can catch a flight back to Chicago from there. We'll leave for Italy from Chicago on Sunday.

Me: We're going to Chicago first?

Kane: *I kind of need to pack.*
Me: *Oh yeah, right, of course. Tell me what time and I can book my plane ticket to Chicago.*
Kane: *Already done.*
Me: *What? How?*
Kane: *I'm all over this. Flight leaves for Chicago Saturday at eleven a.m. which is about an hour after my flight is scheduled to land in Arkansas so we should be good.*

Dear lord this man wastes no time. Which is the exact opposite of Kam who was so laid back at times. In those moments, getting him to do anything was like pulling teeth. I honestly loved that about him though, except when we were trying to plan anything. Hence why our trip we were trying to plan still hadn't happened a month after graduation.

And then the accident happened…

I push the thought away, not willing to let myself go there right now.

Me: *You have to let me pay for myself.*

Even though I know I don't have the money to pay for everything, I'd feel better if he at least let me pay for my own plane tickets.

Kane: *You're my guest. And before you object again, know that ninety-five percent of this trip will be covered by my contract.*

I think over that for a moment, not sure if that's actually the truth or if he's only saying that so I don't fight him on it. Kam used to always pull the same crap with me. Sometimes it's hard to separate the two in my mind.

Me: *That depends. Is it the truth?*
Kane: *One thing I will never do is lie to you, Elara.*

I stare at that message for several beats, somehow able to envision him saying those words to me. How his dark eyes would narrow in on my face as if I've seen him do it a million times before even though I haven't.

Is it weird that I feel like I know Kane a lot more than I should? Or am I just too busy comparing him to Kamden to see I don't actually know him at all?

The thought is more than a little unnerving.

Me: Good.

I finally type a response, not sure what else to say.

Kane*: I will see you Saturday, Elara.*

Me*: Sounds good. See you Saturday.*

Setting the phone back down on the table, I let out a nervous laugh, not able to wrap my head around what I just did. And even though every part of me is filled with uncertainty, I also can't bring myself to regret it.

Because no matter what happens tomorrow or the day after or the day after that, I never want to look back at my life and feel like I didn't live it to the absolute fullest. I feel like I owe it to Kamden to do something with the time I've been given that he was robbed of.

At the end of the day we never know which moment will be our last. Nothing is guaranteed – especially not tomorrow. Kam's death taught me that above all else.

Chapter Eight
Kane

"Hi, honey. Dad's here if you're ready to eat." My mom peeks her head into my childhood bedroom where I'm lounging on the bed with my laptop resting across my legs.

"Yeah, give me a couple minutes and I'll be down." She nods, giving me a soft smile before disappearing into the hallway.

I hate being home.

Don't get me wrong, I love my parents more than anything but it's so fucking depressing in this house. My poor mother is running on fumes. She barely eats or sleeps and I've caught her crying at least a handful of times in the couple of days since I arrived home to visit. I can't imagine what it must be like for her or my father; losing a child. Sometimes I feel like they wished it was me that had died instead of Kamden. He was the glue, the life, the goofy one that made everyone laugh at the dinner table with his ridiculous jokes and contagious smile. Now it feels empty and quiet and no matter how hard I try, I can't make it better.

Because I'm not my brother.

Elara's face flashes through my mind at the thought and instantly a sick feeling settles into the pit of my stomach.

I've thought about her way too much over the past few weeks.

After the night of the funeral I woke up in an absolute panic. I don't know what caused it or why, but I knew if I didn't get out of here that instant I was going to cave under the weight steadily building in my chest.

I thought maybe once I put some distance between me and this place, between me and Elara, that I would be able to breathe again. I was wrong. It only got worse the more days that passed until I knew I had to see her again.

As soon as I got back into town I went to see Kam, desperate to talk it out. But there she was, just like that day on the beach. It's like something beyond either of our control is pushing us together. Or someone…

I've never been so consumed by a woman before, but I'm having trouble separating if it's her or if it's her connection to my brother that is driving those feelings. And I desperately need to figure that out. Because I feel like I'm all twisted up over her and I have no fucking clue why. I don't even know her.

And it's not like I'm one to shy away from women. If I want something, I go for it. That simple. But with Elara it's different. She's not just any other girl. She's Kamden's girl. And even though he's gone that still means something to me.

I do find some comfort in the fact that the two were never actually together. My attraction to her feels like less of a betrayal somehow. But I still have this nagging guilt that keeps me up at night. Haunted by the voice in my head that tells me I'm only going to make this worse.

Watching her at the funeral was like watching a beautiful tragedy play out in front of my eyes. I was riveted.

Absolutely consumed. I couldn't keep my eyes off of her for more than a few seconds at a time.

It was simply by chance that I ran into her at the beach that day. I went there in an effort to feel closer to my brother. What I found was so much more than that.

There's something about Elara that lights me on fire. I knew it from the very first moment I laid eyes on her that she was something special. But now it goes beyond the physical attraction to a much deeper place – a place that desperately longs to connect to anything.

I guess that's why I invited her to Italy the way I did. I hadn't even nailed down the contract, yet there I was insisting she come with me. And even though she flat out refused, a part of me knew she'd change her mind.

Maybe it's because I feel like I know her, given how much Kam talked about her, or maybe it's because I know, like me, she's desperate for anything to make her feel less of what she's currently feeling. I also think she's just as curious about me as I am about her. It makes sense I guess. The two people who were closest to Kam. We're bound to have some type of connection. Only this isn't just about Kam. At least not for me anyway.

Again, I wanted her the first time I saw her. If not for Kam I would have made a move on her the night of his graduation party. If for no other reason but to have her in my bed. But because I love my brother and he loved her, I backed off.

But everything has changed since then. I'm not even sure I'm the same person as I was back then. So much has happened over the past four years. So much that has changed and shaped the person I am now – recent events included.

When Elara finally text me back last night agreeing to go to Italy with me, part of me was struck with disbelief while the other part of me knew all along she would come. I bought my ticket to Arkansas and both of our tickets to Chicago so fast it's a wonder I didn't end up screwing it up. I knew I needed to do it right then and there, that way she'd be less inclined to back out on me.

I already had the two tickets to Italy. Once the contract was signed and official, I requested two because somewhere deep inside I knew she would come with me. Maybe it was wishful thinking but whatever it was clearly worked.

She has no idea that we will be staying in a little one room flat together, otherwise I may not have gotten her to agree. I'll let that be a surprise once we get there. At that point she'll have no choice but to deal with it.

I close my laptop and lean my head back against the headboard; my eyes falling closed for a brief moment as I take a deep breath in before letting it out just as slowly.

The thought of spending the next four weeks in Italy with Elara has me twisted up like a fucking teenager. I swear I haven't been this anxious or excited about anything pertaining to a girl since I lost my virginity to Rachel Balanie when I was fifteen.

"Kane," my father's voice calls up the stairs, instantly breaking me from my daze.

"Yeah, I'm coming," I holler back, realizing several minutes have passed since my mother had come up to tell me dinner was ready.

****

"So, Kane, I was thinking," my father says between bites of my mother's famous pot roast. "We should take the old boat out this weekend. Maybe get a little fishing in while you're home."

I instantly feel bad knowing I can't.

"I wish I could, Dad, but I'm actually leaving Saturday."

"So soon?" my mom questions, disappointment clear on her face.

"I know. I'm sorry. I got signed for a big contract with an Italian eyewear company that I couldn't pass up. I fly out of Chicago on Sunday so I'll need to give myself time to get home and pack."

"Where are you off to this time?" my dad asks, having always been interested in my line of work.

I wait until I've swallowed the bite in my mouth before speaking. "Italy."

"Right. You said Italian company. I should have guessed." My father shakes his head.

"Well, as you know, where I end up isn't always where the company is based out of so it's a valid question."

"How long will you be gone for this time?" my mother asks, hitting me with a look that makes me feel like the lowest piece of shit on Earth for not being home more.

"About a month," I say, shoveling some potatoes in my mouth in an effort to not have to say more.

"That long?"

"It's not that long, Mary," my dad chimes in, clearly sensing my need of rescuing. To this day my dad is still the only person that can reel my mom in and he can do so without even batting an eye.

"I guess you're right." She smiles softly, shuffling carrots around her plate with her fork. "Oh, I completely forgot to tell you that Elara came by the other morning." The mere mention of her name has my stomach swirling once again. *Fuck, what is it about this girl?*

"She did?" my father questions.

"Three days ago. I can't believe I forgot to tell you." She shakes her head. "I swear my memory is not what it used to be."

"I hadn't seen her at Carol's. Figured I had missed her." My father's expression softens slightly.

"You did. She came over to say goodbye but you had gone into the office that morning. I still can't believe I forgot to tell you." She pauses before adding, "I really hate that she felt like she had to leave."

"I think it's good that she went home. You know how close those two were. There was hardly a place Kamden would go that Elara wasn't right there with him. And then the accident," my father trails off. "I'm sure being here wasn't easy for her."

"I suppose your right. I'm sure gonna miss her though." My mom blinks back tears that well behind her eyes, not a single one falling.

"Me too. I got used to having her around all the time," my father agrees. "I'm sure she'll come visit."

"I hope so. Though a part of me is almost relieved that she's gone," my mother admits quietly, surprising both me and my father. "I guess it was difficult for me. Seeing her all the time knowing my sweet boy didn't walk away from the accident but she did."

"Mom!" I interject, appalled by the words that just left her mouth.

My mom is the sweetest person I know. She loves every single person that comes into our lives and does so with her whole heart. Not because she has to but because she wants to. I don't think I've ever heard her say anything about another person even remotely close to what she just said.

"I'm happy she's alive, of course I am. That's not what I meant. I just, it's just hard for me sometimes." She blows out a breath.

"Elara loved Kam just as much as we all did. How do you think she feels knowing she lived and he didn't?" I question, dropping my fork on the plate, my appetite long since passed.

"Honestly, I can't imagine what that must be like for her," she admits.

"None of us can. We can't even fathom what it would be like to be in her shoes," I grind out, more irritated than I should be given that my mom's comment was not meant to be a dig at Elara. She was simply voicing what any parent would probably feel only weeks after losing a child.

"I know that. Of course I do. I didn't mean it the way it sounded." She seems genuinely sorry about what she said which in turn makes me feel even worse.

"We know you didn't, dear." My dad reaches across the table and rests his hand on top of hers. "We're all a bit on edge. A lot has happened."

"I asked Elara to come to Italy with me." The statement is past my lips before I can completely think it through and in that instant the entire dynamic of the room changes.

"What?" My mom looks at me wide eyed with confusion. "I didn't realize you two knew each other. Why would she be going to Italy with you?"

"Because I asked her to," I state matter of fact. I had planned to tell my parents this regardless but I think maybe my timing could have been a little better.

"And no, we don't know each other that well," I continue. "But I spent a little time with her after the funeral where she told me Italy was somewhere she always wanted to go. Then I saw her again on Saturday as she was leaving town, right after I found out I could possibly be going to Italy. She was at Kam's grave and she seemed so sad. I didn't really even mean to ask her, it just kind of fell out of my mouth."

"And she said yes?" my mother questions.

"Not at first," I admit.

"I don't understand why it even crossed your mind to ask her."

"Elara was the most important person to Kam. I feel like I owe it to him to make sure she's okay. And right now I don't think she is. I think I can help her. And honestly, I think she can help me too."

"Well I think it's fantastic," my dad weighs in. "Elara is like family. It makes me feel better knowing you two will be looking out for each other."

"Thanks, Dad. I appreciate that," I say. Turning back toward my mom, I continue, "It's not what you're thinking, Mom." I feel the need to reassure her even though I know the statement is only partially true. "I just wanted to do something nice for the girl my brother loved."

"It makes sense," she admits. "And your father's right. Knowing the two of you will be looking out for one another does make me feel a little better. Just be careful, Kane. Elara is in a very confusing place right now. I'd hate for you to get hurt."

"I'm not going to get hurt, Mom. We're just friends."

"Things can change rapidly when emotions are running high. You've got a good head on your shoulders, honey. You always have. But sometimes you get a little blinded by the opposite sex." A smile plays on her mouth for the first time all evening.

"That's the Thaler in him." My father laughs.

"You two are too much sometimes." I smile, not able to help myself.

"Just be careful, honey." My mom falls serious once more. "That's all I'm asking."

"I will." I nod only once before standing and excusing myself.

My mother's warning is still ringing in my ears several hours later as I lay in bed tossing and turning, unable to shake the feeling that maybe she's right. Maybe I'm setting myself up to be hurt. Or maybe, and more likely, I'm setting Elara up to be hurt.

"You'd never hurt her." Kam's voice is so clear I would almost swear he was in the room.

"But what if I do?" I voice aloud.

"You won't."

"I might."

"You won't," he insists.

"How can you be so sure?"

"Because you know how much I loved her."

Chapter Nine
Elara

"Can you turn around?" I ask my dad as the airport comes into view, a sudden panic gripping at my chest so tightly I feel like I'm moments away from hyperventilating.

"Turn around?" My father seems confused, glancing to where I'm sitting next to him in the passenger seat of his SUV.

"I can't do this," I mutter under my breath. "I can't do this," I repeat a little louder. "I can't fly half way across the world with someone I don't even know. Why did I think I could do this?"

"Relax, sweetheart. You're just nervous. It's completely understandable."

"This is insane. Why don't you think this is insane?"

"It's not insanity, Elara. It's adventure. It's living." He gives me an amused smile, his eyes meeting mine for the briefest moment before finding the road again. "Besides, you're my daughter. I know you. You're more like me than I think you realize."

"Mom always said I got my fearlessness from you. Though right now I don't feel very fearless." I blow out a breath.

"Did she ever tell you about the time I jumped off the hotel balcony into the pool?"

"Only like a hundred times." I smile, my panic receding a bit. "She wanted to make me understand why it was careless and dangerous to do such things but I think it only succeeded in making me want to do them more," I admit.

"God she used to hate how much of a risk taker I was. Made her a nervous wreck."

"And now look at you; you've gone soft," I tease.

"I've gotten old," he counters. "My body can't do the things it used to do. If I tried jumping two stories into a pool now I'd likely break a lot more than just my arm." My dad turns into the drop off lane at the airport entrance and slows the SUV to a stop.

I knot my hands nervously in my lap.

"You've got this, El. You know as well as I do that you will never forgive yourself if you let your nerves keep you from taking this chance. Life is all about chances, Elara. Chances, choices, memories. These are all the things we get. Don't be afraid to dive in head first."

"Taking chances is what got me in this mess to begin with," I remind him. "It's why Kam isn't here."

"That's not true and you know it. What happened to Kamden was a horrible accident. You can't live your life carrying the responsibility of that weight." He reaches across the middle console and squeezes my hand. "The guilt never goes away." His statement pulls my gaze to his. "That they died and we lived," he clarifies. "But just because someone dies, Elara, doesn't mean you stop living. Kamden would want you to live each day to the fullest, just as your mother would want that from me."

I think on that for a long moment, realizing he's right. Kamden would want me to go. My mother would want me to go.

"You're right," I finally say, forcing a smile to my face. "I should probably head in or I'm going to miss my flight and then none of this will matter anyway." I let out another breath before pushing open the door, the late August heat hitting me like a wave the second I climb out of the SUV.

My dad crosses around the back of the vehicle, retrieving my suitcase from the hatch before joining me on the curb.

Even though I'm sure I didn't pack nearly enough for a four week trip, I hated the idea of having to worry about multiple pieces of luggage along the way. I have enough to make do, assuming that washing machines exist in Italy.

After doing some research I learned that Milan is in its peak summer season right now with temperatures right in the nineties, so most of my clothing is light and doesn't take up a lot of room in my suitcase – so that helped too.

"Call me as soon as you land in Chicago." My father waits until I've nodded before continuing, "And make sure to text me when you're boarding your plane for Italy and then again as soon as you've landed."

"I will," I promise, realizing how nervous my dad seems. "I'm going to be fine," I reassure him, figuring I owe him one after all the reassurance he's offered me over the last couple of days.

"I know you are." He smiles, pulling me into a tight hug. "I love you, Elara."

"I love you too, Dad." I pull back, looking up to meet his gaze. "You take care of yourself," I say, wrapping my hand around the handle of my suitcase.

"Always."

"Bye, Dad."

"Bye, sweetheart." He offers me one more encouraging smile before I turn around and disappear inside the airport.

I take another deep breath and let it out slowly as I look around the space, trying to figure out exactly where I'm supposed to go. I've only been inside an airport once before and that was when I was maybe ten or eleven and had come with my mom to pick up Aunt Carol who had flown in for Christmas.

My mom wasn't much of a flier, and while she had done it a few times when she was younger, she had only flown once that I know of after I was born. So to say this is new territory for me would be a very accurate statement.

I walk around aimlessly for a couple of minutes, not really sure where to go or where exactly I'm supposed to be meeting Kane. He said he would text me where to meet him once he landed but I have yet to hear anything from him.

Spotting a small bar to my left, I decide that a drink wouldn't hurt and quickly cross the aisle to where it sits, accompanied by a handful of round top tables. Sliding into one of the stools at the bar, I order a whiskey from the middle aged bartender, drinking it down the instant he sets it in front of me, just needing something to take the edge off.

"I'll take one more," I advise him. My phone buzzes to life on the bar top seconds after he turns to refill the rocks glass in front of me.

My stomach twists when I see Kane's name flashing across the screen and even though I know I have to answer it, it still takes me a solid five seconds before I finally do.

"Hello." My voice is hoarse from the burn of the whiskey.

"Hey. I just landed. Are you here?" He seems anxious which oddly puts me more at ease. At lcast I'm not alone.

"Yeah. I'm at the bar around the corner from the drop off entrance."

"Perfect. I don't think I'm very far from there now. I'll meet you shortly."

"Okay," I say, ending the call without saying more.

The bartender has finished refilling my drink by the time I remember why I'm here and I instantly snatch up the glass and pour the amber liquid into my mouth. The burn isn't as intense as the first round but it still has quite a bit of a bite.

I feel the heat as it hits my stomach but I don't have much time to think about it before my focus is pulled in an entirely different direction.

"Is this seat taken?" His voice causes my skin to prickle and the little hairs on the back of my neck to stand straight up.

I close my eyes, draw in a breath, before finally turning to meet his gaze. The second I do I'm rendered damn near speechless. *Was he always so attractive?* is the first thought that crosses my mind as I take in his disheveled brown hair and two day old scruff that lines his jaw.

Holy hell.

"Starting early, are we?" He smiles, gesturing to my empty glass when I have still yet to speak even one word.

"I- uh…" I stutter, before finally snapping out of my fog. "I'm a little nervous about the flight. Thought this might take the edge off."

"I always have a drink or two before I fly." He nods to the bartender, pointing to my glass. "She'll have another and I'll have whatever she's having."

"I really shouldn't." I push my glass to the edge of the bar. "I want to be able to walk onto the plane myself."

"I'm sure one more wouldn't prevent you from doing that." He smirks, thanking the bartender who sets a whiskey in front of him before using the bottle to refill my glass.

Kane waits until he's moved on to another customer before speaking again.

"What should we drink to?" he asks, holding up his glass as he angles his body toward mine.

101

"Not sure." I hate how stupid I sound but lord help me this man has me feeling all sorts of jittery and nervous.

"How about to Italy?" he suggests.

"How about to not dying in a horrific plane crash," I counter.

"Yeah, that'll work too." He chuckles, raising his glass.

Without a word I lift my glass and lightly tap it against his.

I watch as he brings the glass to his lips, tipping it back, his Adam's apple bobbing as he swallows down the whiskey. I'm completely transfixed by the sight, still gawking at him when he sets the glass back on the bar and eyeballs the drink still in my hand.

"Are you going to drink that?" He grins, eyes going to the glass and then back to my face.

I smile like I'm not completely losing my mind before tipping the glass back, the third shot warming me even more than the first two.

"Better?" he asks, taking the empty glass from my hand and sliding it to the edge of the bar.

"Much actually," I admit. A slight buzz runs through my veins as I finally feel the effects of the first couple of drinks.

"Good." He smiles and for the first time I realize just how different his smile is than Kam's.

Don't get me wrong, they look very similar, but when I'm not so focused on Kamden, I can see that they don't look nearly as much alike as I had originally thought they did. And oddly enough that doesn't disappoint me like I thought it would.

"We should probably get going. Getting through security can be pretty time consuming sometimes," he suggests, standing.

"Okay." I nod. Sliding off my stool, I grab the handle of my suitcase, dragging it behind me as I follow Kane out of the bar and through the airport.

I've heard horror stories about getting through airport security but surprisingly me and Kane pass through without an issue and reach our terminal in less than thirty minutes.

By the time we board the plane a few minutes later, I'm feeling much more relaxed, thanks in a large part to the whiskey, but also thanks to Kane. For being a little intimidating, he really is pretty easy to talk to once you let your guard down a little.

Kane leads us to our seats, which thankfully are next to each other, and insists that I take the window seat. As much as I appreciate the gesture, I almost think I'd rather sit toward the middle of the plane but, of course, I'm not going to tell him that.

I look out the window nervously as several other passengers file on board. The closer we get to taking off the more anxious I become.

"You okay?" Kane asks, pulling my attention from the window to his face.

"Yeah, fine." I force a smile.

"You sure?" He gives me a lopsided grin. "Because you kind of look like you're about to vomit all over the seat in front of you."

"I'm not going to vomit." I shake my head, wondering for a brief moment if maybe I am going to be sick.

"Seriously, Elara. You look terrified." He reaches into my lap and takes my hand, causing my heart to race even faster than it already was.

"I didn't think being on a plane would be so scary," I admit.

"Wait. You've never flown before?"

"No." I shake my head back and forth.

"How is that possible?" he questions. "I would think a little daredevil such as yourself would love flying."

"I am not a daredevil," I interject. "Yes, I love the rush of doing something exciting… living on the edge if you will. But I am always, always, in control and that's the big difference here."

"So you're a control freak."

"I wouldn't say I'm a freak. Just that I like to be in control of my own body. In here, I'm at the mercy of the pilot and the plane. Two things that I have zero control over. I don't like feeling like I'm powerless."

"I guess I get that." He squeezes his fingers around mine, his thumb tracing slow circles across the back of my hand.

What is it about him touching me that makes me feel so…fluttery? That's not even a word and yet it's the only thing I can think that describes the way I feel right now.

"I just can't believe you agreed to this trip having never been on a plane."

"No time like the present I guess." I shrug, a small smile pulling up the corner of my mouth.

"Well I've flown hundreds of times and I can assure you that you're perfectly safe," he says, finally releasing my hand as he sits back in his seat.

"So we will be in Chicago until tomorrow?" I clear my throat and straighten my posture, praying he doesn't see the glimpse of disappointment that I'm sure flashes across my face at the loss of contact.

"Yes." He swallows and the action draws my eyes to his throat.

Without even realizing what I'm doing, my gaze slowly descends past the v-neck of his white t-shirt to the cut of his broad chest, the definition of his muscle clearly visible through the light, thin fabric. I have to physically fight the urge to reach out and touch him.

Finally snapping out of my fog, I turn my gaze upward to find him watching me intently. Heat immediately rushes to my cheeks and I quickly look away, knotting my hands back into my lap.

God, I can't even sit next to him without getting all squeamish. How the hell am I going to last a month in Italy with him?

Before the thought has time to fester, the captain's voice comes across the intercom announcing that we are about to take off. In an instant, every other thought comes to a screeching halt. The earlier tension and anxiety I felt returns with full force as I grip both of the arm rests.

"Hey." Kane's voice is soft, pulling my gaze to his. "Deep breaths." He coaches me as the plane starts to move – taking a deep breath in and then waiting until I do the same before slowly letting it out.

I follow his lead, pulling in air when he does and then releasing it at the same time.

Just as I feel myself beginning to relax, the plane starts to lift and in that instant my stomach feels like it turns completely upside down. Pushing my head back against the seat, I turn to watch the ground disappear below us from my view out of the window.

I don't even realize I've grabbed Kane's hand until I'm squeezing it so hard my own begins to throb.

"I'm sorry." I finally let go as the plane levels out and I no longer feel like I'm seconds away from dying.

"It's okay." He offers me a reassuring smile. "You should have seen Kamden the first time he flew."

At the mention of his brother's name the nauseous feeling from earlier returns. It's not that I don't want to talk about Kam, of course I do, but there's so much guilt that comes along with every conversation we have about him.

"Oh yeah?" I push past the knot in my throat and force a smile.

"He threw up before we even made it down the runway." He chuckles, losing himself to the memory.

"He didn't?" I find myself suppressing my own laughter, somehow not all that surprised by what he's telling me.

"Oh he did." He nods. "All over my mom's shoes."

"Oh god."

"It was pretty funny."

"How old was he?"

"Eight or nine maybe."

"Poor kid." I try to imagine Kam at that age but for whatever reason I can't seem to picture it and the thought bothers me more than I expect it to.

"He got over it. He never really took to flying but he wasn't scared after that. I think it was the unknown that got to him."

"I can understand that."

"Can you?" He studies me for a long moment before finishing his thought. "Because I have a hard time picturing the girl who dove off *Viper's Cliff* being anything but intrigued by the unknown."

"God, did Kam tell you all the stupid stuff I did?"

"Pretty much." He smiles.

"Well, I'm not that girl anymore." I shake my head, my eyes going back to look out the window.

"That's a shame," he says after a long moment. "I think I would have liked that girl."

"You wouldn't have. She caused more problems than she was worth."

"My brother didn't seem to think so."

"Yeah, and look where he is now," I snip. In an instant the realization of what I said hit me like a ton of bricks. "I'm so sorry." I turn to meet Kane's dark gaze. "I don't know why I said that."

"It's okay, Elara. You're allowed to be angry." His understanding and patience is both reassuring and frustrating.

I don't want him to be understanding with me. I want him to lash out. Tell me how everything is my fault. Blame me the way I know he should.

"Do you ever talk to him?" He rests his head back against the seat, his eyes never leaving mine.

"All the time," I admit.

"Me too." He smiles to himself.

"What do you talk about?" I mirror his actions, resting my head against the seat, turning toward him.

"Now that I can't tell you."

"Why? Because you're talking about me?" I tease.

"Maybe," he admits, not an ounce of humor on his face.

The flutter hits me hard and it's a wonder that I don't melt into a puddle on the floor right here and now.

"What do you talk about?" He quirks a brow. "Me?"

"Maybe." I play coy, offering him only a smile before turning my gaze back out the window.

Chapter Ten
Elara

The flight to Chicago is quick. We're only in the air a little over an hour before we are landing. I didn't expect it to be quite so smooth but with the easy small talk stretching between Kane and I paired with the effects of the whiskey, which have since passed, it was a very enjoyable experience.

"First time in Chicago?" Kane asks as we sit in the backseat of an Uber, weaving in and out of downtown traffic.

"It is," I say, keeping my eyes out the window as I try to take it all in. I've never been to a city this big before. "It's a lot," I admit.

"Yeah, certainly isn't what you're used to."

"It's beautiful," I acknowledge. "But I still think I'd choose the beach."

"You and me both."

"Then why do you live here?" I ask curiously, turning toward him. "You said you're barely ever home anyway.

Couldn't you get a place on the beach and stay there when you're not travelling."

"I could I guess." He thinks on that for a moment. "But city life is easier, more convenient for work. It gives me more networking capabilities."

"I think if I had the opportunity to do what I love and still live where I love, I'd make it work regardless."

"Yeah, well." He shrugs, falling silent for a long moment. "I love North Carolina. But for the longest time I didn't feel like I really belonged there. Hell, I'm still not sure if I do." His gaze goes toward the window so I'm unable to read his expression. "I think that's probably the biggest reason I stayed in the city after graduation. This place feels more home than Baybridge ever did."

"See, that's the way I felt about Baybridge. It always felt more like home to me than Arkansas. Especially after my mom died."

"I'm sorry you had to go through that." He turns back toward me. "Losing your mom," he continues. "I can't imagine how hard that must have been for you."

"It was rough," I agree. "But I had Kam who refused to let me wallow in my loss. I still miss her every day but in some strange way I feel like she's been beside me since the moment she left. I'm sure that probably sounds crazy."

"Not at all. I feel the same way about my brother."

I have to resist the urge to reach across the middle of the seat and take his hand. I'm not sure if it's because I sense he needs that reassurance or if it's because I do. Either way I decide against it. Touching Kane does weird things to me and right now I'm attempting to keep a clear head.

I'm still trying to figure out how to respond to his comment when the driver slows to a stop outside of a building that has to be at least twenty stories tall.

"Ready?" Kane asks as he pays the driver.

"Yep." I quickly climb out of the back of the car, crossing around to the trunk to retrieve my suitcase. Kane joins me at the back of the car, grabbing his own luggage before leading me toward the front door of the building.

After crossing through a small lobby that reminds me more of a hotel than an apartment building, Kane leads me to the elevators that sit just off the right down a wide hallway.

For having such easy conversation on the plane and car ride over, you would think things wouldn't feel quite so tense when the elevator doors close behind us. But tense is the only way to describe how I feel at this very moment.

I swear I hold my breath the entire sixteen story ride up.

"How long has it been since you've been home?" I ask, feeling like I need to say something as I exit the elevator and follow Kane to the end of the hallway. I wait behind him as he fishes out his keys and unlocks the door.

"I flew directly to my parents' from L.A. so I guess it's been a while." Pushing the door open, he waits until I've stepped inside before following me in, locking the door behind him.

"It's not a ton of space but it suits my needs just fine," he says as I look around the gorgeous apartment.

I don't know what I expected but I can tell you that this was not it. I think I was imagining something more dark and brooding – like Kane himself – but this is anything but.

The entire room is light and airy with off white walls and light blues and grays accenting the open space. There's a decent size kitchen on the far right of the room with gray countertops and white cabinets. The kitchen flows directly into a small dining space that houses a round glass top four person table with a French door directly next to it that opens up into what appears to be a small balcony.

The room bends in an L-shape. The living room sitting in the far left curve, decorated in theme with the rest of the apartment. There's a two piece gray couch and loveseat in the center of the room accented with blue pillows, a large fireplace along the back wall with a television mounted above it, and another French door that opens up to the outside making me realize that the balcony is much bigger than I had originally thought.

Kane gives me a tour, taking me down a small hallway where the guest bedroom and bath are housed. After depositing my suitcase on the queen bed and taking a quick look at the space I'll be staying in for the night, I follow Kane next door into the master suite.

Stepping into Kane's bedroom feels oddly personal. While every part of me wants to stand here and study every detail of the space, after staring at the large king bed for several long seconds, imagining what it would feel like to be wrapped in the sheets with Kane's body hovering over me, I find myself muttering how nice his apartment is and quickly backing out of the room.

There may be a lot of baggage surrounding Kane and me, but the fact still remains that I'm only human. And being in such close proximity to a man like Kane Thaler is definitely a testament to my will power.

"Are we able to go out there?" I ask, gesturing to a set of French doors as we reenter the main living space. I feel like fresh air might help clear my mind a bit.

"Of course." He waits until I step out onto the balcony before following me outside.

The temperature here is warm but it's nothing compared to the Arkansas heat and I take a moment to appreciate the breeze as it whips through my hair. The view is astounding. I swear you can see most of the city from up here.

The balcony is long and narrow, stretching the entire length of the living and kitchen space. There are a couple outdoor chairs and a small table in the middle but other than that it's completely bare. Though it makes sense why he wouldn't keep anything outside considering he's barely ever here.

"This place is incredible, Kane," I tell him, needing to reestablish the comfortable existence I felt between us earlier.

"It's good for what I need." He shrugs, leaning against the railing next to me.

"I can't believe this place sits empty all the time. If I paid for a place like this I'd probably never leave."

"I prefer to be anywhere but here most days," he says, his dark eyes locked on the city below.

"Why? I thought you liked the city."

"I do. I just, I don't know." He shakes it off, not finishing his thought. "You must be starving." He turns toward me, completely shifting gears.

"Now that you mention it, I am a little hungry." I let him get away with the change of subject because eating right now sounds too good to pass up.

"You feel up to going out or would you rather order in? I would offer to cook but I don't have anything here to make."

"You cook?" I raise a questioning eyebrow at him.

"Is it that hard to believe that I would know how to cook?" he questions, crossing his arms in front of his chest.

"A little, yeah." I laugh.

"I happen to be a very good cook."

"Well I guess you'll have some time to prove it to me," I point out, remembering that Kane will be my traveling companion for the next four weeks. Another excited burst of energy flutters through me and I find myself smiling even though I don't mean to.

"You should do that more often," Kane says, uncrossing his arms.

"Do what?"

"Smile," he says, wearing a pretty fantastic smile of his own.

I want to say something, come back with some witty comment or joke that shows I'm completely unaffected by his admission. When in reality I feel like my heart is about to beat out of my chest, and I come up empty handed.

"Come on." Kane turns, pulling open the door, essentially saving me from myself. "There's quite a few places that deliver so you can pretty much have any kind of food you want." His hand grazes the small of my back as I step past him into the apartment.

"What do you recommend?" I ask, trying to ignore the way that one innocent touch makes me feel, which is easier said than done.

"Are you a fan of Thai food?" he asks, crossing into the kitchen to pull open a drawer, laughing when I curl my nose and shake my head.

"Okay, no Thai food." He pulls out a folder and sets it on the counter in front of him. "What about Chinese?" I shake my head again, joining him on the opposite side of the island that divides the kitchen from the dining room.

"Here." He opens the folder and slides it across the bar to me.

It's filled to the brim with every kind of menu you could possibly imagine and while everything sounds amazing, I'm not sure if I will actually be able to bring myself to eat or not. Even though I feel hungry, my stomach has been a knot of nervous energy since I woke this morning and very little, other than the short lived buzz of the whiskey, has been able to relax me.

I pull out a few menus, looking at the different array of options laid out in front of me, deciding almost instantly that there's no way I'm going to be able to make any kind of decision right now.

"How about pizza?" I offer something familiar.

You can never go wrong with pizza, right?

"I've always heard how amazing Chicago deep dish pizza is. Might as well try it while I'm here," I quickly add.

"Sounds good to me." He takes the folder back from me once I close and extend it to him. "I'm going to get this ordered, then run down the block and grab some drinks. What can I get for you? Soda? Water? Beer?"

"I could drink a beer." I chew nervously on my lower lip, wishing I could get my nerves to level out a bit. I feel so up and down and all over the place right now. It's actually pretty mentally exhausting.

"Beer it is. You'll be okay for a few?" he asks, tucking the menu under his arm before sliding his cell phone into the back pocket of his jeans.

"I think I'll survive," I tease. "I would actually really love to take a shower if that's okay."

"Of course. Towels are in the closet in the hallway. It should be stocked with everything you'll need."

"Okay, thank you."

"I'll be back soon."

"Okay." I offer a small wave before turning and quickly making my way down the hall toward the guest bedroom.

****

By the time Kane returns I'm finished with my shower and curled up on his couch in my favorite plaid pajama shorts and faded Southern State t-shirt scrolling through Facebook on my phone. Truth be told I'm not big on social media but with nothing else to keep my mind occupied I've resorted to distracting myself with everyone else's drama.

114

"Hey." Kane smiles as he deposits a couple bags on the island in front of him. "I forgot to ask what kind of beer you like. I hope Blue Moon is okay."

"Blue Moon is perfect." I push the wet strands of blonde hair over my shoulders and reach out, taking the beer that Kane's holding out to me.

"Feeling better?" he asks, opening his own beer before taking a seat on the loveseat directly across from me.

"Tons," I admit, feeling like the shower was able to wash away a little of the fog that seems to have been settled over me for most of the day.

I had to take a few minutes alone to remind myself that Kane is Kamden's brother and while I may be out of my mind attracted to him, that's not why I'm here. Of course that was way easier to convince myself of when he wasn't sitting right in front of me wearing the insanely sexy smirk he's currently throwing in my direction.

"What?" I question, suddenly self-conscious under his gaze.

"You just look really cute." He tips his beer back and takes a long pull.

"Cute?" I repeat, not sure how to take that statement.

"It's a compliment, El." He chuckles.

It's not lost on me that this is the first time he's called me El – what nearly everyone calls me. It makes me feel good that we've at least crossed into somewhat friendship territory. At least enough that he feels comfortable not using my full name.

"I just, I've never seen you like this. Wet hair, pajamas, no make-up."

"You've seen me a lot worse," I interject, slightly embarrassed when I think about how I broke down in front of him several times over the course of that first night we spent together. God I was such a hot mess then. Not that much has changed really. I've just gotten much better at pretending.

Kane opens his mouth to say more but is silenced by a hard knock to the front door, followed by the ringing of his doorbell.

"Coming," he hollers, smiling at me as he climbs to his feet and quickly crosses toward the door.

It's less than a minute before he reappears, dropping a large pizza box, a couple plates, and some napkins on the glass coffee table in front of me.

"Dinner is served," he announces proudly, this time taking the seat next to me rather than across from me.

We spend the next hour eating pizza – which is probably the best pizza I've ever eaten in my life, drinking beer, and watching *Beat Bobby Flay* on Food Network. I was surprised to learn that he actually loves cooking shows and taught himself how to cook when he was in college by watching shows like Iron Chef and Baking Championships.

It's strange how I feel so comfortable with Kane sometimes and other times I feel like I've touched a live wire and can't seem to get my heart to beat in a normal rhythm again. And while I still feel the energy buzzing through me as we sit next to each other on the couch, it's not as pronounced as it was earlier which I'm grateful for.

I have to find a way to push past the way Kane makes me feel. I don't know if it's the obvious physical attraction or if it's because he intimidates the hell out of me for some reason. But whatever it is I have to get over it. There's no way I will last four weeks out of the country with this man when I can barely control myself in the same room with him for one evening.

I have to remind myself that there was a time when I felt this way for Kamden too. Though things with Kam were so much different. I didn't feel quite so overwhelmed by the way he made me feel nor was I as on edge as I am with Kane. But then again nothing about Kane feels comparable to my relationship with Kamden.

Kam had a way of making me feel at ease, comfortable with who I was. Where Kane makes me feel squeamish and self-conscious. Kam would tease me constantly where Kane is much more serious. And while I sometimes see glimpses of Kamden in Kane, it's clear that they are, or were, very different.

I just wish I could separate the two somehow. Then again I'm not sure if I would be more or less comfortable around Kane if I could. Because, I don't know what it is about Kane that has me so all over the place.

Yes, he's gorgeous. But he's also not the first good looking guy I've been around so it can't be that. Then again he's probably the most attractive man I've ever seen so I guess that's not really a fair comparison.

I don't know what, but there's something there. Some invisible bond that I feel like tethers us together and to be honest, I'm terrified of what that might mean. Because I'm scared to get too close to Kane. Not only because I'm afraid to get too close to anyone after losing Kam but also because I don't want to hurt Kane the way I'd hurt Kam.

I decide to call it a night just after nine o'clock. The heavy pizza combined with three beers and not enough sleep has me feeling seconds away from dozing off while sitting up.

Unfortunately I'm wide awake the second I slip under the expensive sheets and end up spending the next several minutes lying in bed looking at the ceiling wondering how the hell I actually ended up here.

It still seems like a dream. All of this. Kam being gone, me being here with Kane. It all feels wrong and yet oddly right at the same time.

Kane's bedroom door closes about thirty minutes later, followed by the sound of his shower turning on. I close my eyes and imagine what his reaction would be if I snuck into his room and slid underneath the hot streaming water with him.

Would he push me away and tell me to leave? Or worse… Would he pull me into his arms and beg me to stay?

My eyes shoot open and I quickly shake off the thought. God, what is wrong with me? It's not like I'm a prude or anything but thinking of Kam's brother that way feels wrong on so many levels.

Though it's no wonder why my mind would go there considering how long it's been since I've been with someone. Maybe that's my problem. Maybe I just need to get laid as my friend, Abby had told me on the phone a couple days ago when I confided in her about how off kilter Kane makes me feel.

I mean I'm twenty-two and my sexual experience is limited to Mike Webster, who I dated for three months my junior year of high school, and Jack Taylor, who I slept with after my mom died in an effort to make myself feel anything other than the soul crushing sadness I couldn't shake.

When I hear Kane's mattress creak through the thin apartment walls my urge to go to him becomes almost overwhelming. It would be so easy to walk into his room, climb under the covers with him, and ask him to make me feel something again, but I know I can't risk it. Kamden is gone and Kane is the only person in the world that makes me feel close to him. I can't risk screwing this up because my libido has all of a sudden decided to work again.

I don't know how long it takes before I finally doze off but my sleep is choppy and restless once I do. A constant nagging feeling eats at the pit of my stomach all night.

It's just after six in the morning when I finally give up and crawl out of bed, throwing on the only hooded sweatshirt I brought with me before quietly padding through the apartment and out onto the balcony.

I sit there for the next hour watching the sun rise, promising myself that I will let whatever this is go, all the

118

while trying to convince myself why I should. The old Elara would go for what she wants and isn't that why I'm here? To find her again.

Then again the old Elara was secretly in love with her best friend and it took her nearly seven years to admit it to him, so maybe she didn't really go for what she wanted after all. It's strange how when it comes to something like bungee jumping I don't blink an eye but then when it involves real feelings I run away like a terrified child.

Maybe I should be less focused on finding the girl I used to be and more focused on discovering the girl I am now. No one goes through what I've been through and comes out the same person on the other side. I think it's time to accept that the old me is gone. She died that day with Kamden. Unfortunately for me, I don't have any real clue who took her place.

Chapter Eleven
Elara

Two years ago

"Damn it, El. If you don't hold your pretty ass still I'm going to come over there and sit on top of you," Kam warns, holding his camera up to his face as he looks through the view finder and snaps another picture

"I'm sorry but this hurts." I cover my face with my hands as the tattoo gun continues to prick the flesh directly above my right hip bone. "I don't understand why you have to take pictures now. Can't you wait until it's done?"

"This is your first tattoo, butter bean. I need to capture the moment." He moves the camera away and hits me with a wide smile.

"I'm pretty certain I won't need a picture to remember this." I look down at the burly man covered head to toe in tattoos, better known as Tulk, as he moves the ink gun back and forth, his hand dangerously close to touching my naughty bits.

"You say that now, but twenty years from now you'll be glad I took pictures of everything," Kam disagrees.

"I think some things are better left un-captured." I lay my head back in the chair and look sideways at Kam.

"It's going to look amazing." He bounces on his heels, zooming in on the almost finished product before snapping another picture.

"Well it better look as amazing as yours or I want my money back." I flash a grin at Tulk who simply grunts and continues on. "I still can't believe I let you talk me into this."

When Kam suggested we get tattoos I never dreamt we'd get matching ones, but then I saw the amazing piece he had designed and instantly I knew I wanted it too. It's a feather that has a small section missing from one side where it's broken off and turned into five tiny birds flying away. He says it represents life. I like to think in some weird way it represents the two of us.

"It will," he reassures me.

"I'm thinking maybe I shouldn't have picked such a painful location." I cringe when the needle hits a really sensitive spot.

"You could have done it on your arm like I did." He gestures to the top of his forearm that's wrapped in plastic.

"If I didn't think my dad would kill me for doing this, I probably would have. This way he'll likely never see it."

"Unless you're wearing a bikini."

"Well lucky for me I don't wear bikinis in front of my father."

"Lucky for me you do wear them in front of me." He lifts his eyebrows suggestively.

"You're ridiculous." I laugh, earning me a stern 'be still' from Tulk.

Kam hits me with a wide grin and I swear he becomes a hundred times better looking when he smiles at me like that.

You would think after five years of friendship I would be immune to his charms, but alas, I'm anything but immune.

"Okay." Tulk pulls the gun back and wipes across my skin, pulling my focus back to him. "I think we're all done." He straightens his posture before reaching behind him to grab a hand held mirror, extending it to me.

"Oh my god." I cover my mouth with the hand that's not holding the mirror, still in complete and total shock that I actually went through with this. "I love it." I smile up at Kam who once again has his camera focused on me.

"It looks amazing, bean. I told you it would."

Looking back down at the tattoo, I angle the mirror so I can get a really good look at it. It's perfect. Everything that I hoped it would be. And what's even better is that it really means something to me.

"Now I'm a part of you forever." Kam steps up next to me as Tulk rubs some ointment on the tattoo and slaps a piece of plastic wrap over it, taping up the sides so it will stay.

"You'll be a part of me forever anyways," I counter, taking his hand once everything is covered and allowing him to pull me upright.

Kam smiles, tipping his face down to drop a kiss to the top of my head before pulling me to my feet.

****

Present Day

"Elara." My eyes shoot open and I quickly look around, disoriented and confused. The reminiscence of the dream still heavy on my mind as reality slowly starts to filter in.

I blink several times, trying to shake off the image of Kam's smile as my hand instinctively goes to the front of my right hip. I wish it was just a dream. Dreams I can handle. It's the memories that haunt me. The ones that play out like I'm still there, experiencing the moment as if it's actually happening, and then having to wake up to the same gut wrenching truth – that Kam is gone – then all I want to do is slip back into that dream world somehow. The one where Kam is still alive, smiling at me the way he always used to, snapping away on that damn camera that used to annoy the hell out of me but is now one of the things I miss the most.

"Elara," I hear again, the voice able to successfully pull me from the fog, like a beacon calling to me as I try to find my way out of the sea.

"Hey," I say, my eyes finally focusing enough to find Kane's gaze.

He's sitting in the seat next to me, tilted forward slightly so he has a full view of my face. "You fell asleep." He smiles, gesturing to the window on my right.

I sit up straighter and look outside, surprised to see we are much closer to the ground than when I dozed off. "How long was I asleep for?" I ask, my gaze going back to him.

"About seven hours."

"Seven hours?" I question, a bit shocked I was able to sleep so soundly given my surroundings.

"I hope it's okay I let you sleep. I didn't want to wake you. You looked so peaceful."

"No, it's okay." I stretch out, turning side to side to try and work out the stiffness in my back. "I guess I didn't sleep very well last night."

"Well considering you were awake before the sun even came up, I would expect not." He gives me a knowing look before adding, "We should be landing really soon."

"I can't believe we're actually here," I say, once again looking out the window at the green world beneath us.

"Italy." I smile to myself. "It's even more beautiful than I imagined."

"Just wait until you get to see it up close."

"How quickly do you have to get to work once we arrive?" I ask abruptly, turning back to face Kane.

"I'll need to be in the office first thing tomorrow morning," he says, clearly seeing the disappointment on my face that I try like hell to hide. "But we can do a little sightseeing this evening after we get settled. Then tomorrow evening I'm taking you on a beer tasting tour."

"Beer tasting tour?" I question, not sure I've ever heard of such a thing.

"It was the first thing I did the first time I came to Milan. It's a great way to get out and experience the city a little. They have microbrews all around and a guide will take us on a walking tour where you'll get to try different beers and appetizers. They take you right along the canal too which is honestly like a scene from a movie."

"Sounds incredible."

"It really is," he agrees. "I can also make arrangements for you to visit Manarola in the next few days."

"You don't have to do all that. I can manage on my own."

"No offense, Elara, but you're in a strange country for the very first time. It would make me feel a lot better if you let me help you navigate your visit here."

"You could always come with me," I say, but not really sure if I meant to.

"To Manarola?" he asks, a small grin playing on his mouth.

"Have you ever been?"

"I have not."

"Then you should come. It will be something new for the both of us."

"I'd like that." His smile widens. "We could make plans to stay a weekend there so you can really get the true feel of the area."

"Sounds perfect." I smile, the fluttery feeling in my belly becoming even more prominent.

****

"Well, this is it." Kane opens the door to the apartment we will be staying in, waiting for me to step through the doorway before following me inside.

I pause in the foyer, taking in the small space. It's modern and clean but also full of Old Italian charm which I'm very happy to see. I was hoping to get the full Italian experience and it's clear that is exactly what I'm going to get. The door ways are incredible arches and the wall that runs along the back of the living space is covered in deep red wallpaper that for some reason screams Italy to me. The furniture is stark white with end tables that look like something out of an art gallery

There's a small two person table pressed against the outside wall of the kitchen and one doorway that sits at the back of the room. The space can't be more than five hundred square feet total, unless the bedrooms are bigger.

"I've stayed here the two times I've been in Italy." Kane drops his suitcase to the side and crosses to the left where a small galley kitchen is tucked away in the corner. He continues to speak after he's disappeared inside. "I know it's small, but it's a central location and as you saw from the drive in, it's surrounded by tons of restaurants and shops. I could have gotten something bigger," he says, re-emerging from the kitchen with two bottles of water. "But I thought you'd appreciate this location more." He hands me one of the bottles when he reaches me.

"It's perfect." I smile.

"Just wait until you see the bedroom. The view from the window back there is amazing." He puts the bottle to his lips and takes a long drink.

"Bedroom?" I question, not missing the way he says it as in singular.

"There's only one bedroom here," he admits, seeming completely comfortable with this.

"One?" I choke.

"Relax." He chuckles, setting his water on the small door side table before hoisting his duffel bag over his shoulder and grabbing the handle of his suitcase. "I can sleep on the couch," he adds, carrying his luggage to the back of the room and disappearing inside what I can only assume is the *one* bedroom.

Not sure what else to do, I grab my suitcase and drag it through the apartment toward the bedroom as well. When I step into the doorway, Kane already has his suitcase open and is hanging shirts in the closet which is really more of a wall with hanging racks and shelves, completely open to the rest of the room.

I open my mouth to say something but become momentarily distracted when I catch sight of the large window, or rather the view out of that window. It takes up almost the entire back wall of the room, giving off a perfect view of the canal.

Abandoning my suitcase in the doorway, I make my way to the window, not able to tear my gaze off of the incredible sight before me.

Italy. I'm actually in Italy, I think to myself, for the first time actually taking it all in.

"Amazing, isn't it?" I jump when Kane's voice sounds directly next to me.

"Incredible," I admit, slowly turning to find his gaze locked on me.

"I'll need to keep all my things in here and of course, we will have to share the bathroom." He points to a door behind me. "But you can have the bed."

"That's not necessary. I'm happy to take the couch. Besides, you're way taller than me. You'd likely hang half way off that tiny thing," I object.

"I've slept on worse." He chuckles like he's remembering something funny before quickly adding, "Besides, you're my guest. What kind of host would I be if I forced you to sleep on the couch?"

"And what kind of guest would I be if I made you sleep on it?" I counter.

"It's fine, Elara." He grins. "Really."

"Kane," I say as he turns to walk away.

"Not up for discussion, Elara. The bed is yours."

I'm seconds away from suggesting that we share it but quickly snap my mouth shut, knowing how absurd that would be. Even though it is a queen bed and we could both easily fit, I honestly can't imagine sleeping next to him and not doing something I would very much regret after the fact.

So instead I say nothing at all, watching him exit the room moments later without another word.

It takes me all of fifteen minutes to empty out my suitcase, hanging the few outfits I brought with me right alongside Kane's much fancier looking wardrobe that consists mainly of black suits, light colored collared shirts and ties – all of which I know to be for work. I trail my hand down the arm of one of the suit jackets, my mind wandering back to the only time I've seen him in a suit – at Kam's funeral.

"Hey." Kane's voice startles me. I quickly drop the jacket sleeve, bend down to pick up my toiletries from my bag, and do my best to pretend like he didn't catch me oddly touching his clothing.

"Hey," I say, straightening my posture once I have my cosmetics bag, shampoo, conditioner, body wash, and all my other girly things balanced in my arms.

"I was thinking I'd take a shower. Then maybe we could go out for dinner in a little bit," he offers, continuing to speak as I step into the tiniest bathroom in the world and deposit all my things on one of the built in shelves above the toilet.

"I'd like that," I say, emerging from the bathroom seconds later. "But you'll need to give me time to shower as well. I feel like I've been in these clothes for days," I say, looking down at my black yoga pants and gray baseball tee. I wanted to be as comfortable as possible for the eleven hour flight here but now I feel rather frumpy.

"Of course. Why don't you go first and I'll make a few phone calls while I wait my turn."

"Okay," I agree, letting out a small breath when he nods once and disappears from the doorway.

Quickly crossing the space, I close the door and slide the lock before dropping my back against the old weathered looking wood.

I'm pretty sure my heart has not beat properly since the second we stepped into this tiny space and I'm already wondering how in the hell I'm going to be able to exist with Kane in such close proximity for the next four weeks.

I have a feeling I may have bitten off way more than I can chew.

Spotting my cell phone on the edge of the bed where I dropped it, I remember I need to let my dad know we landed safely. Using the reminder to distract myself, I quickly type out a text and head for the shower.

I take way longer than I should, making sure my apple butter scented body wash touches every single inch of my body at least twice. As if I can somehow wash off the effect Kane seems to be having over it.

When I exit several minutes later, I hear Kane on the phone in the other room, only I can't understand a word he's saying. Walking to the door, I press my ear to the crack and listen closer, realizing that the reason I can't understand him is because he isn't speaking English. Kane speaks Italian?

I wish the thought didn't warm my cool skin but something about listening to the way the words roll from his mouth so beautifully, so sexy, makes him somehow even more attractive. I listen for several long seconds, taking deep breaths to try and steady my pounding heart, before I finally decide I can't listen anymore.

As if I wasn't already fighting off the urge to throw myself at him, now I'm just plain torturing myself.

I dress quickly, slipping on an off the shoulder pale yellow sundress that lands just above my knee. It's one of those dresses that can be worn with just about anything and can be easily dressed up or down depending on how you accessorize. My mom always said it's not about the outfit itself, but about how you accent it that makes all the difference.

And she would know. She always dressed so beautifully. Even when she was working around the house doing laundry or cleaning, she always looked stunning.

I keep my hair tied up in the towel while I use the long free standing mirror in the corner of the room to apply a little makeup. I keep it simple; a little eyeliner, some light mascara, and the tiniest blush to my cheeks to give me a little color. Having not spent that much time outside this summer, my skin is starting to lose the golden tan that I usually have pretty much year round.

Running a quick blow dry through my long hair, I leave it down, quite pleased with how the natural wave gives it some body. My hair is pretty hit or miss. Sometimes it looks amazing with just a quick brush, other times it takes me an hour with an iron to get it to do what I want. Thankfully today was not one of those days.

Deciding to spruce up my outfit a little, considering I have no idea where Kane is taking me, I partner the pale yellow dress with a long silver double chain and simple drop earrings, before sliding into my favorite silver sandals to finish off the look.

I'm still looking at my reflection in the mirror when a soft knock sounds against the door.

"Come in," I say, the door opening seconds later.

Kane's expression hardens as he catches sight of me in the mirror. His eyes darken as they trail up my body before finally meeting my gaze in the reflection. If I had any question that the attraction I feel for him was one-sided, it would now be gone. The look he's giving me tells me something much different.

As if realizing his mistake, he looks away, turning to drop his phone on the bedside table.

"We're going to need to get going soon if we want to have some daylight left," he says, not looking in my direction.

"Okay. I'm finished." I turn away from the mirror, grabbing my own cell phone before quickly stepping past him.

"Elara." His voice stops me just as I reach the door. "You look beautiful." His dark gaze meets mine and I swear that one look causes my entire world to tilt on its axis.

Chapter Twelve
Kane

"You look beautiful." My words are followed by complete and utter silence.

She's staring at me; lips parted, cheeks pink, a million things running behind those incredible ocean blue eyes of hers. I didn't expect such an innocent comment to completely stun her. Then again, there was really nothing innocent about it.

She *is* beautiful.

Hell, she's more than just beautiful. I can't recall ever getting weak kneed over a woman but that's exactly what happens to me every time Elara looks at me. And she's damn near bringing me to my knees with the way she's looking at me right now.

It takes all the willpower I have not to pull her to me. Not to take her face in my hands and taste the sweetness of her plump lips – to feel her melt into me the way I've pictured she would a million times over the course of the last twenty-four hours.

"Thank you." She finally breaks eye contact, offering me a soft smile before quickly exiting the room, her scent staying with me long after she pulls the door closed behind her.

Fuck me…

****

"So, tell me more about your plans for the future," I press, spooning a bite of gelato into my mouth.

I took Elara to one of the most incredible restaurants in the area where you can pretty much order just about any Italian food your heart desires and she ordered the plainest, most basic thing on the menu–spaghetti. Which prompted the conversation of all the foods she hasn't tried, one very important one being gelato. Who hasn't tried gelato, was my one and only thought. So, of course, I decided it was something I had to remedy immediately.

"I don't really know that I have plans." She doesn't meet my gaze as she swirls the spoon in the frozen mixture.

"Come on, Elara. Everyone has plans. What did you want to be when you were a kid?" I try another angle.

She thinks on that for a long moment, her eyes shifting up to meet mine. "You'll laugh." A small smile graces her lips.

"I won't," I promise.

"You will," she counters.

"Well, there's only one way to find out. Try me."

"You first," she challenges, scooping a bite of gelato into her mouth. "You were right by the way. Incredible." She practically moans as she swallows.

I'm momentarily drawn to that action, the one small sound that sends my mind reeling in a completely different direction.

"I..." I clear my throat and refocus. "I guess my top pick was to be a pilot. Either that or I wanted to join the military."

"Seriously?" She quirks a brow at me.

"What?" I shoot back, not able to hide my smile.

"You don't strike me as a military man."

"Why's that?" I counter, trying to hold my serious expression when I see her squirm slightly.

"You just seem more..."

"More what?" I cut in when she pauses. "I'm getting the impression here you think I'm too pussy for something as intense as the military. You might be wounding my manhood a bit," I say, completely stone faced even though on the inside I'm finding this quite humorous.

I expect her to try to explain herself, apologize even, so when she bursts out laughing I'm not really sure how to react.

"Is something funny?" I cock my head to the side and narrow my gaze at her, fighting the smile threatening to split across my face.

"I'm sorry. I didn't peg you for a man that throws around words like pussy. Just caught me off guard is all." She bites her bottom lip in an effort to keep herself from smiling.

"What kind of man did you peg me for?" I ask, leaning forward, placing my elbows on the small table between us.

"I don't know. You seem really serious. And your kind of intimidating," she tacks on the last part.

"I'm intimidating?" I question, not really sure how to take that.

"You know, like you just always seem, god I don't know what I'm trying to say." She blows out a breath. "I guess you would have made a good military man. Perhaps a drill sergeant. You would have been amazing at that job."

She's rambling and fuck me if it isn't the most adorable thing ever.

"You done now?" I chuckle when she finally stops speaking, not able to suppress the smile stretching across my face.

"Yep. Officially mortified. We good now? Can I go home?" She hitches her finger toward the door.

"You're not getting off that easy. You still have to tell me what you wanted to be," I remind her.

"I wanted to be a trapeze artist," she mutters, quickly shoving another bite of gelato into her mouth and slowly swallowing.

"What was that?" I hold my hand to my ear like I didn't hear her.

"A trapeze artist," she says a little too loudly, drawing the attention of the older couple sitting to our right. "In the circus. Okay?"

"You don't have to yell it," I tease, loving the light shade of pink that reaches her cheeks.

"Shut up." She huffs.

"So a trapeze artist, huh? Somehow that doesn't really surprise me."

"Are you making fun of me right now?" She glares daggers in my direction.

"Babe, if I were making fun of you you'd know it," I say, not missing the way her blush deepens at my choice of words.

"Whatever." She brushes it off, clearly diverting.

"Okay, so clearly trapeze artist didn't work out," I observe.

"Clearly." She rolls her eyes and sits back, crossing her arms in front of her chest.

"So then was writing always your second choice."

"I don't know. Maybe." She pauses before continuing, "When I was in high school I became obsessed with old movies and even more fascinated with how the entire process works. How they brought something to life with nothing more than putting pen to paper, producing an amazing story. I guess it stuck." She shrugs.

"Hence the English major."

"Yep." She nods, uncrossing her arms to take another bite of gelato.

"What about outside of that?"

"Outside of what?" she questions after she swallows.

"Outside of career choices. You're still pretty young, there has to be things you want to do."

"You're almost as young as me," she counters.

"You'd be surprised what a difference three years can make. And that wasn't my point anyway. How about marriage and kids? Is that something you see in your future?" My turn in the conversation gets her attention and within seconds she's abandoned her spoon in her cup of gelato and has her hands knotted in front of her on the table.

"Yes? No? Maybe?" I question when she makes no attempt to answer.

"I think I'd like to get married one day," she offers, finally meeting my gaze. "What about you?"

"Yeah, I think eventually. Maybe once I've nailed down a more consistent employment and can be around long enough to actually have a relationship."

"I see." She twists her fingers together but doesn't look away.

"Kids?" I ask.

"No." She shakes her head, her answer surprising the hell out of me.

"No, you don't want kids?" I clarify.

"No, I mean yes, I do. But no, I can't."

"What do you mean you can't?"

"Just what I said, I can't."

"You can't have children?" I soften my voice.

"Nope." She lets out a slow breath. "I got really sick when I was little and almost died. We didn't know until many years later but the medication they gave me caused

135

irreversible damage to some pretty key areas." She gestures to her abdomen. "Therefore, no kids."

"Wow." I sit back, not really sure what to say. "I'm sorry that happened to you," I offer.

"Don't be. I accepted it a long time ago."

"Do you think you'd ever adopt?"

"Maybe." She shrugs. "I guess it would depend on my situation. But right now I'm nowhere close to considering anything like that."

"I didn't suspect you would be," I offer, wishing she'd meet my gaze.

"So, anyway. What about you? You see kids in your future." She finally looks up, clearly trying to hide the emotion this conversation has stirred.

"I think I'd like to have one or two," I admit.

Something shifts on her face. Something I can only read as disappointment, but it's gone as quickly as it appeared and I'm left wondering if maybe I'm just looking for things that aren't there.

"Tell me something you've never done that you've always wanted to do?" I change tactics, sensing the urgency for a lighter topic.

"Visit Italy." She smirks.

Smart ass.

"Something you're not currently doing," I counter. "Something off the top of your head."

"Skydive," she says after thinking on it for a moment.

"Really?" I smile.

"Well, that's something I used to want to do," she adds.

"But not anymore?"

"I don't know." She shrugs, blowing out a breath.

"If I took you to go skydiving right now would you do it?" I challenge.

"I don't know," she repeats.

"Why don't you know?"

"A year ago I would have said yes with no hesitation but now, I don't know. I guess maybe I'm scared."

"What are you scared of?"

"Death," she blurts.

"We're all scared of death, Elara."

"I wasn't. I was only scared of not living. I pushed everything to the limit. Was afraid of nothing. Until..." She trails off.

"Until Kam," I finish her sentence.

"Until Kam." She nods, sadness filling her face.

"You know he wouldn't want that, right."

"Wouldn't want what?" She looks at me, her forehead drawn in confusion.

"He wouldn't want you to change who you are."

"Who I am is the reason he's dead."

"Who you are is the reason he loved you," I interject.

"Can we please not do this?" She scoots her chair back and stands abruptly. I immediately follow, dropping a few bills on the table before exiting the small shop behind her.

"Elara." I snag her arm as she turns to walk away.

"I can't talk about him, Kane." She whips around, tears welling behind her eyes. "I know I should. I should want to talk about him. I should want to remember him. But it hurts too much. I can't do it."

"You can." I place my hands on her shoulders to steady her. "It's the only way you're going to deal with it. You have to talk about it. About him. You can't close off and pretend like the accident didn't happen, like Kam isn't gone."

"I know he's gone," she bites. "I'm not pretending the accident didn't happen. I was there, remember? I won't be able to erase that from my memory for as long as I live. So no, Kane, I'm not pretending anything. I just can't talk about him like it's okay because it's not okay."

"Hey." I pull her to my chest, locking my arms around her shoulders. Maybe I pushed her too hard too fast.

137

It helps me to talk about Kam, to remember him as he was, but it clearly isn't the same for Elara. At least not yet.

"I'm sorry," I whisper into her hair, feeling her relax against me the moment I do. "We don't have to talk about it. But, Elara, one of these days you're going to have to and when you're ready, I hope you know I'm here."

"I do," she says against my chest, her arms wrapping around my middle. "I'm sorry too. Sometimes I just can't deal."

"It's okay," I reassure her, dropping my cheek to the top of her head, not ready to let go just quite yet.

"I'm sorry I ruined our evening." She breaks away too soon for my liking and I'm forced to take a step back.

"You didn't ruin anything." I reach up and brush a hair away from her cheek.

Her body tenses at my touch but she doesn't step away from it.

"I kind of did," she counters.

"Well, maybe a little." I grin, pulling the exact reaction from her I was hoping for.

"Such an ass." She fights a smile as she spins on her heel and takes off up the sidewalk.

I wait until she's several yards away before informing her, "You're going the wrong way."

She stops, looks around, realizes she has absolutely no idea where she's going before turning back in my direction, a slight pout on her mouth.

"I repeat, ass," she mutters loud enough that I can hear her before she stomps back in my direction.

"You're really cute when you glare at me like that." I chuckle as she walks right past me, her shoulder bumping into me as she does.

"Good, then I'll be sure to do it more often," she quips, throwing me another glare when I step up next to her, matching her stride.

I can't help but tilt my head back on a laugh that I simply cannot suppress. This girl. I swear to God I don't know what I'm going to do with her. One minute she's seconds from tears, the next she's faking anger. I'm almost afraid to see what comes next and yet oddly excited at the same time.

"Stop laughing at me." She tries to fight her smile as she bumps her shoulder gently into mine.

"I can't help it. You're funny," I deadpan.

Her lip twitches once before her own sweet laughter fills the air.

"You are not at all what I expected, Kane Thaler."

"I'm hoping that's a good thing," I say, dropping my arm around her shoulder before tucking her into my side.

I don't even mean to do it; it just happens so naturally. One minute I'm walking next to her, the next I'm pulling her to me. And once she's there, the fuck if I'm letting her go.

"The jury is still out on that one." She smiles up at me and I swear it takes everything in me not to lean down and press my lips against hers.

"Is that so?" I say instead, flipping my gaze back up to watch where we're going. Mainly because I know with complete certainty that if she keeps looking at me I *will* most definitely kiss her.

"It is." I feel her nod.

"Anything I can do to help my odds?" I joke.

"I'll let you know if anything comes to mind." I can hear the smile in her voice but I keep my eyes focused forward. "Damn, I really was going in the wrong direction," she adds when the apartment building we're staying at comes into view. "Here I thought maybe you were just trying to screw with me."

"I would never do that." I drop my arm from her shoulder, throwing her a wink before climbing the front steps. I pull open the front door, holding it for Elara until she steps past me into the foyer of the building.

"Did I ever tell you how much I despise stairs?" She looks up at the narrow staircase in front of us.

"I could always carry you," I offer with a wide smile on my face.

"You're so much more like him than I realized." I can tell the moment it leaves her mouth she wants to take it back, but before I can even think to respond she quickly adds, "Race you to the top."

With that she takes off up the stairs so fast she's already half way up the first set before I've even moved an inch.

It takes me no time to catch her. Her five-four frame is no match for my six foot one. My legs are long enough to easily take two steps at a time and I quickly pass her with very little effort.

"No fair," she yells after me. "You're legs are way longer than mine."

"You're the one that challenged me, remember?" I laugh, slowing down enough that I don't get too ahead of her. "Perhaps you should have thought it through," I call behind me.

"Again, ass," she yells through the stairwell, her footsteps not coming as quickly as before.

"You gonna make it?" I stop at the top of the sixth floor landing and look over the railing. She's still a good floor and a half down.

"Does your offer to carry me still stand?" She stops for a brief moment, taking a deep breath before continuing her climb up.

"That depends, would it help my case?" I holler down to her.

"With the way my legs are burning I would say most definitely," she says breathlessly.

Clearly she doesn't actually think I will do this, because when I appear in front of her, hoisting her into my arms and cradling her to my chest, she cries out in surprise.

"Kane. I didn't think you were serious," she objects as I head back up the stairs I just came down.

"I'm pretty sure I told you, El, I won't ever lie to you. I said I would carry you and carry you I will." I catch her smile out of the corner of my eye but I keep my focus on the stairs, not wanting to trip with her in my arms.

"How about now?" I ask, depositing her on her feet in front of the apartment seconds later.

"How about now?" She looks up, eyebrows drawn together.

"Jury still out?"

The smile that stretches across her face damn near does me in.

"Getting close I think." She winks, shimmying past me into the apartment.

And if I didn't know it before, I sure as hell know it now. I am in some serious trouble…

Chapter Thirteen

Elara

"You about ready, El?" Kane calls from the living room.

"Be right there," I holler back, throwing another outfit into my bag.

We've been in Italy for six days now and while I was apprehensive about all of it, most of all our sleeping arrangement, it's actually been quite nice. Kane has been nothing short of amazing and thus far my time here has been life changing.

Every morning after Kane leaves for work, I head out on an adventure, exploring a part of this beautiful city. The days are for me, the nights I spend with Kane. He's taken me to a new restaurant every evening since we arrived. He's been teaching me about the different foods and even managed to get me to order something other than spaghetti.

And now, like he promised, he's taking me to Manarola for three days. To say I'm over the moon would be the understatement of the year. I haven't felt this excited about anything since the accident and to know I'm still capable of feeling this kind of happiness gives me hope that maybe my future is not as bleak as I once thought.

Of course that excitement might have quite a lot to do with the man whose eyes I meet as I walk into the living room, trying to not act like the giddy smitten teenager I feel like anytime I look at his gorgeous face.

I mean seriously, it should be a crime to be as good looking as Kane is. He's perfection. From his thick brown hair, to his breathtaking dark eyes, to that knee weakening smile, and body that screams *plaster me on every magazine in the world*, it's all I can do to keep a clear head and not completely lose it–which I've nearly done more than once this week. Especially when he walked out of the bathroom two mornings ago in nothing but gym shorts, giving me my first real taste of what is hiding underneath his clothes.

Dear lord, I couldn't bear to look at him for more than a second for fear drool would start pooling out of my mouth. It's not just his looks, either. Sure, he's still serious most of the time, and intimidating as hell. But I'm also finding he's really quite sweet, thoughtful, and does an amazing job of making me smile nearly every time I'm with him.

Things have changed between us over the past few days too. Slowly, we've settled into some semblance of friendship, though I can't say it's like any friendship I've had before. Because deep down I don't want to be his friend. I want to be something much more.

It's not lost on me that this was how I felt about his brother. Then again, I was able to be Kam's friend despite my feelings. For seven years I stood by and watched as he dated other girls, never taking my chance. But for whatever reason, this thing with Kane feels different. As in I can't imagine watching him date other women or only ever being his friend, which leaves me feeling both confused and guilty.

Guilty that I waited so long to tell Kam how I felt when I'm already fighting back the urge to tell Kane that I'm attracted to him. Confused because if I can't see myself just being his friend then what the hell am I doing here?

Kane has given me no reason to believe he feels anything even similar to how I feel. Then again, maybe that's not entirely true.

I catch him staring at me sometimes. Not in a normal way you might look at someone that's your friend, either. But in a way that makes my skin feel like it's been touched by a live wire. And it's in those moments I find it the hardest not to launch myself at him.

How did I get here? How after just a week is he already under my skin so deeply that I can't seem to shake him?

I came here to find myself. Instead what I'm finding is that Kane Thaler is even more irresistible than his brother. And there it is… Guilt.

"You good?" Kane brings my attention up to him and only then do I realize I've been standing here for several moments without saying or doing anything.

"Yeah, sorry. Just running through my mental check list to make sure I have everything I need," I lie.

"Well, if you happen to forget anything, we can always stop somewhere." He crosses the small space toward me and takes my duffel bag from my shoulder, sliding it on to his.

See what I mean… *Sweet*.

"We really should get going. I'd like to get there early to avoid traffic if at all possible."

"Okay." I nod, glancing around the space before turning my attention back to him. "I think I'm ready," I hesitate, actually going through the check list in my head this time.

"You sure?" He chuckles.

"Yes." I meet his gaze and smile. "Let's go."

****

144

Kane rented a car for our trip to Manarola. A medium size semi-sporty car. A Renault Captur. Something I had never heard of or seen before today.

We're about half way through our drive, windows down, soft music playing on the radio, when I feel Kane's eyes on me for probably the hundredth time. I shift in my seat, keeping my eyes glued out the windshield.

"I'm really glad you decided to come on this trip with me," his voice low. Then out of nowhere his hand touches mine.

I jump slightly before looking down to where he turns my palm upright, sliding his fingers in between mine, entwining them. Staring at our hands that are now joined, I make no attempt to pull mine away. Looking from our hands to Kane, I'm graced by a small grin on his face, his eyes never leaving the road.

"Yeah..." I stutter, remembering what he said before his touch wiped everything else from my mind. "Me too." I look back down at where are hands are, my heart doing something funny in my chest while my stomach feels like it has hollowed out into an enormous open pit.

"Relax, babe." He glances in my direction and gives me a lopsided grin.

There's that word again... *Babe*.

"I am relaxed," I counter after several moments of silence.

"Your posture says otherwise." He flicks his eyes to mine for the briefest moment, his smile not faltering for even a second.

I open my mouth to argue but realize he's right. I instantly make a point to sink back down in the seat, though I don't feel any more at ease in doing so.

"So what do you want to see first?" His fingers tighten around mine, pulling my gaze to his. "When we get to

Manarola," he clarifies, his eyes bouncing back and forth between me and the road.

"I haven't really thought that far ahead," I admit, wanting desperately to pull my hand away so I can think clearly, yet not wanting to ever take it away at the same time.

"You said your great grandparents lived right by the water, yeah?"

"Yes," I barely manage to get out past the knot in my throat.

My god this man does something to me that I just can't explain. It's like I can't keep a single thing straight in his presence and this fact has only intensified given that he's currently holding my hand.

What exactly is happening here?

That's what I want to ask him. I want to know if he feels it too. The zing of chemistry between us, the pull of something more. I'm convinced he does, *he has to*, and yet I'm afraid he doesn't. Then again, I might be more afraid that he does.

"I'm not really positive on that, but from what I've gathered from pictures I believe so," I eventually add.

"We will have to stop by and visit."

"Visit what?" I question, not sure what he's talking about.

"Where your great grandparents lived." He flashes me an amused smile and I swear my heart flips in my chest.

Why does he have to be so beautiful? Why can't this be easy? Come to Italy, reconnect with myself and my roots, and gain a good friend in the process. That's what I wanted. A friend. Someone who understood what I'm going through. Someone I could offer some understanding too as well.

Instead I find myself off in la la land, dreaming about Kane's mouth and hands and every other part of him I haven't been able to stop staring at.

"We can't. Someone else owns it," I say after composing myself.

"And?" Kane questions, his gaze fixed on the road.

"And you can't walk up and knock on someone's door and expect they will let you inside their house."

"Says who?"

"Says any sane person alive. Would you let someone into your house?"

"If the reason was valid, yes I would."

"There's a valid reason for letting complete strangers into your home?"

"We're not in America, babe."

Babe... God I wish he would stop saying that word. Every time he does I feel myself slip a little further, my heart beat a little faster, and my stomach knot a little tighter.

"If I explain to them the significance of the house and that it once belonged to your grandparents, I'm certain that they will at least let us in long enough to look around. To experience the place where your great grandparents lived. Where your grandfather was born. Where your father might have been raised had they not moved to the States. This is a part of your history, Elara. It's important."

"I still don't think they'll let us in," I counter, trying my best to focus on that and not his mouth which I can't seem to stop staring at.

"We'll see." His eyes briefly glance my way and I quickly pull my gaze from his mouth to meet his dark eyes.

"I guess we will." I force an easy smile before turning my gaze back out the window, praying to the heavens above that we get there soon.

I'm not sure how much longer I can sit in the close confines of this car with Kane. Not with the way he keeps looking at me, the way he keeps squeezing my hand—not for one second releasing it, or the way his incredible scent fills the space. It's all I can do to keep myself rooted in my seat, knowing that once I act, there's no going back.

Kane is all I have left of Kam and no matter how twisted up he has me inside, I'm not ready to risk losing that just yet. Another hour in this car and I might have a different answer...

****

"You're kidding me, right?" It's the only thing I can say as I step into the small bedroom Kane booked us at a local B&B.

"Just wait until you see the view." I hear the smile in his voice as he steps up behind me, his body so close to mine I can feel the heat radiating from it.

"The view? Kane, look around," I say, spinning to face him. "There's only one room. The whole thing is one room," I explain, feeling like any rational person would understand my issue.

"I'm aware." He chuckles, dropping both of our duffels on the full size bed next to us.

My eyes dart around the space again, my heart hammering a million miles a minute. It's one thing to be forced to exist in a small one bedroom apartment. That alone is difficult enough. Now he expects me to spend the next three days in a small bedroom with an even smaller bathroom. Forget about a couch or separate living spaces. Hell, there's hardly room for the small table and two chairs crammed into the corner.

"Where will we sleep?" I ask, my eyes finding his, humor dancing behind them.

"In the bed," he says like it should be obvious.

"But there's only one bed," I object.

"Again, I'm aware." His smile widens.

"This isn't funny." I cross my arms over my chest.

"Oh I beg to disagree. This is quite funny."

"Are you laughing at me?" I say when his shoulders silently shake. "We can't sleep there." I point to the bed.

If it was a king maybe I could see making it work. I could stuff pillows between us or something. But it's not even close to that size. We will be lucky if we can lie together and avoid touching.

"Elara." Kane's expression falls serious and he takes a full step toward me, essentially closing what little space existed between us. "You mean to tell me that you never shared a bed with Kam?" He cocks a brow.

"That was different." I shake my head.

"How's it different? He was your friend. I'm your friend. It shouldn't be any more complicated than that. Unless there's something you want to tell me," he pauses, pushing my hair over my shoulder. His hand grazes the side of my neck causing goose bumps to erupt across my skin.

"I…" I start to speak but am too frazzled by his nearness to gather my thoughts enough to respond.

"I promise it will be fine. If it makes you feel better I will sleep on the floor."

"You can't sleep on the floor," I immediately object, gesturing to what little floor space exists.

"I'll manage," he insists.

"I'm not letting you sleep on the floor."

"Well you seem pretty hell bent on not sleeping together in the bed either."

"That's not it," I start, only to be cut off by him before I can finish my statement.

"Then what is it exactly?" he asks, his dark eyes boring into mine.

"I. I."

"I promise I will be on my best behavior." He holds his hands up between us. "Not one part of my body will touch yours, Elara." he announces and disappointment instantly floods through me.

What the hell?

I shouldn't be disappointed, I should be relieved. So why do I suddenly feel like someone just told the eight year old me that there's no such thing as Santa?

Then he does something so unexpected my breath hitches and an entirely different sensation runs through me.

He leans forward, his face mere inches from mine, and quickly adds, "Unless you ask me to. Of course."

With that he grins, announces he's going to get food, turns on his heel, and marches out of the room.

I don't know how long I stand there, paralyzed, unable to think let alone move, before his head appears in the doorway, a knowing grin spread across his handsome face.

"You coming or what?"

****

While I was able to shake off the encounter with Kane in the bedroom, it never strayed far from my mind. After doing a little sight-seeing along the way, we finally stopped and ate at a small local restaurant that specializes in wines, fruits, and cheeses. And while all three were amazing, nothing could top the incredible view of the sea from our table on the outdoor terrace.

After eating, we walked for a good two hours but it felt like much less. Time with Kane passes so easily that sometimes I have a hard time keeping a grasp on it. By the time we arrive back at the small bed and breakfast sandwiched between two tall brick structures, it's nearly dark and while I feel wide awake, my body feels exhausted.

It takes everything in me to climb the two flights of stairs to our room and once there, the only thing I want to do is to climb into a hot bath and soak for three hours solid. Unfortunately our bathroom is no more than a tiny sink, a toilet, and the smallest shower I've ever seen.

The conversation between Kane and me was easy and flowed freely while we explored the city, but the second the door closes behind us the earlier tension returns full force. Or at least for me it does. Kane seems completely at ease, moving around the small space like he doesn't have a care in the world.

"You wanna grab a shower first?" He looks up from his duffel on the bed to where I've barely moved since entering the room.

"Um, yeah. That would be great." I instantly jump into action, deciding that a shower might help clear my head a little.

Grabbing my bag, I quickly disappear inside the bathroom without another word. Once the door is shut behind me, I'm barely able to move around enough to pull the things I need out of my bag. I really should have taken out the things I planned to use and left the bag in the room, but I was so eager to get away from Kane I didn't think it through.

Even still, I manage okay. I shower first, taking an extra amount of time washing my hair because the hot water feels so good on my skin. Then I set to the somewhat difficult task of brushing my teeth while straddling my bag that I had no option but to leave directly in front of the sink.

After that I dress in a pair of plaid pajama shorts and a pale pink tank. And even though I never sleep in a bra, I decide that given my present company it's an absolute must. Normally I would refuse to wear such little clothing in the presence of another, but given how hot it is here and that the room is cooled by nothing more than a fan jammed into a small window, it's likely I will bake if I put any additional layers on.

When I reenter the room, my blonde hair laying heavy and damp down my back, an instant chill runs through me and it has nothing to do with the breeze flowing in from the

151

open door leading out to the terrace. But everything to do with the man standing in that doorway, arms crossed in front of himself as he leans casually against the frame.

Stepping up next to him, I feel his eyes on the side of my face but I keep my gaze forward, taking in the incredible view he tried to tell me about earlier. We're elevated high up in the valley, an incredible outstretched view of the sea provided. The moon hangs high in the sky, illuminating the water in the most breath taking way.

"Well, at least you were right about the view," I say without actually meaning to.

"I think you'll find I'm right about a lot of things." He turns toward me, one side of his mouth pulled up in a playful smirk.

"Adding cocky to the list," I mumble, smiling to myself.

"What was that?" His smirk stretches to a full blown smile.

"I'm keeping a list," I inform him casually, turning my gaze back out to the sea.

"Keeping a list?" he repeats.

"Of all the things I'm learning about you."

"And what's on that list so far."

"Nope. It's a secret." I shake my head, flipping my gaze to see his eyes filled with amusement.

God, he really is way too good looking for his own good.

"Elara," he warns, taking my shoulders as he turns me toward him. "You can't tell a guy you're keeping a list on him and then not tell him what's on said list."

"You can't handle it," I tease, feeling oddly at ease and like my heart is going to beat out of my chest at the same time.

"Try me."

"Asshole." I bite my bottom lip as he lets out a low chuckle.

"Keep going."

"Oddly sweet."

"I'll take it," he continues to comment.

"Surprisingly thoughtful."

"I'm starting to like this." He chuckles again.

"Super intimidating."

"Got that already." His smile holds its place and my heart beats a little faster.

"Cocky."

"So you've recently said."

"Way too good looking for your own good." His eyes take on this sort of twinkle at my admission.

"You think I'm good looking?" he teases, rocking back on his heels.

"Shut up. You know you are." I roll my eyes. "Or did you miss the part where I called you cocky?"

"Oh no, I got that. But I want to go back to the good looking part." He takes a step toward me and I take a matching one back.

"Stop looking at me like that," I warn, recognizing that look in his eyes. It's the same look Kam always got before he'd tickle me or throw me over his shoulder and toss me in the pool.

Kane has the same look on his face right now and because of this, I take another step backward, my back meeting the door that opens up to the terrace eliminating my ability to go any further.

"Like what?" He cocks his head to the side and takes another step toward me, caging me between him and the door.

"Like you're about to pounce."

"Pounce?" He cocks his head to the side and laughs.

"Pounce," I repeat.

"I've been making a list about you too; do you want to hear it?" he asks, continuing before I can answer one way or the other. "Loyal. Funny. Sweetest fucking laugh I've ever

153

heard." He leans in closer, his lips almost touching mine. A simple push up on my toes is all it would take and my mouth would be on his. "Breathtakingly beautiful," he continues, his eyes darting to my lips and then back up to my eyes.

"I'm going to kiss you now, Elara. So if you don't want me to, now's your chance to say so." His words paralyze me and even though I feel like I should say something, *anything*, I can't seem to force one word out.

"Three." His eyes are locked on mine, his gaze unwavering. "Two." He dips in closer. I can feel his breath on my face. "One."

Then his lips are on mine, soft and sweet. Testing. Tasting. My body zings to life and I have to fight the urge to dive my hands into his hair and kiss him harder. Instead I stay rooted to the spot, also testing, tasting, letting myself explore the most sensual kiss I've ever shared with anyone.

But then as quickly as it started, it's over. Kane pulls back and drops his forehead to mine, his breathing uneven and his eyes so dark they look black as they hold my gaze.

"Tastes like a fucking dream," he mutters, his mouth still so close to mine I can feel his words vibrate against me.

It takes me a moment to realize he's adding to his list and I'd be lying if I said I'm not eating up every word as he says it.

But then just like that, the moment is broken. He straightens his posture, looks down at me for a long moment, and quickly turns and disappears inside the bathroom. Leaving me standing there, looking after him and wondering what the hell just happened.

Chapter Fourteen
Elara

I feel the bed sink next to me as Kane climbs in. I won't deny the disappointment that seeps through me when he rolls to his side, his back facing me, and doesn't say a word. But with that disappointment also comes relief. I don't trust my head or my heart right now, especially after that kiss. A kiss I can still feel lingering on my lips even though it's been well over thirty minutes since it happened.

If Kane's behavior afterward tells me anything, it's that he's just as conflicted about whatever is happening between us as I am. Sometimes I can't get the fact that he's Kam's older brother out of my head. Other times I find myself forgetting they have any relation at all.

Because even though Kane and Kam are very similar in a lot of ways, the more time I spend with Kane the more I realize that they are two completely separate people and comparing them is not fair to me or either of them.

And as much as I tell myself that I'm glad Kane chose his current position, the longer I lay here staring at his back, the less I'm able to believe the lie. I want to reach out and touch him. I want to wrap my arm around his middle and snuggle up behind him. I want to roll him over and finish what we started earlier. But instead I do none of those things. Not a single one.

It takes me a long time to find sleep and when I finally do, I dream of nothing but dark eyes and soft lips pressed against mine.

****

I wake with a start, blinking against the bright sun that filters into the room through the open terrace. I push up on my elbows, catching sight of Kane's bare back as he leans against the rail looking out over the sparkling sea below.

Was he shirtless when he crawled in bed with me last night?

I try to rummage through the memories but can't seem to pinpoint one way or another. It was dark and I never touched him, so I guess I wouldn't exactly know. I will say this, if he did sleep next to me with no shirt on, I'm sure as hell glad I didn't notice.

I allow my eyes to trail down his firm, sculpted back. This man has a body that says he spends hours in the gym and yet from what I can tell, he hasn't touched one since we've been here. Then again he's always up and dressed well before I am. Maybe he visits the little gym at the apartment complex where we're staying before I get out of bed. Who knows?

God I'm a total slacker.

Throwing back the covers, I quickly climb from the bed. It creaks under the movement and by the time I get myself upright, Kane has turned toward me, a small smile pulling at his lips.

Okay, so he's not upset like he seemed last night. That's a good sign.

"Mornin', babe." He raises a coffee cup to his lips and takes a small sip as he rests his shoulder against the door frame.

Mornin', babe. My knees instantly go weak.

"Morning," I force out, pointing to the cup in his hand. "Where can I get me one of those?"

"Downstairs." He smiles. "Why don't you get some clothes on and we can go down and grab a bite to eat. They've got quite the spread down there."

"You didn't go down like that, did you?" I point to his bare chest, thinking of all the women he probably passed that had to grab onto something to keep themselves upright at the sight of him.

"And if I did?" He cocks a brow at me.

"Then you probably gave poor Ms. McGreevy a heart attack." I grin, referring to the sweet woman in her late sixties who owns the B&B.

"She didn't have any complaints." His smile widens and the flutter in my stomach hits me with a force that nearly knocks me backward onto the bed.

"I'm sure she didn't," I mutter, my eyes scanning the length of him. "Even still, I'm not going anywhere with you until you put on a shirt."

"Why? By the way you're looking at me I'd say you rather enjoy the view." He's joking and I'm not sure if he realizes just how true his statement actually is.

"Yeah, my point exactly," I say, surprising us both before quickly stepping into the bathroom and closing the door, determined not to embarrass myself any further.

****

Kane doesn't mention the kiss from last night and neither do I, even though it's all I've been able to think about since it happened.

We enjoy a beautiful breakfast that includes fresh fruit, biscuits, bread, and about five different flavors of jam. And of course the coffee, which is absolutely to die for. I've never had such delicious coffee and I told Mrs. McGreevy so before we headed back up to our room. A truth that seemed to thoroughly make her day.

"How long do you think it will take you to get ready?" Kane asks the moment we reenter our room and the door closes behind us.

"Why? You got somewhere to be?" I question, lifting my bag off the floor and depositing it on the bed.

"*We* have somewhere to be," he corrects.

"Where?" I ask, this being the first time he's mentioned any real plans.

"It's a surprise." He smiles at me and another whoosh runs through me.

"I hate surprises," I inform him, mainly because it's true.

"Something I knew about you already." He nods.

"And yet you planned a surprise anyway?" I question, looking up from the contents of my bag to him.

"I like to go against the grain." His smile spreads and try as I may, I can't fight my own from spreading across my lips too. "Now, how long do you think it will take you to get ready?" he repeats his earlier question.

"I don't know." I shrug. "Twenty minutes."

"Perfect." He nods, passing by me to retrieve his bag from the opposite side of the bed. "Wear something comfortable. Shorts or jeans. Tennis shoes for sure."

"Okay." I eye him warily, wondering what on earth he has up his sleeve.

After the way he went to bed last night I wasn't sure what I'd wake up to this morning. I'm happy to see that whatever happened after that kiss seems to have passed, but now I'm even more anxious than I was before. Mainly because all I can think about is kissing him again and that is so not good.

Within two minutes he's already slipped on a pair of jeans and a plain gray tee, looking like a million dollars with next to no effort while I'm still trying to decide what the hell to wear.

"You're down to eighteen minutes," he says, stopping right next to me. His deodorant or cologne or a combination of the two instantly washes over me and I find myself closing my eyes for the briefest moment while I breathe him in.

God he smells so good.

"Seventeen," he says, standing much closer now.

My eyes snap open and I suck in a sharp breath from his sudden nearness.

"Well I can't get ready with you standing in my face," I spit out, proud of myself for holding my crap together.

"Sixteen and a half." He grins, dropping a light kiss to my temple before quickly stepping into the bathroom. My god this man…

Whiplash doesn't even begin to cover the way his behavior is making me feel. Hot, cold, hot, cold. And to think, I've got nearly three more weeks of this before we're scheduled to go home.

And what's even worse, just the thought of leaving makes me want to curl into a ball and sob uncontrollably. I'm nowhere close to ready to go home. Honestly, I don't know if I ever will be.

****

"I don't think I can do this." Looking up at Kane, I'm fearful I might lose the contents of my stomach at any moment.

"Come on, Elara. You said you've always wanted to try it," he reminds me, gesturing to the small plane to our right.

"*Did*. Did want to try it. As in don't anymore."

"You're just nervous. Come on, it's going to be incredible," he assures me, turning toward our instructor for the day without giving me a chance to say more.

After nearly an hour of instruction and watching a short video which–thank god–was available in English, we both suited up and climbed aboard a small plane with two other divers who would be doing tandem jumps with us.

The whole time I kept telling myself there was no way Kane would go through with this. In my mind I kept envisioning Kam who would always talk me out of doing anything even remotely dangerous. But as I've come to realize very clearly over the last few days, Kane is not like Kam in this regard. And as the plane levels out and everything starts to unfold, I realize very quickly that he is in fact going to jump and apparently, so am I.

Kane smiles next to me, giving my hand a soft squeeze of encouragement as the instructors prepare us for our jump.

"Kane–" I start but he instantly cuts me off.

"You wanted to find the old Elara," he reminds me, his voice loud so I can hear him over the noise of the plane. "She's still in there. I know she is. This is how we do it. You don't tip toe, you don't hide. You throw yourself out of a plane and remember what it is to be alive." With that, he turns and within seconds the door opens and he disappears through it, leaving me with nothing but his words whirling around in my head.

I don't even process the events happening around me. All I know is when Scott, my tandem diver, hollers *ready* into my ear, I feel like my heart is seconds away from exploding.

I want to scream no, tell him I can't do this, but my words are ripped back into my throat when he leans forward and all of a sudden we are free falling through the open sky. It takes me several seconds to find my ability to breathe, the sudden fall sucking the wind right from my body. But eventually I do. Eventually I find more than just my breath.

The feeling hits me full force. The same feeling I spent my whole life chasing. The pump of the adrenaline through my veins. The rapid thumping of my heart in my chest. The feeling of being alive.

I close my eyes and open my arms, smiling into the force of the wind that presses against my face. This is what I've been looking for. This is what I've been missing. This is it. And Kane knew it. Somehow he knew exactly what I needed and he knew without ever having to ask. He knew this because he paid attention. Because he listened to Kam when he spoke about me and because he'd been listening to me for days.

My heart swells with this knowledge. The knowledge that even despite everything I've been through and everything I've done, there's someone on this Earth that still cares enough to listen. That cares enough to pay attention. That cares enough to want to help me heal as badly as I want to heal him.

As Scott instructs me on the land, I see Kane standing several feet away. I brace for impact, certain I'm seconds away from eating the earth, when Scott leans back and his feet hit the ground running.

I'm pulling at my straps trying to get free the moment we come to a stop. Urgency that I haven't felt in a very long time is driving through me. Scott helps me shed my restraints and the instant I'm free, I'm sprinting across the open field toward Kane.

He can see my smile before I reach him. I know because his smile matches the one I'm wearing. I don't slow down when I get close. Instead I launch myself into Kane's arms

161

with so much force he stumbles back a good two feet before finally regaining his balance.

"That was incredible," I squeal, legs wrapped around his waist, arms locked around his neck as I stare into his dark eyes.

Then I do something I never thought I'd find myself doing. I lean forward and press my lips to his. Not soft and careful like last night, but a full on frontal assault, our tongues tangling and hands roaming. Every part of my body is high on adrenaline from both the jump and the man whose arms it feels almost too good to be in.

Kane finally breaks away, his breathing ragged, his eyes darker than they've ever been as they find mine and hold tight. "Elara."

"Thank you." I drop my forehead to his, one hand on each side of his face.

"I'd do anything to have you look at me the way you're looking at me right now," he says, straight to the point, no bullshit.

"The jury is in," I mutter against his lips, dipping my face back down to press a light kiss to the corner of his mouth. I know he knows exactly what I'm talking about.

"Is that so?" He pulls back and meets me with a heart stopping smile. "And what's the verdict?"

"So much better than I expected."

If I thought the smile he was giving me moments ago was heart stopping, then the one he's giving me now is powerful enough to stop the world from spinning.

"I'm not done yet," he tells me, gently setting me to my feet as Scott and Rick approach where we're standing.

I don't have time to learn what's next because shortly after we're picked up in an old pickup truck and taken back to the airstrip we took off from. Kane holds my hand the entire time, smiling at me whenever our eyes meet.

By the time we're back in the rental and heading toward our next destination, I feel like I've died and gone straight to heaven. And while it's impossible not to get caught up in everything happening around me– Kane, Italy, skydiving, all of it–a small part of me is still hanging onto the hint of guilt that has buried itself deep in the pit of my gut.

I'm starting to believe it will always be there and I'd be lying if I said I didn't deserve worse than that. But even with such dark thoughts seeping in, they don't put a marginal damper on my day. And that has everything to do with the man sitting next to me.

The man whose smile makes me blind to the world. The man whose kiss makes me feel something I have never felt before. The man whose eyes are currently locked right on mine, telling me he feels it to.

Chapter Fifteen
Elara

"So, how was it?" I hear the smile in my dad's voice.

"It was incredible." I sigh, leaning against the railing of the terrace. "I still can't believe you and Kane did that and neither one of you said a word."

After skydiving, Kane treated me to the most incredible lunch at a small outdoor eatery before leading me two blocks away to a group of houses all bunched together at the top of a hill. I didn't realize where we were at first. That is until I saw it. The tall yellow house that my mother posed for a picture in front of all those years ago.

Apparently Kane had called my Dad a couple days after we arrived in Italy. After pulling some strings, Dad was able to track down an old friend who got him in touch with the new owner of his grandparents' old house. A small frail looking woman by the name of Everett, who readily agreed to let us visit after Dad explained to her what it would mean to me.

"I like him," my dad interjects without commenting on my statement. "He seems like good people."

Kane's ears must have been burning because he chooses this very moment to push his way through the door, a takeout bag in one hand and a bottle of wine in the other, his smile lighting up the room the moment his gaze meets mine.

"Yeah, he is," I admit, my focus trained on Kane. My stomach is a mess of butterflies as I watch him deposit the food and wine on the small table in the corner before stalking toward me.

"You sound good, honey," my dad regards, pulling me from my haze. I try to snap out of the fog Kane always seems to cast over me.

"I feel good," I admit, turning when Kane steps up next to me and drops an arm over my shoulders, his lips instantly connecting with my temple before his gaze goes out to the view of the water.

"Good. I knew this trip would be good for you."

"Per usual, you were right," I tell him.

"I don't think I'll ever get tired of hearing those words." He chuckles and it instantly brings a smile to my face.

"To stand where she stood," I say, redirecting the conversation back to the main reason I called him–the trip to my family's old house. "It felt like she was right there with me," I admit, emotion swelling in my chest like it had the very moment I stood on those steps and looked up at that yellow house on the hill.

"Because she was," he says moments before I hear his hand slide over the phone and his muffled voice speak.

"Dad?" I question, unsure of whom he could be talking to.

"Sorry, honey."

"Who were you talking to?"

"It was nothing. Just Jenson next door asking a question."

"Right," I say, thinking he could have come up with a better excuse than Jenson, who never speaks to anyone, asking him a question outside when less than three minutes ago he claimed to be in the kitchen making stir fry.

165

"Is Kane there right now?" My dad switches gears and my eyes immediately shoot up to the man standing next to me, his muscular arm draped around me.

"He is," I confirm, smiling when he looks down and meets my gaze.

"Put him on, would you, dear?"

"Uh, sure." I hesitate for a moment before handing the phone up to Kane who instantly drops his arm from my shoulders and takes the device, holding it to his ear.

"Sam." Kane greets my father like they're old buddies and my expression turns even more confused. "Yeah. Uh huh." He pauses, listening to my father. "She did." He chuckles, smiling down at me. "Absolutely. Will do." He responds to something else, his gaze falling to me seconds before he says, "Bye, Sam." And disconnects the call.

"What the hell?" I shoot up at him, taking my phone out of his hand.

"What?" He grins, chuckling as he follows me inside the room.

"Sam? You and my father are on a first name basis now?"

"Well, that is his name, Elara." His laugh deepens, clearly amused.

"You know what I mean. And what the heck? You didn't even let me say goodbye," I point out.

"He said he needed to go. Told me to tell you he loves you and you'll talk soon." He crosses to the table and slides into one of the rickety chairs, gesturing to the other one before speaking again. "Sit." It's not an order, more like a gentle request.

"I'm still mad at you." I huff, dropping down into the seat across from him.

"I didn't realize you were mad in the first place, so I certainly don't understand why you're *still* mad."

"Smart ass. It's going on the list," I say pointedly.

"After the day I've had, not even your lists are going to damper my mood."

"The day you've had?" My heart does a little flip in my chest and my false agitation quickly evaporates.

"I got to jump out of a plane for the first time in my life, only to be attacked in the best way possible the minute my feet were back on solid ground." My cheeks heat up and I know pink is spreading across my face even though I can't see it. "And after that, something changed," he continues. "The wall was gone and for the first time I got to see you. You, Elara. Not the person you try to pretend to be or the one you think you need to be. But you. The real you. And damn if you aren't even more beautiful than I ever imagined you'd be." My breath hitches in my throat and I honest to god have no words to say.

Not a single one.

So I blurt the first thing that comes to mind, "You gonna open that bottle or what?" I point at the wine still sitting unopened in front of him.

He gives me a knowing smile.

"Anything for you." He tips his chin and gets to work on uncorking the bottle before pouring a generous amount of red wine into both of our glasses.

I lift mine and instantly suck a large gulp back, needing something to calm the nervous energy pulsing inside me. I don't know when or how things changed so rapidly. One minute we're strangers on some crazy trip across the world. The next we're laughing and smiling like it's always been this way.

"So what did you get?" I point to the bag between us, which smells so delicious it's a wonder I'm not salivating.

"Pizza."

"Pizza?" I question. "All the incredible places you could have gotten food and you picked pizza?" Despite how good it smells, I curl my nose.

"This isn't just any ol' pizza, babe. Just wait." He pulls two containers from the bag and opens both in front of meOne appears to be a small veggie style pizza topped with a variation of tomatoes, peppers, and mushrooms. The other has fresh herbs, spinach, and something crumbly over the top. Both look incredible and my stomach instantly grumbles. Okay, so maybe pizza wasn't the worst call in the world.

Kane laughs at my reaction as I moan around my first bite of the herb pizza and then each bite after that. He's right, it's not your average pizza.

I smile and enjoy his company more than usual once the wine starts to take effect. Not that I don't always enjoy his company, but the buzz of the alcohol relaxes me more and I'm able to enjoy him without all the other noise in my head.

I swear I could listen to Kane talk for hours on end and never get bored with a thing he says. Broaching the subjects of ex-girlfriends was the only time I became slightly uncomfortable during the course of the evening, but only because the little green jealous bug in my belly wouldn't stop dancing.

Needless to say that conversation ended quickly, but not before I learned that he has never had a serious relationship and while he has dated here and there, he hasn't met anyone that stuck enough to move into what he considers a "real" relationship. Secretly I hope I can change that but then quickly second guess myself for even thinking it.

It's after midnight before we finally decide to call it a night, by which point my eyelids are so heavy it's a wonder I've been able to keep them open this long. While it's been one of the best days of my life, it's also been emotionally draining. Kane makes me feel so many various emotions that by the time my brain is able to process even half of them it's already overheating and starting to shut down.

I exit the bathroom after washing my face and brushing my teeth, wearing a similar pair of pajamas as the night before.

Kane is already in bed, stretched out on his side, no shirt, eyes locked on me. *Great.* As if it isn't hard enough to control myself around him, he now has his beautiful chest and abs out on display and I swear it's like each ripple of muscle is calling *"Touch me"* with every step I take.

Not sure how to proceed, I hesitate at the edge of the bed.

Last night was easy. Kane shut me out and turned his back on me. And while it bothered me at the time, I now secretly wish he'd do the same thing tonight so I wouldn't have to stand here looking at him, trying to convince myself of all the reasons this is such a bad idea.

"Come here," Kane says, sensing my hesitation. He reaches out his arms and I find myself instantly going into them.

He pulls me into a deep embrace, my back to his front, his face nuzzled in my hair, arm locked tight around my waist.

I'm surprised by how easy I find myself relaxing. How quickly sleep starts to muddle my head. How incredible it feels when he whispers in my ear, "Night, babe," seconds before I peacefully doze off, thinking there's nowhere else I'd rather be than exactly where I am.

****

I wake abruptly when a cool breeze whips over my body. Blinking into the early morning light, it isn't until I look around that I realize the breeze is coming in from the open terrace where Kane is once again standing, bare back to me.

His stance is easy, relaxed. I can tell immediately that he's lost somewhere inside his head. Mainly because when I climb out of bed he doesn't turn toward me like I expect him to. Deciding a visit to the bathroom can't wait, I quickly slip inside and do my business – brushing my teeth and splashing some water on my face before re-entering the room to find Kane still standing in the same spot as before. Only this time when he hears me, he turns, a slow grin pulling up the corners of his mouth.

"Mornin'."

"Good morning." I grab a throw blanket from the foot of the bed and wrap it around my shoulders before going to him. It may be hot during the day but the morning air is crisp with the cool breeze coming in off the water.

He opens his arms for me and I go right to them, breathing in his scent the moment he wraps me in his embrace.

"You sleep okay?" he murmurs into my hair, turning our bodies so we're facing the water.

"I did. You?"

"Better than I've slept in a very long time."

I don't know why but his admission does something funny to my insides. Maybe because I like to think *I'm* the reason he slept so good. Like maybe somehow I bring him the same semblance of peace that he brings me.

"Good." I lean my head back and smile up at him. Within seconds his lips find mine, brushing them in a whisper of a kiss that sends my heart once again galloping full throttle inside my chest.

"What's the plan for the day?" I ask when he pulls back and turns his gaze back out to the sea.

"It's our last full day here. I thought maybe we could just see where the day takes us."

"I like that plan." I tighten my arms around his middle and squeeze.

"You hungry?" he asks, his hand trailing lazily through my hair.

"Starving," I admit.

I'm one of those people who's ready to eat breakfast five minutes after waking up. I've always been that way, even when I was really little. Kam used to say I was inhuman – that people need at least an hour to wake up before they eat. I always gently reminded him that just because he needed that long did not mean everyone else did.

"I spotted a little restaurant on the corner while I was out getting pizza last night. Thought we could swing in there this morning, get some coffee and a muffin before figuring out the day."

"Sounds perfect," I say, before adding, "Can I ask you a question?"

"Of course." His hand is still in my hair and I instantly rethink what I'm about to say. If I ask what's on my mind, I'm sure it will most likely put a damper on this perfect morning, but because I'm me and the queen of word vomit, I ask anyway.

"What exactly are we doing here?" I lean back slightly just in time to see his expression shift, a shadow passing through his eyes which disappears almost instantly.

"I don't really know," he answers after a long beat.

"I just mean…" I hesitate. "You know what, never mind." I step out of his embrace and quickly go back inside the room, going straight to my duffel bag.

"Elara?" Humor is clear in Kane's voice and when I flip my gaze up to him, I'm surprised to see he's smiling. "What are you doing?" He looks at my duffel bag before turning his gaze back to my face.

"Getting clothes to change into," I say like it should be obvious.

"I mean, why are you all the way over there when you should be right here?" He points at the spot directly in front of him.

"If we're going to go to breakfast I have to get dressed," I say, slightly embarrassed that after one incredible day together I'm already pushing him to know where this is going when I'm not entirely sure I know where *I* want it to go yet.

"Elara," he repeats, his smile firmly intact. "Come here." He once again points to the ground in front of him.

Letting out a slow exhale, my feet shuffle toward him before my mind has time to process the action. The next thing I know I'm back in his arms, my cheek pressed to his bare chest.

"I don't know why I asked that," I admit, keeping my arms at my sides.

"I do." He drops a kiss to the top of my head before tipping my face up to look at him.

"You do?" I ask..

"You're wondering the same thing I am. Is this about Kam or is this about us?" His expression falls serious, his hand snaking around the back of my neck to hold my head firm so I can't look away. "And the truth is, Elara; at first I worried it *was* about Kam for me. A way for me to feel closer to him because well, you make me feel closer to him. The night before last, after I kissed you, I realized it had nothing to do with Kam and that made me feel so guilty I couldn't even look at you afterward."

Well I guess that explains him shutting me out.

"But then yesterday, when you launched yourself at me and kissed me, all I could think was guilt be damned because there was no way I wasn't going to explore this with you. Whatever this is." He runs the back of his other hand down my cheek, his thumb skirting against my bottom lip.

"It isn't about Kam for me," I admit, but quickly continue, "I mean, at first it was. But now, I don't know. Yesterday when I looked at you, you were no longer Kam's brother. You were Kane. And I liked what I saw."

"Then keep your eyes open, babe, because it's about to get a whole lot better." His smile once again graces his face just moments before he's bending down and laying a light kiss to my lips.

"Guilt be damned," he mumbles against my mouth before deepening the kiss. His tongue sweeps against mine in the most delicious motion making my knees wobble slightly.

When he pulls away moments later I'm breathless, captivated, and completely consumed by a man I barely know and yet can't seem to get enough of. And while there's still that knot in the pit of my stomach, the one that tells me I shouldn't be allowed to feel this way, it's currently being silenced by a pair of incredible dark eyes looking at me in a way I'm quite certain no one has ever looked at me.

My stomach and my heart flip flop in unison.

Oh boy.

Chapter Sixteen
Elara

It's been a week since we returned to Milan from Manarola. A week filled with countless heart flips, butterflies galore, and a newly forming tingle that starts at the back of my neck and works its way down to my toes every single time I look at Kane.

We've taken things extremely slow, learning more about each other with each passing day. He kisses me regularly…as in all the time. But our physical relationship has not gone past that. Unless you count spooning, because Kane Thaler is one hell of a spooner.

Needless to say he upgraded from the couch to the bedroom the day we returned from our three days in Manarola and he's been there since. There's something so incredible about him being the last person I see, the last voice I hear, the last touch I feel before I fall asleep. And then I get to wake up and experience every sensation all over again. It's become my new favorite way to start my day.

Music's coming from the apartment as I climb the last staircase, so I pause outside the door to listen.

James Bay.

Did I mention he has stellar taste in music too?

Surprised that he's already home from the office, given that it's only four-thirty, I quickly push my way inside, depositing two shopping bags on the floor next to the door before spotting Kane in the kitchen.

He's shirtless–*of course he is*–and barefoot, his suit pants low on his hips doing some really good things for his ass. Not that he needs any help in that department. *It's hot in the small apartment,* is what he always says when I ask him why he never has clothes on. I think he walks around like this on purpose because he likes the reaction it gets from me.

I stand in the doorway of the small kitchen for several seconds watching him stir something in a pot before he finally senses my presence, clearly not hearing my entrance over the music blaring through the small apartment.

"There she is." He grins, popping a lid on the pan before peeking into the oven.

"What are you doing home already?" I ask, giggling when he pulls me into his arms and drops a kiss to my mouth.

"Wrapped up early. Thought I'd surprise you with dinner."

"Now that you mention it, you have yet to wow me with these so called cooking skills you claim to have. About time you put your money where your mouth is." I pull back and give him a teasing wink.

"You just wait, Miss Menton. I'm going to knock your socks off."

"I'm not wearing any socks," I point out, looking down at the flip flops on my feet.

"Would you rather I say it'll knock your panties off?" His voice drops low, lips sweeping against mine. "Because that can be arranged."

My body instantly gets tight and a slow ache forms in my lower belly. I have to take a few calming breaths to pull myself together. I've told myself we need to take things slow, but when he looks at me the way he's looking at me right now it's all I can do not to tackle him right here on the kitchen floor. Kane stirs something in me; a desire I've never felt toward another person.

"You talk a big talk, Thaler," I tease, needing to lighten the mood.

"I walk a big walk too." He winks, taking my hand in his before stepping back and twirling me under his arm.

My head drops back on a laugh when he pulls me back to his chest and starts swaying slowly back and forth to my favorite song on this album, "Move Together".

My laughter doesn't last long. Like the song, Kane's movements are slow and sultry. His hand grazes slowly down my back, his lips trail up the side of my neck, his hips sway back and forth against me as he effortlessly moves us around the small kitchen.

All I can do is hold onto him, fearful that if I let go my legs won't be able to support my weight. That's what he does to me; he turns my body into mush and my mind even more so.

"Elara." His whispered words at the base of my throat send a rush of need through my body.

Tangling my fingers in his hair, I lift his face to mine before pressing my lips firmly against his. He instantly deepens the kiss, his arms wrapping around my waist as his tongue sweeps through my mouth.

An involuntary moan slips past my lips and he swallows it whole, pulling me off my feet so the only choice I have is to wrap my legs around his waist, my arms locking around his neck.

Backing me into the refrigerator, his mouth continues to move against mine. When his fingers slide up my shirt, touching the bare skin of my side, something inside me snaps.

All I see is Kane.

All I smell is Kane.

All I feel is Kane.

All I want is Kane.

My hands find the back of his neck as I pull him closer to me, my fingers digging lightly into his flesh as the *want* coursing through my body starts to take hold. I feel like I can't get him close enough. I want to feel him everywhere.

"I want you," I say against his mouth.

"Elara," he groans, pulling back slightly to look at me.

"I want you," I repeat with more force. "I want this."

I see the conflict behind his dark eyes, the battle he's trying to hide. But when I lean forward and whisper a small "please" against his lips, uncertainty is instantly replaced with something darker. Hunger. Desire. Need. It's only seconds before his lips are on mine again and he's moving with me still in his arms, guiding us through the small apartment with complete ease.

He pushes his way through the bedroom door, but I'm already too preoccupied to care where we are. The only things that matter are the way his body flexes as he lowers me to my feet and the way his hands skirt up my bare back as he pulls the fabric of my shirt over my head and deposits it on the floor. My bra is next, his fingers against my flesh causing prickles to pepper down my arms as he slides each strap down before tossing it to the side.

He steps back and looks at me for a long moment, appreciation shining through his dark eyes. Just the sight has my skin blistering from the heat of his gaze. And then he's moving, slowly lowering himself onto his knees in front of me.

I'm in complete amazement, watching him unravel me like he's done it a million times before. His fingers go to the waist band of my jeans, unbuckling and sliding them down

177

my legs in one fluent movement. He kisses the top of each thigh, running his nose along the seam of my panties before slowly standing.

He kisses me sweetly before guiding me onto the bed, my back coming to rest atop the thick comforter.

I watch as he stands before me, hear his rapid breathing as he leans forward and slowly removes my last article of clothing.

My entire body goes rigid as he spreads my legs open, allowing his eyes to trail across my now bare exterior. I don't shy away from his penetrating stare. Instead I embrace it. Encourage it. I want him to see all of me, have all of me.

I see the flash of recognition cross his face when his eyes find the tattoo on my hip but it's gone as quickly as it appeared.

I hear the buckle of his pants and the rustle of fabric as they fall to the floor, but my gaze remains locked on his face. On the way he's looking at me–making every part of my body ache with the need for his touch.

He crawls up the bed, the heat from his body making tiny beads of sweat form along the back of my neck as he settles his weight on top of me.

He pushes my hair from my face, his lips once again finding mine as he kisses me deeply. I jump slightly when his hand slides between us and settles between my legs. When his fingers push inside of me, all coherent thought seems to leave my body.

I become greedy, lifting my hips to meet his hand as he pumps his fingers inside of me. The effect his touch has on me, the pleasure causing my body to pool around his hand.

"Please," I whimper when he pulls his hand away, leaving me unsatisfied and wanting so much more.

"Please?" His mouth settles over mine again as he gently pulls my bottom lip into his mouth. "Tell me what you want, Elara," he whispers against my lips.

"You. I want you." My words are pleading, begging even.

I've never had a man's touch control me the way his does. I feel each flicker of movement across every surface of my body.

"Please," I whimper again when he slides his hard length against me, his face hovering inches above mine.

"Is this what you want?" he asks, grinding down harder.

"Yes," I hiss, digging my nails into his shoulders.

"This?" He continues to tease me, lining himself at my entrance but making no move to do what every part of my body is aching for him to do.

"Now, Kane," I practically scream, my frustration mounting

This seems to snap what little restraint he has left and he immediately plunges inside of me, both of us crying out from the intensity of our bodies coming together. Pulling back, he slams into me again, pulling yet another scream of pleasure from my mouth.

I try to hold back. The moans and whimpers that seem to keep flowing from my mouth, but I can't. He's pulling everything from me, making me feel every ounce of pleasure as he thrusts harder and harder inside of me.

It takes minutes—or maybe it's only seconds—before the warmth starts to work its way through my lower belly. Kane senses my heightening desperation and pushes my legs further open, pounding into me so deeply I swear I feel him everywhere.

"Kane," I cry, my body so overcome with pleasure I'm not sure how to control myself.

His mouth finds mine as he swallows my cries of pleasure; the earth seeming to literally fall out from beneath me. My body explodes around him, and I swear I have never felt anything so intense before in my entire life.

It comes in waves, washing over me, warming every single inch of my body until I can feel the effects to the very tips of my fingers and toes. Kane makes me feel every ounce of my pleasure as he continues to thrust inside of me, pulling every last bit of desire from me that he can. My body is shaking, trembling from the aftermath of what has to be the most incredible orgasm I've ever experienced.

Kane's movements start to become less controlled, frantic even, and then he lets out a deep groan, pumping inside of me several more times before letting himself go.

When he stills inside of me, he pulls back slightly and hits me with the most incredible smile, the action doing funny things to my heart. His lips find my cheek first, then my forehead, followed by the tip of my nose before he finally presses them gently against my own.

I continue to pulse around him as he sweetly kisses my mouth, his tongue sliding against mine as his hand pushes the tangled mess of hair away from my face.

There are so many things I need to say, so many things bubbling to the surface that I have to bite back. I want you. I need you. I'm falling so hard and fast that I'm terrified if I let go I'll go careening out of control.

Of course I can't say any of this, certain it would freak him out. Hell, I'm freaked out. How is it after less than three weeks my feelings are already so strong? I can't explain it, can't rationalize it, but I also can't deny the truth.

I'm falling in love with Kane Thaler…

****

"You have the same tattoo as Kam," Kane says, his head on my stomach, his fingers tracing the outline of the permanent ink on my hip.

"I do," I murmur, my hand lazily playing with his hair.

180

We haven't left the bed in over an hour, at least *I* haven't. Kane left briefly to shut off the oven, announcing moments later that I ruined his dinner. When I asked him if he was complaining he grinned and dove back into bed with me. And that's where we've stayed.

"We didn't plan it that way," I continue when he doesn't reply. "Kam designed it and as soon as I saw it, I knew I wanted it too. I guess it sounds kind of corny, getting the same tattoo as my best friend, but it meant something to him, therefore it meant something to me."

"I don't think that sounds corny at all." He kisses the tattoo which instantly sends a wave of emotion washing over me. "You have this piece of him. Something that's permanent. Something that will always be there. Nothing corny about that."

Feeling the heavy shift in the room, I instantly divert from talking about Kam.

"What about you? Do you have any tattoos?" I ask, biting my bottom lip when he looks up at me and hits me with a sultry smile.

"You wanna explore and find out?" His eyes get dark and before I can react he's shifted next to me and somehow managed to slide me on top of him.

"What do I get if I find something?" I play along, loving the heat that floods his gaze.

"Whatever you want, babe." He groans when I lean forward and press my lips to the base of his throat.

"Whatever I want?" I speak against his warm flesh, loving the way his throat bobs when he takes a hard swallow. "I think I like this game." I nip at his collarbone; pretty certain he's going to like it too.

****

Four Years Earlier

"Are you having fun, bean?" Kam asks, his voice low in my ear as he moves me gently across the makeshift dance floor his parents set up in the backyard for his graduation party.

"I am," I admit, pulling back to smile up at him.

"Even though my parents hired quite possibly the worst band in existence?" He chuckles, gesturing to the side where a four person band plays from the large stone patio a few yards away.

"They aren't that bad." I crinkle my nose at him.

"You only think that because half the music they've played is eighties shit."

"There is nothing wrong with the eighties," I object.

"Everything was wrong with the eighties," he disagrees, his gaze going over my head to something behind us.

"Everything okay?" I ask, noticing the shadow that crosses over his face.

"Yeah." He shakes it off, refocusing on me. "Marie is hanging all over my brother... Again. You'd think she'd get the hint already."

"The hint?" I say, not familiar with the situation.

All I know is there is no way I am turning around to see what he's talking about. No way, no how. I've met the dark eyes of Kane Thaler one too many times over the course of this evening. And if I'm being honest, I'm not sure I like that every time I look at him his gaze is locked on me. I don't know if he's sizing me up, trying to figure me out for his brother's sake, or if it's something more. And while I can't explain it, I can't deny that my gut instinct is that it's something more. I just don't know what.

"Marie has been chasing Kane around since we moved here. They've never been any more than friends and he's

tried letting her down easy several times. But last year, they got drunk at a party and Kane ended up sleeping with her."

"Oh lord," I mutter, already knowing where this is going.

"Yeah." He gives me a knowing look. "Needless to say she woke up the next day convinced they were going to be together."

"Let me guess. It didn't work out as she had hoped."

"Not even a little," he confirms. "And what's worse, he left town shortly after and avoided taking her calls, so she kept showing up here asking if we had heard from him. I felt really bad for her but at the same time I wanted to shake her and tell her to wake the hell up. Kane is Kane. She knows him, knows how he is. I don't know why she expected anything more from him than exactly what he did."

"Kamden Joseph, are you telling me your brother is a player?" I cock a brow, having never heard him talk about Kane's love life, or lack thereof, before.

"I wouldn't say he's necessarily a player. I think he means well. But then again, the line of broken hearts he's left behind him might say otherwise. I can't even count on two hands how many girls showed up here either crying or raging pissed while Kane was in high school." He chuckles, shaking his head.

"Somehow that doesn't surprise me," I admit, dragging my teeth along my lower lip.

"No?" He cocks his head and smirks.

"He kind of seems like a player," I admit. "And I've only been around him a couple of hours. There's just something about him. Something that reads 'untouchable'."

"And that's the appeal," Kam confirms. "Girls chase after guys like Kane. The ones who seem unobtainable. It's like some messed up game." He shakes his head. "Confuses the hell out of me."

"Of course it does." A small laugh passes through my lips.

183

"What's that supposed to mean?" He hits me with a serious expression but his hazel eyes are full of humor.

"You're incapable of playing games, Kam. You are one of those 'what you see is what you get' kind of guys. And I adore that about you," I quickly tack on. "No bullshit. No lies. You're just you."

"I think you're giving me too much credit, bean."

"I think you're not giving yourself enough," I shoot back.

"Always sees the good." Kam smiles, shaking his head before pulling me back flush to his body as the song shifts from a slow song to one a little more upbeat, but still with a slow enough tempo that our current position on the dance floor doesn't seem completely out of place.

I rest my cheek against Kam's chest, smiling when Kris and Mary go whirling by; Kris spinning his wife around the dance floor like they've done it a million times before. Then again they probably have, considering the Thaler's have been married for nearly twenty-five years.

That and I know for a fact Mary has been dragging Kris to a late night Salsa class every Thursday for the last eight months. Kam says his dad complains about it every chance he gets but because it's important to Mary, he keeps going.

My gaze falls to the other people around us as Kam glides us along the dance floor. Hailee, Kam's cousin, and her boyfriend Jimmy. Drake and Carrie, two of Kam's close friends from school. Some other classmates whom I've met but can't for the life of me remember their names.

And then suddenly I'm looking into the same set of dark eyes I've found myself looking into several times over the course of the night. A shiver runs through my body as Kane holds my gaze, his expression unreadable.

God, what is it about this man that has had my stomach in knots a good portion of the night? I try to

184

ignore the way his eyes on me makes me feel and turn my head, resting my other cheek on Kam's chest just as his arms tighten around me.

"I'm really glad you were able to make it tonight, El," Kam speaks into my hair.

"Like I'd miss it." I pull back to smile up at him.

"I just... You've been through a lot this year. I know this isn't easy for you." I know instantly he's talking about my mom.

"Don't." I shake my head, tears instantly pricking the back of my eyes. "I can't talk about it here, Kam."

"I'm sorry. I shouldn't have said anything." He brushes the pad of his thumb over my cheekbone.

"It's fine." I force a smile. "Really," I reassure him. "I just don't want to ruin this night for you."

"You could never ruin this night." He smiles softly.

"Melting into a puddle of tears in the middle of the dance floor might serve to prove you wrong," I say as a joke, but deep down I know that it wouldn't take much to send me there.

"Refer to my earlier statement." His thumb moves from my cheek down my jaw, and in that moment it takes everything in me not to push up on my toes and kiss him.

I can't of course. Because no matter what Kam says, that would most definitely ruin the evening, and perhaps even our friendship.

I blink, quickly dropping my face back to Kam's chest. My gaze once again collides with Kane's, who's dancing with Marie, a petite dark haired girl with big brown eyes and full lips. She's really quite pretty and I can't help but wonder why he doesn't see that in her. Or at least not enough to give her anything more than a drunk induced one night stand.

I instantly feel sad for her. Kane is beautiful. Well, in the manly sense of the word. Every inch of him is carved perfection; from his dark hair to his even darker eyes, to the

185

*incredible curve of his jaw which is currently clenched so
tight I wouldn't be surprised if his face hurt.*

*My eyebrow shoots up in question, letting him know I
see him and I'm more than a little confused by why he's
glaring at me like I've rubbed him the wrong way when in
reality we've barely spoken.*

*He turns for a moment before once again facing me.
His expression is slightly softer but his eyes are no less
intense. His gaze jumps to the side of Kam's face and then
back to me before he abruptly steps away from Marie and
quickly exits the dance floor.*

*I watch him walk away before my eyes dart to Marie
who seems even more confused than I do. Poor girl.*

*Shaking my head, I refocus on Kam–the reason I'm
here–and do my best to shove his sexy as sin but jerk
brother out of my head. I've already got enough on my
plate right now. I don't need to waste my time obsessing
over someone I likely won't see again for another three
years–considering that's how long Kam and I have been
friends and this is the first time I've ever met him.*

****

I wish I could say that was the last I thought of Kam's
brother. I wish I could say I forgot him the moment he
walked away, but that isn't true. The expression he wore
when he looked at me across that dance floor had been
burned into my retinas and I couldn't shake the feeling
that left me with.

It took several days before the effects of that night
finally faded away. But even as they did, even after Kane
returned to Chicago and things returned to normal, I
would still wake in the middle of the night seeing those
eyes.

A part of me thought maybe it was just his obvious
good looks. You'd have to be blind not to be effected by a

man that looks like Kane Thaler. The same could be said for Kam as well. But somewhere deep down I knew there was more.

I guess you could say I was drawn to Kane from that very first night. A pull I didn't understand stayed with me for years to come. It lived in the background, simmering just out of sight and it wasn't until I was staring into those dark eyes again years later that it all came back like a gust of wind, sucking the air straight from my lungs.

Only I wasn't the same girl. When our eyes met over Kam's casket I knew none of it mattered anymore. I was heartbroken–devastated–not sure how I was going to go on living knowing I'd never see Kam smile again. Never get to count the blue and green speckles in his eyes or hear him call me butter bean. Knowing his sweet laughter would never fill my ears again, I felt nothing but an empty void where my heart used to be.

Until suddenly it started beating again...

I open my heavy eyes to find Kane's gaze locked on mine, his face hovering just inches above me.

"You were dreaming." he murmurs, brushing his lips lightly against mine. "What were you dreaming about?" he asks, rolling me to my side so my face goes to his chest.

"You," I admit, hanging on the cusp of sleep, not entirely sure if I'm actually awake or still dreaming. "It's with you now," I mutter as I slip back under.

"What is?" I hear him in the distance.

"My heart."

Chapter Seventeen
Elara

"Tell me something about you I don't know." I trail my fingers gently along Kane's bare chest as I lay next to him in bed, tucked into the crook of his arm.

"Like what?" he asks, his fingers playing with the ends of my hair.

"Like anything. Just something I don't know."

"That's pretty vague, babe." He chuckles, the rumble under my cheek a welcome one. "I hate the color red. There, how's that?"

"Okay not really what I had in mind, but wait," I pause, just now processing what he said. "What do you mean you *hate* the color red?"

"Just what I said, I hate the color red," he repeats, voice thick with humor.

"Like it's your least favorite color or the sight of it actually bothers you?"

"Both." He slides his hand down my bare arm causing goose bumps to erupt across my skin.

"Hmm." I think on this for a moment.

"You're mentally running through your wardrobe right now, aren't you?" His laugh deepens and for the tiniest moment my mind tricks me into believing it's Kam lying next to me. Not because I want Kane to be Kam but because what he said was something Kam would have said.

"You know me too well already." I push my previous thought away.

"Well, how deeply impacted is your closet by this news?" God I love when he talks and I can hear the smile in his voice.

"That I can think of, not at all. I mean, I'm sure I have something red somewhere but it's not a great color on me."

"I can't imagine a color that doesn't look good on you."

"Perhaps I should slip into something red and put that to the test." I prop my head up, resting my chin on the back of my hand atop his chest so I can look at him.

"Do you have anything red here?" He cocks a brow down at me.

"No, but that doesn't mean I can't buy something," I counter.

"You would." He grins.

"Tell me something else."

"What else do you want to know?"

"Everything."

"Everything." He chuckles. "How about we go with one thing at a time?"

"Fine." I huff, pushing up into a sitting position before turning my body so that I'm facing him, twisting my legs Indian style in front of me.

I let my eyes soak in the sight of him; propped up on a stack of pillows, one arm draped behind his head, hair a mess, eyes sated, his incredible chest and stomach on full display. My god, he really is way too good looking for his own good.

"You were saying?" he prompts when my eyes still haven't left his torso.

I blink, my gaze going to his face to see he's wearing a cocky smirk. Yep, he definitely knows where my mind was right then.

"Favorite band?" I shoot off the first thing that comes to mind.

"Backstreet Boys."

"Favorite mov... Wait? What did you just say?" My eyes widen in surprise.

"Backstreet Boys," he says like he couldn't be more serious.

"You're kidding," I say disbelieving.

"Of course I am." He finally cracks, laughing at the shocked look on my face. "Babe, Backstreet Boys, really? Do I look like the kind of man that dances around singing 'Bye, Bye, Bye'?" He impersonates the hand gestures.

"That's not the Backstreet Boys." I fight to control my laughter.

"My point exactly." His easy smile does something wonky to my insides and I find myself struggling to keep hold of the conversation at hand when all I really want to do is climb up his body and have a repeat of last night, this morning, and this afternoon.

"So who is your favorite band then?"

"If I had to pick just one I think I'd go with Manchester Orchestra."

"I approve." I nod, causing his smile to spread.

"I didn't realize I was being judged on my answers." He narrows his gaze at me, his expression humored.

"Just keeping a running tally." I shrug, seconds before his incredible laugh moves through the room. With a wide smile on my face, I continue, "Favorite food?"

"That's hard." He thinks on it for a moment. "I'm going to go with pasta. Pasta of any kind."

"So what you're saying is you're a carb whore."

"A what?"

"A carb whore," I say like that's a term regularly used in the real world.

"I eat pasta a lot. If that makes me a carb whore then fuck it, I'll own that title." His grin stretches across his face, the action giving his eyes almost a sparkle.

My heart thuds in my chest.

"How do you eat a lot of pasta and still look like that?" I point to his abs.

"It's called the gym, babe."

"Shut up." I lay a light smack to his hard stomach. "I know you work out… Obviously," I say after a thick swallow. "But even if I spent ten hours a day at the gym I don't think I could eat pasta regularly and maintain any sort of decent figure."

"Guess I'm lucky." He winks.

"Men," I groan.

"Are you done asking me questions now?"

"You're not that lucky."

"Well then please, Miss Menton, continue," he says like I'm some client in a board room rather than the woman in his bed.

"Hmm. Let me think." I tap my chin like I'm thinking really hard, causing Kane to chuckle. "How old were you when you had your first kiss?"

"Twelve," he says with no hesitation.

"Twelve?" I gawk at him.

"Kate Malbourne. Behind the shed at her parents' house," he says matter of fact.

"Twelve?" I repeat.

"How old were you?" he asks, turning the question on me.

"Not twelve," I clip. "I don't know, I guess I was fifteen or sixteen."

"You don't remember how old you were?" He seems to find this humorous.

"It wasn't the greatest experience of my life. It was quite mortifying actually. I try not to think about it," I ramble.

"Was it that bad?"

"Worse." I sigh. "He bit my tongue."

"He what?" He slides up into a sitting position, not even trying to hide how funny he finds this bit of information.

"He bit my tongue," I repeat.

"Babe, when you say he *bit* it..."

"I mean, when I stuck my tongue in his mouth he bit down...hard."

"Oh my god." Kane holds his stomach, laughter roaring through him.

"Screw you, jerk." I shove at him. "I don't think he meant to do it. I think he was a little over excited and clamped his teeth down when I stuck my tongue in his mouth. Anyway, it was his first kiss too so I guess I shouldn't have expected much."

"I'm surprised you didn't swear off kissing right then and there."

"I would have if it weren't for my friends promising me that what happened to me *never* happened to anyone else. Eventually I figured it had to get better than that."

"And did it?" He rests his back against the headboard, eyeing me knowingly.

"You already know the answer to that one," I tell him before quickly redirecting the conversation back to him. "First time you had sex?"

"Fifteen. Rachel Balanie."

"God. Fifteen?"

"That's actually not that young, especially for a teenage boy," he informs me. "How old were you?"

"Seventeen. Mike Webster."

"Did he bite anything he wasn't supposed to?" He raises an eyebrow at me.

"Oh my god, I shouldn't have told you that story." I shake my head, not able to hide my smile even though I try like hell to.

"Can't take it back now."

"I'm aware." I hit him with an evil glare–one that I know he sees right through.

"Is that your attempt at mean muggin'? Because I gotta tell you, babe, it's not working." He laughs when I once again smack his stomach.

"Asshole," I say dramatically.

"Have you ever been in love?" Kane's question is so out of left field it takes several long moments before I've recovered enough to form a response.

"Have you?" I counter.

"No," he answers simply. "You're turn," he prompts when I make no attempt to say anything.

"That's a complicated question with an even more complicated answer."

"I'm sure I can keep up."

"I don't know," I finally answer on a long sigh.

"You don't know?" He arches a brow at me, his confusion apparent.

"I mean, I loved Kam. For years I thought I was in love with him. I never loved anyone else. He had my heart and didn't even know it. But now..." I trail off, not sure how to put the next part into words.

"Now what?" Kane leans forward, disconnecting my hands that I've unknowingly knotted in front of me.

"Now I'm not sure if I was in love with him or if I just loved him so much I thought I was. Does that make sense?"

"Yes and no." He answers truthfully.

"I loved him. I still love him, but things are different now."

"What changed?"

"You." I say seconds before his hand comes up to cup my face.

"Do you remember what you said to me last night?" he asks, his thumb tracing along my bottom lip.

"About what?"

"You woke up in the middle of the night and you said something to me. Do you remember what you said?"

"I said something to you last night?" I question, my stomach hollowing out as I try to rack my brain for any hint of what he's talking about. Only I come up blank.

"Mm hmm." He leans forward so only a couple inches separate our faces, his hand sliding around to the back of my neck. "You told me it was with me now," he whispers, eyes locked on mine.

"I told you *what* was with you now?" I croak, barely able to force the words out past the lump in my throat.

"This." He places his other hand flat against my chest, directly over my heart. "You said this is with me now. And I have to know, Elara, did you mean that or was it meaningless ramble in the midst of sleep."

While I didn't mean to say that to him, I also can't deny the truth behind it. I buried my heart with Kam – or at least I thought I did – yet now I find it in the hands of someone else. And not just any someone but Kam's older brother.

He's the reason I find myself questioning how I felt for Kam. Because the way I feel about Kane is so much more intense, consuming, raw, and powerful. It's the kind of feeling I feel with my entire body and not just my heart. He's everywhere, weaved into my very core.

In no way does how I feel for Kane lessen the love I had for Kam, but it definitely has forced me to take a closer look at what I thought love was.

"Babe." Kane drops his forehead to mine. "Just tell me," he urges, almost pleading.

"I think I'm falling in love with you," I blurt. When he doesn't respond, I quickly move to explain." I know it seems crazy. I know it hasn't been long. And your Kam's brother. And. And. God, I'm probably freaking you out right now," I ramble. "Would you stop looking at me like that and say *something* already?" I snap when he pulls his face back, looking at me, his expression unreadable and eyes dark as night.

"You love me?" he finally says, one side of his mouth twitching.

"What do you think?" I counter, relief flooding through me when that twitch turns to a full blown smile.

I don't get out another word. Kane's lips are on mine in a flash and before I know it I'm on my back, pinned beneath him.

"Kane, I…" I start to speak but lose my words when he slides inside of me.

"Look at me, Elara," Kane demands, stilling once he's completely filled me. "I've never met anyone like you." He pulls out slowly and slides back in before saying, "I knew from the first moment I saw you." Out and back in. "You're so fucking beautiful." Out and back in. "So fucking beautiful." He looks down at me.

"Kane." I lift my hips, urging him to move. He takes my cue and picks up speed but still keeps his movements controlled, his gaze not breaking mine as he moves above me.

My vision blurs and my body shakes and within minutes I'm already chasing after a release that's dangling right in front of me. Every thrust brings me closer. Dark eyes, lips, jaw, neck, chest. I let my eyes soak in the beauty of the man who's not only opened my eyes but also opened my heart.

I didn't think I could love so easily after Kam but here I am, diving in head first. If losing Kam taught me anything it's that you never know what tomorrow will bring. I spent too much time worrying over my feelings for Kam to ever really explore them. I won't make that mistake again.

Kane is here. Flesh and blood. Body and soul. He's right here with me, inside of me. And I'll be damned if I take even one ounce of that for granted.

It's not an everyday occurrence to feel this strongly for another person. I've been around long enough to know this. So no matter how terrified I am, no matter how down right petrified, I'm going to put myself all in and let the waves take me where they will.

That very thin thread holding me in place shreds away and I fall apart beneath Kane, his name a whispered repeat on my lips as my body pulses around him. His release follows directly after mine and within moments he collapses, the delicious weight of him cocooning me in, making me feel safe for the first time in a very long time.

"You, Elara Menton." Kane lifts his head so that his face is hovering directly above mine. "Are the most fearless person I've ever met. And I don't just mean because you had the guts to come on this trip with me or because you let me drag you thousands of feet in the air and convinced you to throw yourself out of a plane. I mean because when I asked you something, something most people would have been scared to admit, you laid it right out there. No bullshit. No games. I asked you a question and you told me the truth."

"I'm done keeping my feelings inside," I admit softly. "I've done it once before and I don't ever want to do it again. I can't change the past, but I can control how that changes my future."

"Fearless." He smiles, laying a soft kiss to my mouth before pulling back. "I think I fell in love with you the very first time I saw you." His admission has my heart thudding so hard in my chest there's no way he can't feel it. "You were so beautiful. Wearing that light pink dress; your hair pinned up on the sides and left long down the back. I remember watching you all night thinking my brother was quite possibly the luckiest man on the fucking earth."

"Kane," I start, but he keeps talking.

"I thought about you, ya know. After that night of the party. I thought about you more than any man should think about a woman. Especially a woman he barely knew and who was very much spoken for by his brother."

"I thought about you too," I admit, not saying more.

"When I saw you at the funeral, fuck, Elara, even in my grief seeing you was like having sunlight on my face for the first time in days. You made me feel like I could breathe. And that made me feel..."

"Guilty," I finish his sentence, already knowing what he's going to say because I felt the same way.

"I'm done feeling guilty. Whatever this is, whatever is happening between us, I want to keep exploring it. I want this with you. And if I'm being honest, I think Kam would want this for the both of us."

"So do I," I admit, tears pricking the back of my eyes.

"I'm in so fucking deep," he mutters softly against my lips, brushing his mouth against mine.

"Me too," I whisper back.

With that, he kisses me harder and everything I was feeling minutes ago somehow grows a million times over, swelling inside my chest.

Kam Thaler shattered my heart when he died. I never dreamed anyone would be able to piece it back together. But Kane is. Day by day. Minute by minute. Second by second. He's bringing me back to life.

Chapter Eighteen
Elara

"I thought you were coming home two weeks ago," Aunt Carol says as I stretch out on the couch, phone to my ear.

We've been in Italy a total of six weeks now. I was packed, dreading the trip home, and feeling quite emotional that our time here was coming to an end when Kane walked in and announced he got extended.

At first I wasn't sure what that meant for me but directly after telling me his contract was given another four weeks, the next thing he did was ask me to stay. Of course I said yes and then we ended up making love on the tiny kitchen floor.

I think it's safe to say we've made good use of the small space. Honestly, I think I'm gonna miss our tiny little apartment when we leave. It's been like a dream being here with Kane. And even though I know we still have two more weeks, I'm not ready for it to be over.

"We were supposed to but Kane got a four week extension," I answer, refocusing on the current conversation.

"And you decided to stay?" she questions.

"I did."

"And?"

"And what?" I question.

"Elara Rose, don't you play games with me. Tell me everything. I haven't spoken to you in weeks."

"I talked to you last week," I remind her.

"Yes but *he* was there and you couldn't speak freely. Is he there now?"

"No, he won't be home for at least an hour or two."

"Perfect. Now spill."

"There's not a whole lot to tell," I start, not knowing why I bother. Aunt Carol knows me well enough to sense the ridiculous smile I'm wearing as I say it.

"Uh huh." She waits before adding, "Now tell me the truth."

I spend the next twenty minutes pretty much telling her every single detail of the last six weeks. Six of the best weeks of my entire life. I don't leave anything out. When I say I tell her everything I mean *everything.* Right down to the incredible sex that happens daily, if not multiple times a day.

Half way through my rambling, I close my eyes and imagine it's my mom I'm talking to. I wonder how she'd respond. What she would say over how insanely happy Kane makes me. Would she approve? Would she think it's too much too fast? Or would she respond the same as her sister? Supportive and happy for me.

I'm certain it would be the latter...or at least that's what I choose to believe.

"It sounds like a dream." Carol cuts into my thoughts and I realize tears have formed behind my eyes.

"It is." I sit up, shaking off the heavy feeling suddenly sitting on my shoulders. "He is a dream, Carol. I can't even begin to explain it."

"I'm so happy for you, El. You deserve to be happy. My sweet girl. You've lost so much. I know I don't need to remind you of this. But there is one thing I have to ask."

"Then ask," I prompt.

She pauses for several long beats, before continuing, "Please don't take this the wrong way, but do you think your feelings for Kane have anything to do with the fact that he's Kam's brother?"

And there it is, the one question I asked myself the first two weeks we were here – convincing my attraction to him had everything to do with Kam only to learn it had absolutely nothing to do with him and everything to do with Kane.

"I came on this trip because he was Kam's brother. Because I felt like if anyone could understand my pain it was him. Because he made me feel closer to Kam. But Carol, this isn't about Kam anymore. This is about me and Kane and what he makes me feel. I can't explain it. I can't even try to put into words the emotions that overtake me every time he walks in the front door and hits me with that lopsided grin of his. I swear I feel like my heart nearly beats out of my chest when he looks at me a certain way. No one has ever made me feel that way. Not even Kam."

"I just had to ask," she offers softly. "But it sounds like you know what you're doing."

"Well I don't know if I'd go that far." I laugh. "But when it comes to Kane I've never been more certain of anything."

"I just worry about you is all."

"You don't need to. I'm happy. God, I'm insanely happy. And while yes, some of that happiness is overshadowed by everything that's happened in the last few months, it's still there. I didn't think I could feel this way again. I just wish I could shake the guilt I feel knowing that I do," I admit.

"You have nothing to feel guilty for, Elara. Kam died. You didn't. You can't live *your* life carrying the weight of *his* death. There's no doubt in my mind that Kamden loved you more than anything else. He worshipped you, Elara. The last thing he would want is for you to feel guilty for letting yourself be happy. I'm sure that's true for Kane as well. He loved you both. And you know as well as I do that Kam always put the people he loved first."

"I know," I agree softly.

"Then focus on that. Let yourself live, honey. Let yourself love. Freely. Wholly. With everything that you have."

"I'm working on it." I sigh, knowing I've come a long way since three weeks ago when I told Kane I was falling in love with him. And while we haven't talked about it again, we both know it's there. He doesn't have to say he loves me for me to know he does. I can feel it.

"So you're coming home when?" Carol abruptly switches gears, something she does often, especially over the phone.

It's a wonder we've been on the topic of Kane as long as we have. Carol has a way of bouncing from one subject to another and sometimes does it so frequently it takes me a minute to realize we're talking about something different.

"It's supposed to be two weeks from tomorrow."

"Supposed to be? As in, if Kane gets extended you're going to stay?"

"Depends on how long the extension is. Though I don't expect that to happen. Kane says there's not much left for him to do and he can't see them keeping him around longer than they need to considering they're paying an arm and a leg to have him here."

"So two weeks then."

"Two weeks," I confirm.

"And how do you feel about that?"

"Good and bad," I admit. "I'm ready to be home–to see you and dad–to reestablish some sense of normalcy in my life. But I hate the thought of leaving here. I'm afraid that once we leave the bubble we've been living in these past few weeks things will change."

"That's an understandable concern. Something you'll just have to work through when the time comes. Real life has a way of making a muck of things. It's up to you not to let it."

"Sound advice from the woman who's let life muck up every relationship she's ever been in," I point out, knowing she can hear the humor in my voice.

"Just thank god you are not like your Aunt." She says it like she's praising the heavens and I instantly envision her standing in her kitchen, free arm raised to the ceiling as she says it.

"I don't know, I think being like you would be a pretty great thing."

"You're too sweet, but totally misguided." She laughs.

At that very moment, Kane walks into the front door, his eyes finding mine in an instant. My heart flips in my chest at the sight of him. Dark suit, hair combed back, tie loose around his neck. Dear lord this man…

"El, you there?" I hear Carol's voice in my ear and quickly snap out of my fog.

"Yeah, sorry. Kane just got home," I say, looking at the clock to see he's home earlier than I expected him to be.

"Oh well then I'm gonna let you go. I gotta get to the store this morning before it gets too late," she says, reminding me of the time difference between us. It's late afternoon here but still morning there.

"Okay, sounds good. We'll talk soon," I say, sitting up just in time to see Kane shrug out of his black suit jacket and drop it on the back of the chair before stalking toward me.

"Love you, El."

"Love you too." I barely get the last part out before Kane has my phone in his hand, pressing end before dropping it on the side table next to the couch.

"Hey now," I object playfully, letting out a soft cry of surprise when he leans down, latches his hands behind my knees, and hoists me into his arms. I instantly wrap my arms and legs around him, pressing my forehead to his.

"Hey." He smiles against my lips before laying a soft kiss to my mouth.

"Hey," I practically whisper. "You're home early."

"Couldn't get out of there fast enough." He kisses me again. "All I could think about was coming home and taking my girl out on the town." Another kiss, this one more than just a soft press of his lips to mine.

"I think I like the sound of that." I smile against his mouth.

"But first I need something." He drops his face into the crook of my neck and inhales deeply. "God you smell so good."

"Glad you think so." I lean my head back to give him better access to my neck, his lips sliding across the base. "What was it that you needed?" I ask when he makes no attempt to clarify.

"Babe." It's the only thing he says before his hand finds its way into my hair and he's pulling my mouth back to his.

"I see." I giggle, getting the bigger picture. "Lucky for you I'm in a giving mood," I tease, running my tongue along his bottom lip.

"You're always in a giving mood," he reminds me, leaning forward to deposit me on the couch, his body coming down to rest on mine as he settles between my legs.

"Only for you," I point out, gasping when he grinds down against me, a spark of desire lighting fast–the fire instantly spreading through my body.

"That's my girl." I feel him smile against my lips.

It doesn't take long for things to escalate. With Kane I can go from zero to sixty in a matter of seconds. One minute we're kissing, the next we're ripping off clothes like they're on fire.

At some point I end up on top of Kane, pressing my weight down against him as I take him deep before pulling back up. I love this position. I love watching his face. The mixture of pleasure and frustration as I bring him to the brink over and over. Watching his expression change when I know he's close and stopping just before he gets there.

It's a fun game. One he's played with me more times than I can count over the last three weeks. It's about time I get a chance to return the favor. It's torture. I know it is. But it's also the sweetest kind. Only problem is, I'm not just torturing him.

"El." Kane stares up at me, eyes hooded, bottom lip clenched between his teeth.

"What?" I ask innocently, grinding my hips downward in a little circular motion. "I thought you liked this. Delayed gratification is what you called it last time, was it not?"

"You're pushing your luck, babe," he warns, narrowing his gaze at me.

"Am I?" I repeat the circular motion again, watching his eyes close for the briefest moment.

The next thing I know I'm on my back and Kane has me pinned beneath him, my arms above my head, his weight pressing me into the cushions.

"Just remember you asked for this." With that he pulls back and slams into me so hard I move at least six inches up the couch. My hands find the armrest and I flatten my palms against it to hold myself in place just as he rams into me again.

His thrusts are rough, punishing, and while I love every second of it, it makes it clear that he's been holding back on me.

I lift my hips, welcoming his sweet assault, loving the way the pleasure and pain mix together in a way that has me screaming out my own release within seconds. Kane follows shortly behind, collapsing down on top of me moments later.

"That. Was. Amazing," I breathe out, trying to slow my heartbeat.

"I'm sorry I was so rough." He doesn't move his face from my neck.

"I'm not."

"Did I hurt you?" He kisses the base of my throat.

"In the best way possible," I say, placing my hands on both sides of his head and guiding his face upward. "You've been holding out on me," I tell him, watching concern melt into an incredible smile.

"Fuck falling." He pauses. "I've already hit the bottom."

"Kane."

"I'm serious, Elara. You've got me so fucking tied up I can't even concentrate at work. All I can think about is you. Coming home to you. Being with you. You're damn distracting, woman." He peppers kisses up my jaw.

"The same can be said for you." I grin, pulling his mouth down to mine.

"I mean it, El." he mutters against my lips before pulling back, his dark gaze finding mine. "I don't want to leave," he admits.

"Neither do I."

"I don't want anything to change this thing happening between us."

"Neither do I," I repeat.

"Promise me it won't. Promise me it won't change."

Looking into his incredible eyes, for the first time I realize that past his tough exterior and intimidating nature, he's just as scared as I am.

"I promise," I say, rubbing my nose against his. "I promise," I repeat, lifting my head to press a soft kiss to his chin. "I promise." I move my lips to his right cheek and then his left, finally ending up back on his mouth.

"I love you," he mutters against my lips before once again deepening the kiss.

My heart explodes inside my chest, beating so viciously it's a wonder I don't go into cardiac arrest. My hands are shaking when I thread them through his hair and hold him tightly to me, never wanting to lose the feeling that is singing across every inch of my body.

Chapter Nineteen
Elara

Have you ever had something so incredible happen in your life that you can't help but wonder if it's actually real? Sometimes when I step back and look at Kane I can't help but feel like I'm going to blink and suddenly be back at the funeral, staring at him over Kamden's grave.

It's like you see in the movies. One moment bleeds into another but then at the very end the main character wakes up and realizes their mind created this whole reality in a matter of moments. A reality that seemed endless, like it stretched on forever, when only a couple minutes had actually passed.

"Elara," Kane says, tightening his hand around mine. "You okay?" he asks.

Looking up at him, I reply, "Yeah. Fine." I smile, resisting the urge to stop and kiss him given the amount of people around us.

Kane surprised me for our last day in Italy by sweeping me off to Rome via the high speed train system they have here in Italy. The entire day has been like a fairy tale and I mean that in every sense of the word. The only thing we're missing is maybe a glass slipper and some talking mice.

We've seen ancient runes, the Colosseum, thrown coins in the Trevi Fountain, eaten some of the most incredible street food, and Kane somehow managed to arrange a private tour of Cinecitta Studios where some amazing classic movies were made, which of course was right up my alley.

Now, as we walk hand in hand through the heart of Rome, all I can think is that nothing will ever feel this good again. There's no topping this for me. Every single moment I've spent in this country has been beyond what I could have ever dreamed. Hell, I'm ready to pack up and make the move permanently. Then again I think Italy would lose a lot of its appeal if Kane wasn't here. Because no matter how much I have loved being here, it's my time with him that means the most.

"You sure?" Kane looks down at me, my answer clearly not very convincing.

"Yeah."

"You seem a million miles away."

"Just thinking." I gently knock my shoulder against him, plastering on a smile.

"You don't wanna leave." He doesn't ask, he already knows I don't.

"I really don't," I admit, letting out a slow breath. "I mean, look at this place. It's like existing in a completely different world. There's so much history and culture. The people are amazing. I love every single thing about being here."

"It is beautiful," he agrees. "But beautiful places exist everywhere, you just have to stop and actually look around."

"Look at you getting all philosophical on me," I tease.

"It's not about the place for me," he says, grinning down at me before turning his gaze forward. "It's about the moments and the people I get to experience them with."

"*People*." I arch a brow.

"Well in this case, person," he corrects, shaking his head. "And you say I'm the smart ass."

"You are a smart ass."

"Well, you are too. Guess we're both smart asses."

"Guess so," I concede.

"I'm sure you're anxious to see your dad." He goes back to the subject at hand, trying to put a positive spin on things, clearly sensing the decline in my mood.

"Yeah, I miss him but I'm used to going long periods of time without seeing him. We've lived apart for the last four years. Now stop trying to find reasons for me to be happy about leaving tomorrow."

"So bossy." He chuckles.

Silence stretches between us for several long moments and I bite down the urge to ask him what comes next. Will we return to our normal lives? Me to Arkansas and him to Illinois? Will we promise to visit each other as often as we can but then go weeks without actually seeing each other because he's off on a contract somewhere? And what if he expects me to go with him or worse, what if he doesn't want me to? Truthfully, I'm scared of what his answer will be to any of these questions.

"Kane," I say even though I've made the decision not to broach the topic yet.

"Yeah." He looks down at me, his hand squeezing mine.

"Never mind." I chicken out.

"Tell me what you were going to say." He slows, pulling me to the far side of the walkway so that we aren't blocking anyone from going around us.

"It's nothing." I stare at his chest, feeling an overwhelming sadness settle down on me.

What the hell is wrong with me? Is it normal to feel so emotional and unsure when Kane has done nothing but prove to me over and over again that this is what he wants.

That *I* am what he wants? Why do I suddenly find myself second guessing everything?

"Clearly it's something." He places his hand under my chin and lifts my face upward. "There she is." He smiles when my eyes meet his. "Elara, you can tell me anything. You can say anything. You can ask me anything. Nothing is off limits here."

"I was just…" I trail off, trying to figure out the right way to say it. "I was just wondering what happens when we get home."

"What do you mean?" He tucks a chunk of hair behind my ear, leaning his shoulder against the brick building next to us.

"I mean, when we get home. What happens?" I pause, watching his brow furrow. "You live in Chicago. I live, hell I don't know where I live. I guess technically Arkansas though North Carolina still feels more like home," I ramble for a moment before refocusing. "You travel a lot for work and are gone weeks, sometimes months at a time. I guess I'm just worried…"

"You're worried that when we get back to the states things will be different," he finishes my sentence for me.

"Aren't you?"

"No," he answers honestly. "I know how I feel, Elara. I know what I want. The location doesn't change that for me."

"But it does change it. Whether you see it that way or not."

"How so?"

"Were you not listening to me two minutes ago? We live hours from each other. You travel all the time. That changes a lot of things. The most important being when we will get to see each other."

"That's easy. Come to Chicago." He smiles when my eyes go wide.

"What?"

210

"I mean it, El. We've been here together for two months, therefore we've already been living together whether the location was permanent or not. I don't have all the answers for everything but I do know I want you with me no matter what."

"I can't move to Chicago." I gape at him.

"Why not?"

"Well for one, I have no desire to live in Chicago."

"Not even if I'm there?" He gives me a playful smirk which lightens the mood significantly.

"Stop it," I warn, fighting a smile.

"Stop what?"

"Stop looking at me like that."

"Like what?" He fakes innocence.

"Like, you know, like you're looking at me." I huff.

"I think you're losing it a little bit, babe." He chuckles, reaching out to cup my face. "I don't have all the answers but we *will* find a way to make this work. If you won't move to Chicago then I'll move to Arkansas."

"You don't want to live in Arkansas," I challenge.

"You're right, I don't." I can't help but laugh at his response. "But I would live there if it meant I got to be with you every day."

"Now you make me sound like I don't care as much as you do," I whine playfully.

"How so?"

"Because you don't want to live in Arkansas but you're willing to do so to be with me when I basically flat out refused to live in Chicago. Now I feel like an asshole."

Kane drops his hands from my face as his head falls back slightly. His laughter rumbles around us, filling my ears with a sound I could listen to on repeat for the rest of my life.

"You're not an asshole," he gets out on a wide smile. "There's nothing for you in Chicago. I understand that."

"There's nothing for you in Arkansas."

"Yes there is," he disagrees.

"What?" I cross my arms

"You." He grins.

"There you go again."

"Babe, I'm just saying, Chicago has nothing for me either. At least in Arkansas you'd have your dad and I'd have you."

"And what if I wanted to move back to North Carolina."

"Then North Carolina is where we'll go," he states like there's no question.

"And your job?"

"Babe." He places his hands on both my shoulders. "We will figure it out," he says softly, dipping his face down so his is just inches from mine. "I'll move heaven and fucking earth to be with you, Elara. I don't care what stands in our way. I will not lose you. Do you hear me?" He gives my shoulders a slight shake.

"I hear you." I'm finally able to push past the well of emotion that has lodged itself in my throat.

"Good." He kisses the tip of my nose. "Now stop worrying. This is our last night together in Italy and I don't want to spend it arguing over the future."

"We weren't arguing," I provide, a smile playing on my lips.

"Fair enough. Discussing," he corrects himself, turning to tuck me into his side before veering back out onto the sidewalk.

I wish I could say his reassurances make the doubt swimming in my stomach disappear but it doesn't. I continue to stew and worry the rest of the evening while trying my best to also enjoy my time in Rome with Kane.

By the time we board the train back to Milan, I'm both physically and mentally exhausted. It's actually been the perfect day, despite the fact that I've spent most of it on edge and uneasy not knowing what tomorrow holds.

I'm not ready to leave this behind–any of it. I'm just not ready. Then again, I don't know that I'll ever be ready. I guess it's one of those moments where you just have to jump even though you're terrified what you might hit when you reach the bottom.

Kane tucks me into his side the moment we're settled into our seats. I rest my head on his shoulder and close my eyes, letting my mind digest everything that today entailed. The incredible things we did. The way Kane's smile stretched across his face taking in my reaction to each and everything he showed me. The way he held me and kissed me. The way he told me he would move heaven and earth to be with me.

Call me a skeptic but it all just seems way too damn good to be true. I've learned the hard way that if something seems too perfect, it probably is. Kam was perfect. We were perfect...well, in our own little way. And then I lost him.

My family was perfect. My childhood was perfect. And then that perfect childhood was tainted by watching my mom wither away and die of breast cancer at forty-five years old.

Nothing perfect lasts forever. Hell, nothing lasts forever. But isn't Kane worth the risk? What's the famous saying? It's better to have love and lost than to have never loved at all. I think that statement is easier said when you haven't experienced loss the way I have.

Kane has. Kane lost his brother, his only sibling, his best friend, and yet he's unafraid to jump back into life head first. He calls me fearless but I think that title belongs to him. I'm not fearless at all, not really. Deep down I think I'm just as scared as the next person, I'm just better at hiding it.

I don't know at what point I fall asleep, but I wake with Kane's lips against my temple and him saying, "Wake up, sleepy head. We're here."

My eyes flutter open and instantly lock on his gaze.

"Hey." He smiles, brushing my hair away from my face.

"Hey." I blink slowly before adding, "I didn't mean to fall asleep."

"You were tired."

"I guess so." I straighten my posture and look around. "We're back in Milan?" I question, looking out the window to my right.

"Yeah, I didn't want to wake you but they're getting ready to open the doors."

"Wow. I slept that long."

"Almost three hours," he confirms.

"I'm sorry." I rub my eyes with the back of my hands.

"Why are you sorry?" He chuckles like the notion is absurd.

"You must have been bored to death."

"Quite the opposite actually. I had the best view in the house." He takes my hand, entwining our fingers together. "You," he adds before lifting our adjoined hands and kissing the back of mine.

My heart instantly does that little flip flop it always does whenever Kane says or does something that makes me feel like the world has been rocked under my feet.

"Plus you were drooling which was incredibly adorable," he tacks on, his eyes dancing with humor when I immediately move to wipe my mouth with the back of my hand.

"Shut up. I was not," I say, mortified at the thought of him watching me drool.

"Relax, babe." He chuckles, leaning forward to lay a kiss to the side of my forehead. "Totally kidding."

"Asshole," I mutter, shoving playfully at him.

"You should have seen the look on your face though." He pulls back, humor etched into every line of his face.

"Well I'm glad you found it amusing," I snip, crinkling my nose at him.

"Babe." He tightens his grip on my hand when I move to pull it away. "Don't be mad." He grins wider.

"I'm not mad." I turn to face him head on. "But that still doesn't mean you're not an asshole." I watch his lip twitch as he fights to contain his laughter.

"I think we established that a while back. Remember your trusty lists."

"Speaking of my lists, I think I've come up with a couple more things to add to it." I arch a brow at him, letting him know they are not good things either.

"Don't be like that, babe." He chuckles softly before taking his free hand and wrapping it around the back of my neck, pulling my face to his. "You know you love me," he whispers against my mouth before pressing his lips to mine.

And just like that, all is forgiven. And he's right, I do love him.

****

"Do you think we could come back and visit again?" I ask Kane, my head on his chest, his arm wrapped around my shoulders.

It's the middle of the night, but neither of us really seems ready to go to sleep and close the door on this incredible day. As if Rome and everything that accompanied it wasn't enough, Kane made it even better when he shoved my back against the door not seconds after we had stepped inside and dropped to his knees in front of me.

My stomach tingles thinking about the way his mouth devoured every inch of me. From my head, all the way to my toes, there isn't a place his lips didn't explore. Needless to say, we've made the most of our last night in this tiny apartment.

"Of course." Kane kisses the top of my head.

"I mean here, at this apartment. I love this place so much."

"I knew it would grow on you." I can hear the smile in his voice. "You didn't seem too fond of it on that first day."

"I wasn't fond of the fact that there was only one bedroom," I correct him.

"And now?"

"I think you know where I stand now." I slide my hand down his bare torso, loving the way my fingers rise and fall over the ripple of muscle.

"Keep doing that and you're going to know where I stand," he warns when my hand slips beneath the sheet.

"This?" I ask innocently, trailing my fingers feather light across his hard length.

"Babe," his voice low and thick.

"Don't worry, it's my turn now." I push the sheet away and shift my body above him.

My lips start at his mouth before trailing down his jaw, along the base of his throat, kissing each nipple on my decent to his stomach. It takes me a while to reach my destination, the journey slow and torturous, but once I do all bets are off.

Chapter Twenty
Kane

"Hey, mom." I wedge the phone between my shoulder and ear as I toss my suitcase onto the bed. It feels weird being here, back in Chicago. After weeks spent in Italy with Elara, being back in the States feels almost foreign.

"Hi, baby. You make it home okay?" Her sweet voice fills the space.

"We did. Just landed about an hour ago."

"How are you feeling?"

"Exhausted." I sigh, walking to the far window and looking down at the city below.

"I bet."

"Anyway, I need to get some things settled here and stuff, but I wanted to let you know that we made it home safe and sound so you wouldn't worry."

"Of course, honey. You do your stuff and call me later after you've settled in."

"Okay. Sounds good, Ma."

"I love you, Kane."

"Love you too." I click the phone off and turn, spotting Elara leaning against the bedroom door frame watching me:"Hey." I let my eyes trail the length of her. Even in yoga pants and a tank top, hair a messy bun and zero makeup on, she has to be the most breathtaking creature on this earth.

"Hey," she answers, knotting her hands in front of herself.

"You good?" I ask, sensing that something is off with her.

It takes less than three seconds for it to happen. One minute she's standing there, the next she dissolves into tears, her hands coming up to cover her face.

"Elara." I'm in front of her in an instant, pulling her into my arms. "Babe." I rock her gently as she sobs against me, not really sure what the hell is going on.

"I'm sorry," she mutters against my shirt, burying her face in my chest.

"Don't be sorry, baby. Just tell me what's wrong," I soothe, my hand grasping the back of her neck as I hold her to me.

"I don't know," she admits, pulling back to meet me with a tear stained face. "I don't know what's wrong. I just feel…" she pauses, "off."

"Why do you feel off?"

"I don't know. Something just doesn't feel right."

"What can I do?" I ask at a loss. I've seen Elara cry before, obviously, but this feels different. Maybe because before I understood why she was crying and now I have zero idea what's going on with her.

"I need a minute," she says after a long moment, stepping out of my embrace.

"Elara," I call after her as she crosses toward the window I was standing in front of just moments ago.

"I just need a minute, Kane. Okay? I just need a fucking minute." She spins toward me, tears streaming down her flushed face.

"What is going on with you?" I ask, making no attempt to go to her, fearing that might make it worse. "What happened? You were fine a few minutes ago. Tell me what's going on. Let me help you."

"I have to get out of here," she announces abruptly.

With that she crosses the room, shoving past me without meeting my gaze. She's in the living room before I've caught up to her but when she spins toward me it's no longer sadness and conflict that's covering her face, it's pain.

"Elara." I reach her in seconds. "Baby, what is it?"

"Something's really not right." She hits me with panicked eyes, clutching her stomach.

"What is it?" I repeat, starting to panic a little.

Before she can answer me, she buckles over letting out a wail of pain, her arms tightening around her middle.

"Kane," she sobs when I lift her into my arms.

"Don't worry, babe. I've got you." It's the last thing I say before I take off running with Elara secured to my chest.

It takes me less than fifteen minutes to reach the hospital, but by this time Elara is in so much pain she can barely speak at all. It isn't until I lift her out of the passenger seat that I notice blood pouring down her legs.

Oh god.

I have no idea what the hell is going on but that amount of blood cannot be good.

I'm inside the emergency room within seconds, yelling like a lunatic for someone to help me. Seeing the amount of blood that's puddling onto the white tile floor, one of the nurses immediately jumps into action, leading me through a set of doors and down a hallway where she has me deposit Elara onto an examination table.

She instantly curls into a ball, clutching her stomach and crying for me not to leave her.

219

"I'm not going anywhere," I promise, crouching down next to the bed. "Elara, look at me." I wait until her gaze meets mine before continuing. "I'm not going anywhere," I repeat.

"I'm sorry." Fresh tears well in her eyes and I instantly move to soothe her.

"You have nothing to be sorry for," I manage to get out, but not before her eyes flutter close and she goes completely silent.

"What's happening?" I look to the nurse who calmly explains that she's lost a lot of blood and that the doctor needs to examine her. Right then, a middle aged man in a white lab coat enters the room with two other medical personnel following directly behind him.

I'm quickly escorted from the room by another nurse I hadn't even seen come in. I want to refuse to leave, throw myself on top of Elara and tell them they'll have to go through me to get to her, but I know that will only make things worse.

I pace the hallway for what feels like an eternity but is likely less than a couple minutes before Elara is rushed from the room, a four person medical team running alongside the bed she's currently laying on, unconscious and still bleeding.

I hear someone say emergency surgery but I can't process where it came from. I can't do anything but stand here like a frozen statue, not able to process a single fucking thing happening.

A nurse steps in front of me, her voice faint. It feels like she's not the only one talking and I can't process a single word she says. Words like *pregnancy* and *ruptured fallopian tube*. It's all one big blur.

I don't know how long I stand here, staring down an empty hall at the set of double doors where Elara and the team of doctors and nurses disappeared through. A minute ago? Two? Five? I have no real sense of time.

"Sir," I hear come faintly from behind me. "Sir," I hear again, this time moments before the nurse steps into my line of sight. "Sir, can you please come with me? I have some paperwork I need you to fill out."

I nod but don't make any attempt to speak as I turn and follow the woman back out into the waiting area, the word pregnancy flashing in front of my eyes in big bold letters.

How can she be pregnant? She said she couldn't have kids.

And what does a ruptured fallopian tube mean?

Is the baby okay?

Is Elara going to be okay?

These are the things that cloud my mind as I stare down at the clip board in front of me, not fully comprehending. I've only written her name down before realizing I don't know any of the answers to the questions they're asking.

I don't know if she takes any medications, though I can't say I've ever seen her take any. I don't know her family's medical history outside of her mom. I have no idea if she's ever had previous surgeries, though I feel like maybe she would have mentioned that if she had.

Fuck.

I look around me, seeing various people peppered throughout the room and yet oddly enough, not really seeing anyone at all.

I try to refocus, holding the pen back to the clip board where the next question is about history of pregnancies. *Pregnancy.* The word triggers a wave of nausea to run through me and I instantly toss the clip board onto the chair next to me before standing and quickly exiting the hospital.

****

"Is she okay?" It's the first words that leave my mouth when a dark haired nurse approaches me nearly two hours after I watched a team of doctors and nurses roll Elara back into emergency surgery.

"Would you mind following me?" the dark haired woman asks, looking around the room.

"Is she okay?" I repeat, refusing to move until she at least tells me that much.

"She's going to be fine," she says. Relief instantly floods through me. The rest I can deal with, whatever it is, as long as it means I'm not going to lose her too.

I've spent the last two hours obsessing over every moment we've spent together, wondering if this was all we would get. It was the same thing I did when I found out about Kam's accident. I paced, I prayed, and I relived every moment, hoping to god it wouldn't be all I would get. With Kam it was. To be placed into this situation again, this time with the woman I love, it's a wonder I'm still able to stand on my own two feet as I follow the nurse into a small office and take a seat.

"Dr. Bryant will be in to explain everything shortly," she says, nodding once before quickly closing the door behind her. Left alone in the deafening silence, I feel like I'm going to crawl out of my skin at any moment.

Elara is okay. That's the only thought that doesn't have me stalking out of this damn office after waiting a full ten minutes for the doctor to come in and tell me what the hell is going on.

After getting over my panic attack earlier, I placed a call to Sam. I promised him I would let him know the moment I knew anything, so I quickly pull my cell out of my pocket and type a quick message letting him know she's okay and that I'm waiting to meet with the doctor.

When I called him to tell him what was going on he was ready to jump on a plane and fly here immediately. Somehow, I was able to convince him to wait until we know more, though I wouldn't doubt if he's not already on a plane by now. I know if it were my daughter there would be no way in hell I wouldn't be.

I press send on my text message to Sam and look up just as the doctor enters the room. He's shorter than I realized in the exam room. He's also a lot older. Only now do I see the deep wrinkles that frame his round face as he takes a seat across the desk from me.

"How is she?" I don't wait for him to speak before asking.

"Your wife is going to be okay. She lost a lot of blood but we were able to go in and remove the fallopian tube. She's in recovery now."

My wife… It takes me a second to realize why he referred to her that way. I had the forethought to list myself as her husband on her paperwork. The last thing I needed was for no one to talk to me when the woman I love is in danger.

"Thank god." I breathe out another deep sigh of relief but still not able to shake the weight sitting on my chest.

"Your wife experienced an ectopic pregnancy," he continues.

"Which is what exactly?" I cut him off, not waiting for him to continue before asking.

"It's where the fertilized egg implants outside of the uterus. I would say she was approximately six weeks along. Though rare, in some cases this can cause the fallopian tube to rupture, which is what happened here today. That was the source of the blood and why she was experiencing severe abdominal pain."

Six weeks? That means she must have gotten pregnant within the first couple times of us being together.

"I don't understand how this happened though. She's infertile," I say.

"There was a lot of scar tissue on the ruptured fallopian tube, so it may have given a prior doctor that opinion. But her other one looks good. She very well may be able to have a successful pregnancy in the future."

"You're saying she can have children?" I question, in complete shock.

"No. I'm saying it's not impossible," he corrects. "Now, she'll need to stay here for the next couple days so we can keep an eye on her, but I think the worst is behind her and she should make a full recovery."

"When can I see her?"

"She should be in her room now. You can go on up. Third floor. Room 322."

"Thank you so much." I stand, shaking his hand before quickly exiting the office.

It takes me less than five minutes before I'm pushing my way inside Elara's room. It's quiet and dark. The shades are drawn closed and the television is off.

I make my way quietly through the room, stopping to look down at my girl, who even after going through emergency surgery looks so beautiful and peaceful it sends a warm sensation straight through me.

She's sound asleep, lips slightly parted, her hair fanned out on the pillow behind her. There's an I.V. in her left arm and a few monitoring wires hooked to her chest, but otherwise she looks like she would any other day when I would wake up before her and watch her sleep.

"Hey, babe," I say without really meaning to, carefully sitting on the side of the bed before taking her hand in mine. "You gave me quite a scare." I run my thumb up and down the back of her hand. "I thought I lost you for a second there." My insides seize up and the weight of everything that's happened today crashes over me.

Before I know it, tears are welling behind my eyes and spilling down my cheeks.

"I didn't know what was happening," I keep talking. "I was so scared, Elara." I let out a shaky breath. "I know you belonged to Kam first, but I'm not ready to give you back to him just yet. Because you're in here now." I place my free hand over my heart. "You're so deep in here that losing you would rip my heart straight from my chest. I wouldn't survive it, Elara. Thank god you're okay," I say, kissing the back of her hand before releasing it.

I sit here for a long time, watching her chest rise and fall as she breathes, and thanking god every time I see it happen. Eventually I move from the bed to the chair, angling it so Elara is in my line of sight as I stretch my legs out and try to get comfortable.

"Never thought I'd see the day," I hear Kam say, my eyes shooting open to see him sitting on the edge of Elara's bed where I had been only moments earlier.

"Kam?" I question, sitting upright.

"Never thought I'd see the day when a woman would be able to tame the infamous Kane Thaler." He cocks a smile at me, his hazel eyes locking on mine. "Makes sense that it's her." His eyes go to Elara and he looks at her for a long moment before turning back to me. "She's special, this one."

"She is," I agree.

"She's also not as tough as she pretends to be. It's important you know that about her so you understand how to help her through this. She's going to panic and she's going to push you away. It's up to you not to let her."

"She won't push me away," I object.

"She will." He shakes his head. "Trust me on this one, brother. I'm well versed in all things butter bean."

"Butter bean?" I cock my head to the side and fight back a laugh.

"That's what I always called her. She's my bean. The one person that could make me smile no matter what was happening in my life. She was my person. And now, she's yours."

"Kam," I start but he cuts me off.

"I'm glad she chose you. You need someone like bean to keep you in line. And she needs someone like you too. Be good to her, brother. Love her. Give her lots of babies to

225

love. And do me a favor, would ya? The first boy…" He gives me a knowing grin.

"Let me guess, you want us to name him Kamden."

"I mean, if you insist." His grin turns to a full blown smile.

"I miss you," I say, leaning forward to rest my elbows on my knees.

"I'm right here, Kane. I've always been right here. And I'm not going anywhere either. Trust me when I say that if you fuck this up, I will haunt your ass for the rest of your life." He points a finger at me, laughter rumbling through his words.

"I would expect nothing less."

"Time to wake up now, Kane," Kam says, standing. "Elara needs you now. It's time to wake up."

And with that my eyes shoot open and instantly connect with a pair of ocean blue eyes that earlier today I feared I'd never see again.

Chapter Twenty-one
Elara

"I lost the baby?" It's all I say after Kane tells me what happened. I can't focus on anything but that. After years of believing I could never have a child, I had one inside of me and lost it.

I don't care if it was growing in my fallopian tube, it was still a real live baby in there and that baby is gone. Tears sting the back of my eyes and I turn my gaze out the window.

"We did," he says, taking my hand.

"No, Kane. I did," I say without actually meaning to. Anger and defeat outweighing my ability to be rational about this.

"Babe, we can have a baby. The doctor said it's possible. You still have one good fallopian tube and that's enough. We can do this. We can have the family you've always wanted one day. The impossible is now a real live possibility."

"Do you hear yourself? I lost my child hours ago and you're already planning on replacing it like it never existed," I bite out, quickly continuing, "And not only that, but you're getting your hopes up. The likelihood is I will never be able to carry a child. As if I need that pressure. As if I need you telling me how badly you want something with me that I can't give you."

"You're upset," he says softly, reaching for my hand. "I'm sorry. I shouldn't be pushing this on you right now. I just thought maybe it would help. Knowing there's a chance you can have children."

"It doesn't help, Kane. It doesn't help because I know it's never going to happen. So stop saying it. Just stop." I don't know why I'm being so hard on him. I don't know why I'm looking at him and all I feel is my anger and my guilt.

"Elara."

"Can you leave please, Kane?" My chin quivers.

"Babe."

"Leave, Kane," I scream at him. He flinches before his firm mask slides back into place.

"No."

"No?" I question, temper flaring.

"No, Elara. I will not let you make me the bad guy here. I will not let you blame me and I will not let you push me away. I'm staying, whether you like it or not."

My anger shreds and gives way to a sob that rips from my chest, pain flooding through my body as everything seems to catch up with me all at once.

It's less than a second before I'm in Kane's arms and while it's exactly where I want to be, it's the one place I know I don't deserve to be. This is my fault. All of it. Kam. The baby. *Everything*.

I should never have let Kane in. I should have known that eventually what I'd done would catch up to me and now here it is. It's in the knowledge that for a short period

228

of time Kane's baby was growing inside of me and now it's gone. It's in the truth that once Kane learns will result in me losing him too.

So for a brief moment I let him hold me. I close my eyes and pretend we're back in Italy. Crammed into that tiny little apartment, Kane spinning me in his arms, a wide smile across his handsome face. He tells me he loves me under the moonlight filtering in through the open terrace door as he moves inside of me. His lips on my forehead in the morning as my eyes flutter open into the early sunlight.

Every moment flashes through my mind like snapshots. One after the other until so much emotion is flowing out of me I'm sobbing in Kane's arms.

And still I let him hold me. Knowing what I have to do. Knowing what I have to say. I selfishly let him hold me because I'm not ready to let him go just yet…but I know I have to.

"Kane," I say after several long moments, not able to stop the tears but able to calm myself enough to speak.

He pulls back and looks down at me, cupping my cheek in his hand. "We will get through this, Elara," he reassures me with a soft smile which only causes my stomach to twist harder.

"I need you to sit down, Kane," I say, a slight shake to my voice.

"Okay," he says slowly, turning to take a seat next to me on the bed, angling himself toward me.

"There's something I have to tell you." I let out a slow breath, trying to keep my chin from quivering. "Something that will likely change everything."

"Okay." He narrows his gaze at me, not trying to hide his confusion or worry.

"I killed your brother." The moment the words leave my lips his entire expression shifts.

"What are you talking about, Elara?" he questions after what feels like an eternity has passed.

"I killed Kamden. It's my fault he's dead."

"We've been over this. Kam's death was an accident."

"An accident, yes. But my fault none the less."

"Don't do this right now. You're hurting over the baby."

"This has nothing to do with the baby," my voice so loud it echoes around us. "I've been trying to tell you for months that was my fault. I told your parents, my aunt, my dad, and no one would listen. I need the weight of it off of me and no one would take it. No one would let me say what I need to say and eventually it buried itself, became a permanent knot in the pit of my stomach that I've carried with me every single day." I wipe tears from my cheeks. "Kam wasn't the one driving the four-wheeler that day, I was." This gets his attention and he sits up straighter, disbelief in his eyes.

"No, Kam was driving. It said it plain as day on the police report."

"I was the only one who could give a statement. Where do you think they got that information from?"

"You wouldn't lie to the police."

"Well I guess you don't know me very well after all, do you?"

"I don't believe you."

"Do I look like I'm fucking with you?" My voice is borderline hysterical and I have to reel myself back in.

"Why? Why are you telling me this now?"

"Because I need you to know the truth. I need you to know I'm not the person you think I am."

"Or maybe this is your sad attempt to push me away," he grinds out, his expression hard.

"You think I would make this shit up to push you away?" I open my mouth and close it several times, not able to form even one word to continue.

"Say you were driving, and you did lie to the police. Why? Why lie?"

"I didn't mean to," I admit truthfully. "I guess I panicked. I knew Kam was gone," I pause to compose myself. "I didn't want to go to jail."

"Why would you go to jail, Elara?"

"Because I killed him."

"No, you didn't," he grinds out, his jaw clenched tight.

"I'm the reason he's dead. That's the same as killing him."

"Only you know what happened that day, Elara. You're so convinced that you're to blame, yet no one knows the full story. Maybe you're just so hell bent on blaming yourself that you're afraid if you tell another person you might actually have to face the fact that this wasn't your fault."

"But it was," I interject. Shifting to sit upright, pain shoots through my abdomen, causing me to cringe.

"Babe." Kane starts to stand but I hold my hand up and shake my head.

"Please, don't. I have to get this out."

"Then get it out and let's deal with this shit once and for all," he clips, clearly trying to keep his own emotions in check.

"It was my idea to take the four-wheeler out. Kam didn't want to do it. He never liked those things." I knot my hands in my lap. "But like most things, he did it because I asked him to. We rode for a few hours. Mainly down trails and through the creek bed. I let Kam drive because he said he didn't have a death wish." I choke on my words, wiping fresh tears from my cheeks as they spill.

Kane sits motionless next to me, watching me with a pained expression.

"I convinced him to let me drive, promising we could return it and do something else as soon as I got my turn. He conceded but insisted I keep the only helmet. He'd made me wear it the entire day much to my disdain. I wasn't in the mood to argue, knowing there was no way I was going to talk him out of it, so I took the helmet and climbed into the driver's seat."

Closing my eyes, I remember it like it was yesterday.

"He'd said, *don't make me regret this, bean*," I continue to speak with my eyes closed. "*Take it nice and slow. No funny business*, he warned. Only I didn't listen. Instead I did the exact opposite. I whipped the four-wheeler around so fast I nearly threw both of us off before speeding through the field as fast as I could get it to go."

"I can still feel Kam's arms around my waist. Hear his voice in my ear begging me to slow down. But I ignored him. I was determined to show him how fun riding a four-wheeler can be when you're not driving like an eighty year old. I took one hill going pretty fast. We had to have gone a good ten feet in the air. Kam was holding me so tightly I was having trouble breathing so I slowed down enough to tell him one more jump and I promised I was done. He asked me to let him off." I open my eyes to see Kane's dark gaze locked on my face.

"He asked me to let him off and I told him to stop being a baby," I say, choking slightly on my words. "I didn't let him off. I took off toward another hill, hitting it going even faster. Only this time I was too far to one side and the four-wheeler turned. All I know is one minute we were in the air and Kam's arms were locked around me. The next he was gone. I hit the ground so hard it knocked me unconscious even with the helmet on. When I came to several minutes later, I was confused, my arm was killing me, and I couldn't find Kamden anywhere.

"Then I heard it. His voice. It was broken and ragged but I heard him calling for me. I found him almost instantly. He was pinned under the four-wheeler, blood pooling out of his mouth as he tried to speak. I remember trying to lift it off of him. I remember screaming for help. And then I remember Kam saying my name so gentle that I had to look at him. *Come here, bean*, he said. *It's okay,*

232

he said. *Everything is going to be okay*. He was lying there trapped under that four wheeler, bones broken, bleeding internally, and he was reassuring *me* that everything was going to be okay. How messed up is that?" I swipe angrily at my tears, barely able to hold myself together.

"I don't remember calling 911 but I know I did. I don't remember how long it took them to arrive. All I know is that by the time they made it there he was gone. He had started gasping. I held his hand so tight, begging him to hold on but he couldn't. He couldn't hang on." I'm hysterical, gasping for breath, crying so hard I can't see Kane through my tears.

"He told me he loved me. He said, *I love you to the moon, bean*. And then he closed his eyes."

Through my emotions, I can't speak anymore after that. Can't push out another word. All I see is Kam, lying there, blood everywhere, telling me everything would be okay, telling me he loved me.

"I love you to the moon, bean." Those words will haunt me for the rest of my life.

I pull the blanket up to my chin and let myself cry, the sobs racking through me cause me so much physical pain it blurs my vision but I can't pull it together. I can't hold it in anymore. I've been living with this truth, with this guilt, for months, and now it's out there. Now someone else knows the truth. They know what I've done.

The bed shifts and I feel Kane next to me, his lips against my hair.

"My brother loved you more than anything in this world. Even with his dying breath he told you so. Do not disrespect his memory by doing the one thing you know he would never want you to do. This isn't your fault, Elara. I can see why you feel like it is, but it isn't. It was an accident and accidents happen. Sometimes there's not one damn thing we can do to stop them. We can't change the past either. It's time you made peace with that."

And with that he straightens, turns, and quickly exits the room.

Chapter Twenty-two
Elara

Five months earlier...

"You promised we'd do dinner and a movie tonight," I remind Kam, crossing my arms over my chest as I stare at him across the four-wheeler between us.

"I know, bean, but we can do dinner and a movie anytime." He smiles, knowing I can't stay mad at him when he looks at me like that.

"Nope. That's not gonna work this time." I hold my stance, shaking my head adamantly.

"Bean," he says knowingly, crossing around the four-wheeler to stand in front of me.

"Don't you 'bean' me! You're totally bailing on me for some bimbo with big boobs and if you ask me, an abnormally large ass." I pick her apart even though I know the girl in question is gorgeous. Of course she is, as is every girl Kam dates.

He's never been in a serious relationship but he has started dating more over the last couple of years. I smile and *pretend it doesn't bother me but deep down I know it's a lie. A façade for some reason I feel like I have to keep up.*

"Sounds to me like someone is jealous," he points out.

"I'm not jealous. I'm mad. You're leaving me all alone on a Saturday night. What the hell am I going to do now?"

"El, why don't you tell me the real reason you're so upset?"

"I am telling you the real reason."

"I think we both know you're lying." He takes a step toward me, closing the distance between us.

We've done this before – this song and dance – toeing the line between friendship and something more. But something about this feels different somehow.

"I'm not lying." I act confused. When in doubt, confusion works best.

"Bean." He narrows his gaze at me.

"Why are you looking at me like that?" I question, panic rising in my chest.

"Because, you do this every time I have a date. And it doesn't matter if I bail on you for it or not. Admit it, you hate that I go out with other girls."

"I do not. I just don't think they are good enough for you so I'm not sure why you waste your time," I counter.

"As opposed to pining after someone I can't have you mean?" My stomach instantly bottoms out and I have zero response to what he just said. I can take it so many ways but there's only one way that matters and that's what I want him to be saying. That he's pining after me.

"What are…" I start, but Kam inches closer, his words drowning mine out.

"Tell me the real reason you're mad that I have a date tonight, El," he continues to challenge, his face so close to mine I can smell the sweetness of his favorite strawberry gum.

"I already told you," I grind out.

"Tell me again."

"Because you're leaving me high and dry on a Saturday night." I stick to my story.

"Tell me the truth, bean." Both of his hands settle around my biceps and I instantly suck in a shaky breath.

"Kam."

"The truth."

"I can't do this right now." I try to avert his gaze but his hands tighten, holding me in place.

"We've done this for far too long, bean. I'm exhausted and quite frankly I don't want to do this anymore. So I'm gonna ask you one last time to tell me the truth." He pauses. "Tell me why you're upset. The real reason."

My eyes dart back and forth between his. Uncertainty and excitement both dance around in the pit of my stomach. I start to answer, second guess myself, and then move to answer again, only to stop myself.

I hold Kam's gaze for the longest time; studying the tiny specks of blue and green that I've tried counting on more than one occasion.

It doesn't take long before my resolution folds and I say, "You know why."

"Not good enough, bean." Kam shakes his head slowly but a small smile has formed on his lips.

"Because I'm in love with you, okay?" I erupt, the words exploding out of me with so much force that Kam instantly drops his grip on me and I'm able to take a full step back.

"Come again?" Kam's smile is now full blown but there's a darkness to his gaze.

"You heard me," I say, wishing I could take it all back in that very instant.

"Say it again, El." He closes the distance between us again, his hand snaking around my neck as he holds me firm to him. "Say it again," he whispers against my lips.

"I'm in love with you," I say for a second time.

237

"It's about fucking time." It's the last thing I hear before Kam's lips are on mine, soft and gentle, testing me, tasting me.

His tongue slides against mine and I swear my toes curl from the sensation. It's everything that I thought kissing Kam would be like and yet completely different at the same time.

There's a familiarity about it. Like it's something I've done a million times before and yet there's this excited flutter of butterflies in my stomach at the same time. It's hard to explain and yet makes perfect sense all at once. Because it's Kam.

It's only moments before he pulls back and drops his forehead to mine. Disappointment seeps through me and yet I'm also grateful for a second to clear my head and try to process what exactly is happening here.

"I always knew you'd be a good kisser," Kam says breathlessly.

"Took you long enough to find out," I challenge, pulling back to meet his gaze.

"The same could be said for you," he reminds me. "Why didn't you tell me sooner? Fuck, bean, do you have any idea how long I've wanted this?"

"Why didn't you say anything?" My heart thuds violently inside my chest. And while I'm looking into the same eyes I've looked into thousands of times before, it feels like I'm seeing them for the first time all over again.

"I didn't want to lose you," he admits.

"Now you know why I didn't say anything," I counter.

"Is it possible that we've both wanted the same thing this entire time yet we were both afraid to act on it?"

"You tell me."

"It's been this way for me since day one, El. Day fucking one."

"Me too." I shrug, not sure what else to say.

"Come here." He pulls me back to him, kissing me so sweetly I find myself questioning if this is actually real or just the repeat of a dream I've had several times before.

"All these years," Kam mutters against my lips before pulling back slightly. "All these years I could have been kissing you." He shakes his head. "So much wasted time."

"And now?" I say, my voice thick.

"Now I'm never going to stop kissing you." He smiles, the action lighting up his entire face.

"Does that mean your date with ass and boobs is off?" I ask, cocking my head to the side.

"You couldn't pay me to go now."

"If I'd have known all I had to do was kiss you to get you to stop blowing me off for dates, I would have done it a long time ago," I tease.

"Why do you think I kept doing it?" He cocks a brow at me.

"You were testing me?" I question, more than a little surprised when he nods slowly.

"Have been for a while. I needed to know."

"And you knew I'd break?" I question.

"I knew that eventually you'd show your cards. And today, well you did just that. I knew as soon as I said it, seeing the disappointment on your face, I knew it was more than me backing out of our plans. I just needed you to admit it."

"You played me." I shove playfully at his chest.

"I had to know, bean."

"Then why not come right out and ask me?"

"Because I couldn't risk it. Probably the same reason you didn't come clean with me until just a couple minutes ago. We mean too much to each other. Neither of us could risk the other not feeling the same because who knows what effect that would have had on our friendship. I love you, Elara. And while yes, I'm also in love with you, having you

as my best friend was so much more important than the chance to have you as my girlfriend."

"Is that what you think I am now? Your girlfriend?" I say it seriously but I know he can read the humor behind my eyes.

"If that's what you want to be."

"Hmm." I tap my chin, really thinking over my options.

"Shut the hell up and come here." Kam laughs, grabbing my arm and pulling me flush against his chest. "Be my girlfriend, Elara. Let me love you the way I've dreamt of loving you for the last seven years."

Everything seems to slow down around us. There is no time, no space, no world outside of this very moment. How we went from our normal tater tot and butter bean banter to looking at each other like we're seconds away from devouring one another is beyond me. It's like I blinked and everything changed.

"Okay," I say only seconds before Kam's lips find mine again.

"What do you say we get out of here?" he suggests, his hands finding my hips and squeezing.

"Oh no, Thaler, you're not getting off the hook that easy." I pull back and give him a wide smile. "I get one go on the four-wheeler."

"Bean," he starts to object.

"No." I shake my head before he can say anymore. "You've been driving me around all day like we're in some altered version of 'Driving Ms. Daisy.' It's cute and all but I wanna have some real fun before we take this baby back to Travis," I say, patting the seat of the four-wheeler.

"Elara."

"Please, Kam. Just one lap around the trail. I swear that's it."

"Why do I get the feeling you're about to take me on the ride of a lifetime?" he questions, laughter dancing through his words.

"Because I am." I wink, sliding onto the seat.

"Here." He snags the helmet from the ground and moves to slide it onto my head. "If I'm going to ride with you, I at least need to know you're safe." He secures the helmet strap under my chin before finally sliding into the seat behind me. "Don't make me regret this, bean," he warns. "Take it nice and slow. No funny business."

"And here I thought you knew me." I laugh, feeling his arms latch around my waist just seconds before I fire the engine to life and take off like a bat out of hell.

****

Present Day

My eyes shoot open and for the tiniest moment I forget what I'm waking up to. The room dark, I blink my eyes–once, twice–and then it all floods back like a wave crashing over me and instantly I feel like I can't breathe.

I gasp, trying to push the panic away, trying to pull in a breath, but it's no use. My heart pounds so violently in my chest I feel like it's seconds away from exploding and there's not one damn thing I can do about it.

I close my eyes, trying to drown out the noise, the fear, the pain, all the memories. I try to bury it deep but it continues to roll to the surface.

Kane's face flashes through my mind. The pain. The anger. The sympathy. All of the things that his expression held as he sat next to me and listened to me recount the events of the worst day of my life.

And then I see Kam. The way he smiled after he kissed me for the first time. The way he looked at me the same way he always had, yet it was so different at the same time. Then I think about the last time I looked into those hazel eyes. How they faded as he took his last breath. How I knew right then and there it would be the last time I'd ever be able to count the specks of blue and green.

I open my eyes only to close them again. The pain in my stomach from surgery has nothing on the pure agony sitting on my chest.

I can still hear Kane's words like he's standing here repeating them right now. *Do not disrespect his memory by doing the one thing you know he wouldn't want you to do.*

I focus on that thought, knowing even in my current state that he's right. Of course he is. But that doesn't make the action of doing so any easier. Because that means I have to forgive myself and I'm not sure I can do that.

I turn my head to the side and let out a slow, uneasy breath.

It's been hours since Kane walked out on me. Hours. I guess a part of me expected him to come back. The other part of me is not even a little surprised that he hasn't.

What did I expect? That I would lay all that on him and things would go back to normal? God, why am I so amazing at messing up everything good in my life? In that moment I realize my hands are resting on my belly just above my incision where they removed not only my fallopian tube, but the baby that had been living inside of me.

Kane's baby.

The thought brings on a whole new onslaught of tears and I squeeze my eyes shut tighter, hoping to keep them at bay. I know that this pregnancy wasn't a normal one. And I know that the baby had zero chance of survival. But even knowing this, it doesn't lessen the sting of the loss.

"I'm sorry," I say to no one in particular. "I'm sorry I let you down." I look down at my stomach. "I'm sorry I couldn't save you."

I suck in a shaky breath and turn my gaze to the ceiling.

"I'm sorry I couldn't save either of you."

I close my eyes, praying for a response, something...*anything* to let me know that Kam's here. That he can hear me. That he knows how much I love him and how much I miss him every single day. But I'm met with nothing more than deafening silence.

Chapter Twenty-three

Elara

"Elara," I hear my father's voice. It sounds so far away and yet so close at the same time. "Elara," I hear again.

My eyelids feel like they are being held down by weights but somehow I manage to peel them open, one after the other until I am looking into my father's deep brown eyes.

"Dad," I croak, my voice thick with sleep.

"Hi, baby." He smiles, letting out a slow exhale.

"What are you doing here?"

"Kane called me after they took you back to surgery. Hopped on the first flight I could get to Chicago."

"What time is it?" I lift my head, looking for the pitcher of water the nurse left on my bedside table earlier.

"Three in the afternoon," my dad says, reaching for the pitcher, sensing what I'm looking for without me having to say a word. He pours me a cup and then extends it to me.

I take a tentative drink, my throat still sore from the tubes they ran down it during surgery the day before. Once finished, I hand the cup back to him.

"How are you feeling?" he asks, setting the cup on the table before taking my hand in both of his much larger ones, careful not to disturb the I.V. still attached to it.

"I'm okay," I force out, knowing he'll see right through it.

"How are you really, Elara?" He narrows his gaze at me, the wrinkles around his eyes highlighted by the action.

"Honestly, Dad, I'm not sure." I let out a bitter laugh as I try to sit up, but instantly fall back onto the pillow when an angry pain rips up my middle.

"Your body has been through a lot. It's important you give yourself time to heal," he coaxes, fixing the blanket around me.

"It's not my body that's the problem." I turn my gaze away, not able to look at him.

"Your mother and I lost a baby." I turn my gaze back toward him, eyes wide with surprise. "Two actually," he adds, staring at where his hand is holding mine again.

"I didn't know."

"We didn't want you to know." My big, strong father looks up at me with tears swimming in his eyes and it takes everything in me not to fall apart all over again.

"Your mother thought it best," he continues after a long pause. "She was right of course. There's nothing for a child to gain from learning she had siblings that died before they were born. But now…" He squeezes my hand. "Now I feel like you should know. Because no matter how badly you're hurting right now, Elara, I promise it will get better. It will get easier. But honey, I know from experience that it will never go away."

"Tell me what happened," I interject, my voice thick.

"We got pregnant with our first child the year we were married. It was a surprise but a happy one. Everything was going great until one day your mother started bleeding. I rushed her to the hospital right away but it was too late. The baby was gone."

"Dad." It's my turn to squeeze his hand.

245

"The second baby was harder. Your mother was about twenty-two weeks when she went into labor. They weren't able to stop the labor but it was far too early for her to survive. We got to hold her after she was gone."

"She?" I swipe at a tear that streaks down my cheek.

"You had a sister. Malory Everett," he confirms, a sad smile on his lips.

"Malory," I say out loud, trying to wrap my head around all this.

"It was probably one of the hardest things we'd ever been through. Me and your mother. She was sick with grief. We both were. But even through that sadness and loss, she wasn't ready to give up just yet. So after a year, we tried again. And what we ended up with made all the pain and loss worth it. Because we got you. The most precious, beautiful baby girl in the entire world. We didn't forget about what we had lost, but the sadness was eventually replaced with happiness. You did that for us."

"Dad."

"I know it may not feel like it now, but you will get through this. Your body will heal and eventually so will your heart. You just have to give yourself time to get there. I'm not going to lie and say I wasn't a little disappointed when I heard you had gotten pregnant. In my opinion, it's far too soon and you two haven't known each other long enough to be taking on a commitment like that." He looks toward the door and then back to me before continuing, "But I will say you've got one heck of a guy out there, honey. I can tell just by looking at him that he worships the ground you walk on."

"He's still here?" I question without really processing anything else that he said.

"Kane?" My dad's forehead scrunches in confusion.

"He's here?" I question weakly.

"Of course he is." He shakes his head. "Why wouldn't he be?"

"I told him the truth about Kam."

"What do you mean you told him the truth about Kam?" My father seems to be growing more confused by the moment.

"I was the one driving the four-wheeler when we wrecked. Not Kam," I admit for the second time in two days.

"Elara." My dad says my name slowly like he's trying to process what I'm telling him. "Is that why you kept saying it was your fault? Because you were the one driving?"

I nod slowly.

"Oh honey, whether you were driving or not, it doesn't change that what happened was a horrible accident. You've got to stop blaming yourself for that."

"You don't understand," I start to object.

"No, you don't understand," my dad cutting me off, his voice going up the way it always used to when I was a teenager and he had to get onto me about something stupid I did. "Kam died. No amount of guilt is going to bring him back. Kane loves you, Elara. You should see him out there. He's an absolute wreck. It's time to let go of the dead and focus on the living."

"Like you have?" I bite, taking my frustration out on him. "You preach to me about letting Kam go, about moving on with my life, but you haven't let *her* go. You haven't moved on. You act like mom's still alive and at any minute she's going to come strolling in the front door like she's been gone on a four year shopping trip."

"Sam." At that moment I notice the petite woman standing in the doorway. Her eyes flash to me and instant recognition washes over me.

"Lynette?" I question, looking at the woman who's lived next door to my father nearly my entire life. "What, what are you doing here?" I stare at her for a long moment before looking at my dad, meeting his hesitant gaze.

"I, um," she stutters, clearly caught off guard.

"She's here with me," my dad finally speaks up.

"Why would you bring your neighbor with you?" Even as I ask the question I already know the answer to it.

"I just came by to see if you wanted something from the cafeteria," she quickly explains. "But I'm gonna give you two sometime." Lynette quickly backs out of the room as silently as she entered.

"Dad?" I stare at him for a long moment, eyes wide, waiting for him to say something.

"I didn't want you to find out this way." He pinches the bridge of his nose between his thumb and index finger. "I was in such a panic when Kane called me that when Lynette offered to come with me I didn't hesitate to take her up on it. Because truthfully, I didn't want to face this alone."

"Dad." My voice softens.

"I'm not waiting for your mom to come back, Elara. I know she's not. And while no woman will ever replace her, I've found someone that makes me happy. Someone who makes me smile again."

"And that someone is Lynette," I say quietly, more to myself than to him.

"Yes," he continues. "I didn't plan for it, nor did I go looking. But slowly over time our friendship turned into something more."

"How long have you been seeing each other?"

"About six months."

"Six months?" My eyes go wide again. "You've been keeping this a secret from me for six months?"

"I planned to tell you when you came to visit but then the accident happened and you were in so much pain. I couldn't bear to lay anymore on you. You had just started to come back from losing your mom and then Kam." He shakes his head slowly. "It didn't feel like the right time."

"And now does?" I question.

"Well, in retrospect, no. But I needed her here with me and if that meant telling you while you're lying in a hospital bed then so be it. Because at the end of the day being with her makes me feel stronger than I feel without her."

"I guess I get that," I say, my mind drifting back to Kane. "For the record, I'm happy for you. I would've been happy for you six months ago too. I just want you to be happy, Dad. Always."

"I know, baby. I know you do. Maybe after you're feeling better and all this passes, we could get together for dinner; me, you, and Lynette."

"I'd like that." I smile, feeling so many different emotions I'm not sure I have a real grasp on any of them.

"And as far as Kane's concerned, you need to give that man a little more credit. It's clear to see he's in love with you. I don't think you're going to be able to get rid of him so easy."

"I don't know." I blow out a slow breath. "You didn't see the way he looked at me when I told him about the day Kam died." I instantly tear up at the thought.

"I'm sure listening to you tell him what really happened that day was not easy on him. Put yourself in his shoes, honey. He lost his brother. He lost his unborn child. And then sat here and listened to the woman he loves tell him about his brother's final moments. He's not upset with you, honey. He's hurting for you. He's hurting with you."

"He talked to you, didn't he?" I ask, shame and regret hitting me so hard it's a wonder I manage to hold my head up high and meet my father's gaze.

"A little." He nods. "That man out there loves you. Don't push him away because you're scared of losing him. Hold him closer because you don't want to lose him. Things happen. People get sick. People get hurt. People die. Nothing is guaranteed. All you can do is love with your whole heart while god gives you the ability to do so."

"What if I'm not worthy of his love?" I blink back fresh tears that pool in my eyes.

"You are worth that and so much more. Don't ever question that."

"You have to say that because you're my father," I point out, swiping at my cheeks.

"No, I have to tell you the truth because I'm your father. And that, my dear, is about as honest as it comes."

"Thanks, Dad." I force a smile.

"I love you, Elara Rose. You are the one thing in this world that I will always be proud of. No matter what."

"I love you too," I say as he presses his lips against my forehead.

"The doctor said you should be released in a couple of days." He straightens his broad frame so he's looking down at me. "I think you should go back to Carol's."

"Dad," I start to object.

"Arkansas isn't your home. Not anymore. I know you only came back because you were running away from the memory of Kamden, and because I missed you terribly I selfishly let you do it. But honey, North Carolina is where you belong. You know that as well as I do."

"But all my stuff."

"Will be waiting there for you when you get there," he cuts me off. "I've already spoken to Carol. She's taking care of getting all your stuff to her house for when you're released."

"Dad," I start but he once again cuts me off.

"Whatever wall you're trying to build between you and Kane, knock it down. Don't shut him out. I know this happened to you, but honey, it happened to him too. Let him mourn the loss of his child with you. Let him mourn his brother with you. Because whatever pain you're feeling, I can tell you from experience, he's probably feeling it just as strong. Don't let your anger and guilt get in the way of a chance to be happy. You deserve to be happy, my sweet girl. Your mother would want that for you. Kam would want that for you. And before you even think about arguing with me, just think about that for a moment and you'll know I'm right."

"Learned a few of mom's tricks along the way I see." I smile, this time the action coming naturally as I think about my mom and all the things she would say if she were here.

"She may have taught me a thing or two." My dad's smile matches my own but fades almost as quickly as it appeared.

"I miss her," I say.

"Me too." His brown eyes lock on mine and the emotion there damn near rips me in two. "But she's still here. I see her every single time I look at you." He lifts my hand and kisses my knuckles. "Get some rest," he says, likely noticing the way my eyes keep fluttering closed and how hard I have to work to force them back open.

I don't know if it's the medication or that my body is simply exhausted but I haven't been able to stay awake for more than a few minutes at a time since I came out of surgery nearly twenty-four hours ago.

"Dad," I call out right as he reaches the door. I wait until he's turned toward me before continuing. "I'm so lucky to have you as my dad."

"I'm even luckier to have you as my daughter." He smiles and slips out the door without another word.

Chapter Twenty-four

Elara

I wish I could say that my father's advice somehow made everything miraculously better but that simply isn't the truth. Don't get me wrong, him being here has meant the world to me, but between him and Lynette, who's fussed over me more than anyone else these last two days, I feel like I'm suffocating.

Needless to say that when the doctor announced this morning that I would get to go home today, I did a silent little dance in my head at the prospect of getting a little time to myself. Time to process. Time to let all this sink in. Time to figure out how to proceed. None of which are things I can do with my father and Lynette hovering like they're waiting for me to fall apart.

I haven't seen Kane since that first night. I know from Lynette and my father that he's around but for some reason he's opted to keep his distance. I'm just not sure if it's for my benefit or his.

I've tried not to dwell, tried to reassure myself that we'll get through this and that he probably just needs time, but I also can't shake the feeling that maybe he's finally seen the light. Maybe he's finally seen that I'm not the girl he thought I was. Maybe I've lost him forever.

The thought makes my stomach twist so hard that I have to physically fight back the urge to throw up.

Watching Lynette with my dad has made me feel a little better. Just seeing the smile that lights up his face every time she's near is enough to calm the storm inside me. Even if only for a short time.

It's clear to see he cares a great deal for her and her for him. And while the whole thing is still a bit of a shock to me, you'd probably think I'd known all along given how easy we've all fallen into our roles.

I'm sitting on the edge of the bed as my father slides on one of my shoes and then the other. A light knock sounds against the door right as he stands and Kane appears in the doorway moments later.

I suck in a sharp inhale at the sight of him. He's as breathtaking as ever but there's also something so different about him at the same time. His dark eyes are rimmed with red. His normal short scruff is longer and unkempt. His hair looks like he's run his hands through it a million times over; his silky locks wild and disheveled. But it's his gaze that knocks the wind right out of me. The haunted, pained stare I first saw at Kam's funeral is back, only this time it's so much harder to see because I know it's me that put it there.

"Kane," my dad greets him, turning to shake his hand as he steps completely into the room.

"Sam." Kane nods, keeping his eyes on my father. "Would you mind giving me a few minutes alone with Elara?" he asks, looking to Lynette for a brief moment and then back to my father.

"Of course." My dad slaps him on the shoulder before nodding his head toward Lynette, both leaving the room in a silent hurry.

"My dad really likes you," I say to fill the heavy air between us.

"He's a good guy." He nods slowly, his dark gaze finally finding mine after what feels like an eternity.

"I wasn't sure if I'd see you before I left," I say, my voice weakening.

"Neither was I," he admits, blowing out a slow breath.

"Kane, I…" I start but he quickly cuts me off.

"I need you to know that what I'm about to say has nothing to do with what you told me about Kam." His words instantly hollow out my stomach and I attempt to brace myself for what I expect to come next.

"My brother's death wasn't your fault, Elara. But that doesn't mean it was easy for me to sit here and listen to you tell me what happened during his final moments. The image of him pinned beneath that four-wheeler, fighting for air, I haven't been able to shake it."

"I'm sorry."

"Don't be sorry. I needed to know. I'm glad I know. But it made me realize something I didn't want to see when we were in Italy." He pauses, takes a slow breath, then continues, "I wanted you so badly I didn't care that you weren't ready. Or that maybe I wasn't ready either. I ignored the signs. I was careless and selfish and I pushed way too much on you way too quickly."

"No you didn't," I object. "I was there, remember?"

"Yes, I did, Elara," he states firmly. "And this." He gestures around the hospital room. "All of this could have been avoided if I had listened to myself from the beginning. You wouldn't be here. You wouldn't be hurting the way you're hurting. You wouldn't be experiencing yet another loss in such a short span of time. I did that to you."

"No, you didn't."

"I did, Elara. And I can't change it. What I can do is make sure I do right by you from here on out and that starts now."

"What does that even mean?" I question, panic rising in my voice.

"It means I'm going to do what I should have done two months ago. I'm going to put what you need first. You need time to heal, Elara. And I'm going to give it to you."

"What I need is you, Kane," my voice strains as I push to a stand, cringing at the pain in my stomach.

He grimaces at the sight of me in pain and even though I feel like every part of my heart is shattering, a small part of it still swells.

"What you need is to deal with your pain, Elara. I can't be your distraction anymore. I can't be the person you pretend with. I want all of you. The ups and downs. The accomplishments and failures. The good and the bad. I want it all. But until you deal with Kamden's death, and I mean *really* deal with it, I'm afraid I won't get that. I'm afraid I will only ever get the version of you that you want me to see. The one where the pain and guilt are eating you from the inside out and yet you smile and pretend like they aren't there."

"I'm not pretending anything," I bite, letting my anger take the lead.

"You're not convincing anyone, Elara."

"If this is because you don't want to be with me, at least have the fucking courage to say so." I try to fight back the tears that well behind my eyes but within seconds they are streaking down my cheeks.

"I *do* want to be with you." His voice gets louder and I can tell he's fighting to keep himself together. "Jesus, Elara. Have you not been listening to a single thing I've been saying to you for weeks? You think this is easy for me? That I would, that I *could* walk in here and drop you and walk away like it was nothing?" He runs a hand through his hair in frustration. "Fuck!"

"I don't know what you want from me Kane. You want to be with me. You don't want to be with me. Honestly at this point I can't keep up."

"I love you." He steps up directly in front of me, his hands on my biceps, his dark eyes boring into mine. "Do you hear me, Elara? I love you," he repeats more forcefully. "I'm not walking away from you because I want to or because I'm scared. I'm giving you some time to deal with something you should have dealt with a long time ago. I'm not Kam, babe. I can't be his replacement. And until you let him go, I'm always going to feel like I am."

"I never tried to replace Kam. I didn't want this." I gesture between us. "I didn't set out with the intention of this becoming anything. But it did, Kane. Every second I spent with you I fell a little harder, and not because of Kam. But because of you. I fell in love with you, Kane. Not because you're a replacement for your brother but because you're you. Can't you see that? My feelings for you have nothing to do with Kamden."

"I hear what you're saying, Elara. And babe, I can tell you want to believe it. But I think deep down you know I'm right. Maybe I'm not a replacement for my brother, but he still exists between us. Because you refuse to let him go. I didn't see it until two nights ago. Watching your face as you told me about that day is probably one of the hardest things I've ever witnessed. And not just because he was my brother. Because it made me realize that this isn't with me at all." He lays his palm flat against my chest. "It's still with him."

"Kane," I start, but don't get in another word before he cuts in.

"I can't compete with a ghost, Elara."

"You don't have to." My tears stream down my face, panic seizing through my body as I feel my desperation grow. "Please. You told me you'd move heaven and earth to be with me," I remind him.

"I will. But you have to be willing to do the same for me."

"Kane. Please don't do this. Please, I need you." My body gives out at the weight of what I know he's telling me and it's more than I can take.

"I know you do." He cups my cheek, tears swimming behind his eyes. "And I need you. I need you like I've never needed another person in my entire life. You are it for me, Elara. You're all I want. And because of that I have to do what's right for us right now. I can't lose you down the road because there was too much left unresolved. You need to find a way to say goodbye to Kam, Elara. And baby, so do I." He drops his forehead to mine. "Walking out that door will be the hardest thing I've ever done in my entire life."

"Then don't do it," I whisper, my fingers gripping his shirt.

"You know I have to." He pulls back, a tear sliding past his thick lashes onto his cheek. "One day, Elara Rose Menton, I'm going to give you everything you deserve. Love, happiness, a family. All of it. I'm going to give you everything. You will get my everything. Do you hear me?" He tips my chin up and forces me to meet his gaze. "We've lost so much. We both need this. You know I'm right."

"Is this because I lost the baby?" The instant I ask him, I know it was the wrong thing to say.

"Elara, look at me." His hands are on my face, forcing my gaze to his. "What happened here was beyond either of our control. I don't blame you for this. *I don't*. There's nothing you could have done." He lets out a slow exhale.

"I know," I admit, knowing he's right. There's not one single thing I could have done.

"You need time to sort through all of this. I need some time too. But that doesn't change the way I feel about you, Elara. Not for one single second. This is fucking killing me."

"It's killing me too," I whisper, an eerie calm settling down around me.

"But you know I'm right," his voice is soft.

"I do," I admit, feeling my heart shoot apart in a hundred different directions.

"When you're ready, you know where to find me. But not a moment sooner. When you walk back into my life I want to know it's forever. Promise me." He wipes my cheeks with the pads of his thumbs.

"I promise," I manage to choke out.

"Thank you." It's the last thing he says before brushing his lips against mine.

I close my eyes tightly and relish in the feel of him, in the smell of him, in the knowledge that this is all I will get. It's the briefest moment of contact before I feel him step away.

I hear his feet against the tile floor and the distinct sound of the door opening but I can't open my eyes and watch him walk away, knowing that if I do there's no way I'll ever let him leave.

Chapter Twenty-five

Elara

It's been a week since I returned home. One week since I moved back into the apartment above Carol's garage. One week since I last saw Kane, or even spoke to him for that matter. One week since everything fell apart. One week.

To say the last few days have been difficult would be putting it mildly. With my body's natural hormone shift due to the pregnancy and everything going on with Kane, it's no surprise that I feel like I'm going to crawl out of my own skin just about every second of the day.

I wish I could say sleep offers me some reprieve, but so far no such luck. Hell, sometimes my dreams are even worse than my reality. Like the one where Kane never comes back. Or the one where it's him lying under that four-wheeler instead of Kam. And I can't forget about the one where Kane is holding our baby, trying to stay afloat but he keeps disappearing under the water until they both end up drowning right in front of me and I'm powerless to save either of them. I guess nightmares would be a better term for what I'm having.

It only took one really bad one – the one where Kane was trapped under the ATV – before I picked up the phone and called him. He declined the call. I knew he had because it rang twice before his voicemail picked up.

I left a panicked message that I needed to know he was okay. He texted me less than a minute later with one simple message: *I'm okay.*

That's it. Nothing else.

I keep reminding myself that I'm supposed to be taking this time to heal. Up until recently I didn't feel like I needed it. I felt like I had moved on, at least for the most part. I mean, as much as someone can given the circumstances. But now I know I was only pretending that I had. Lying to myself so I wouldn't have to face everything that I buried. Everything that losing the baby brought to the surface.

I don't know how long I've been out walking but when I finally look around I find myself standing feet from the entrance of the cemetery. I wasn't intentionally heading this way so I'm not really sure how I ended up here. I look up at the tall steel gate before turning my gaze beyond it to the small road that weaves through the cemetery.

I haven't been back here to see Kam since the day I left North Carolina nearly three months ago. Taking a deep inhale, I step through the gates, snuggling deeper into my sweatshirt. It's not cold by any means but there's definitely a crispness to the air. A clear sign of colder temperatures to come.

It doesn't take me long to find Kam. He's at the back of the lot next to a large tree that looks like it's older than the cemetery itself. As soon as I reach his headstone I plop down on the ground in front of it, pulling my knees up to my chest.

I don't speak right away. Instead I sit here, staring at his name etched in the stone, wondering what he would say to me if he were here right now. If I close my eyes hard enough I can almost hear him. His voice. His laugh. The way he used to say my name, or rather my nickname.

"Hey, tater tot," I say after a long while, reaching up to lay my palm flat against the stone in front of me. "Sorry it's been so long since I've come to see you. Things have been...well, interesting. Of course you already know all that, don't you? You're probably sitting back, feet up, hands locked behind your head, enjoying the show. You always did find my ability to make such a mess of things entertaining. You're probably having a good laugh at my expense right now, aren't you?" I chuckle bitterly, crossing my legs in front of me before dropping my hands into my lap.

"Nah. You wouldn't have found any of this funny. And you certainly wouldn't have let me lie in bed and wallow for the last week. You would have walked into my apartment, ripped the blanket off of me, and demanded that I get up. And I would have done it. You always did know how to make me listen. Well, almost always." I pick at some of the long pieces of grass that have sprouted up around the base of his headstone.

"You understood me like no one else. I miss that about you. I miss everything about you. But that's one of the things I miss the most. Your ability to know exactly what to say, what to do, how to handle me no matter my mood. You were the only person that called me on my bullshit the instant it left my mouth and even though you would make me so mad sometimes, I could never stay that way. You would smile at me and I would instantly forget about the reason I was supposed to be mad. You knew it too. You knew what that smile would do to me and it worked, without fail, every single time." I smile softly to myself.

"God I wish you were here now, Kam. I wish you could tell me how to fix this. I wish you could tell me how stupid I'm being and to suck it up and put my big girl panties on." I laugh before falling silent. "I wish you could tell me how to

261

let you go," I whisper but my words get carried off in the wind.

Closing my eyes, I lean my face upward to the sky and let the cool breeze whip through my hair.

"Tell me what to do, Kam," I plead to the sky before turning my eyes back to his headstone. "I love him. I don't know how it happened. One minute he was your brother and I wanted to be close to him because it made me feel close to you. And then suddenly it wasn't about that anymore. It was about the way he looked at me. The way his hand would graze my lower back so softly it was barely a touch yet it could set my entire body on fire. The way he would smile at me." I pause, letting the thought hang.

"I think I miss his smile more than anything else right now. The way it would light up a room. The way it would make my heart pound so hard in my chest I was convinced the whole world could hear it crashing against my ribcage. I fell so hard and so fast I didn't have time to talk myself out of it. I didn't have time to rationalize or second guess. I wanted him and that was all I could see... Him."

"And now I've lost him too." I blow out a slow breath. "He says it's because I need time. Time to heal. Time to move on. Time to let you go. Only I don't know how to let you go, Kam. Hell, I'm not even sure I want to. I just need you to tell me what to do. Tell me how I fix this. Tell me how I get him back. Because I can't live without him, Kam, and honestly, I don't want to." I close my eyes again, imagining Kam sitting next to me. I feel his hand close down over mine; feel the warmth of his body as he settles in next to me. I can even hear his words as if he were actually speaking.

"You already know what to do, bean."

"But I don't," I argue.

"Yes you do. You need to face what happened to me, to us."

"I have faced it. I've been facing it every day that you've been gone."

"No you haven't, bean. You've been burying it. Telling Kane was a start. It means you're ready. But you're still holding back. Why are you so afraid to let me go?"

"You know why," I say, remembering the last time I spoke those words to him. It was the day of the accident, when he pushed me to tell him why I was so upset over his date. God I remember that day so clearly and yet it's all blurred together at the same time.

"I do know why. But do you?" I hear him say.

"What if something happens to him?"

"You mean what if you cause something to happen to him," he corrects.

"You always could read me better than anyone else."

I open my eyes and suddenly he's there, staring back at me with those hazel eyes, the blue and green specks catching the sunlight just right making them almost sparkle.

"There she is." He smiles.

"Kam." I choke back a sob, knowing he's not really here but wanting so desperately to believe the lie my mind is telling me.

"You didn't do this, bean. You can't spend the rest of your life focused on what might happen. You don't have that kind of control, no matter how much you wish you did. All you can do is love with everything that you have while you have the chance to do it. I died and you're going to have to find a way to forgive yourself for that. If not for you, then do it for me, bean. Do it for Kane."

"You make it sound so easy." I sniff.

"It's only as difficult as you make it."

"I don't want to let you go, Kam. I don't want to purge you from my life and forget about you. I want you with me, always."

"And I will be."

"No you won't," I accuse, trying to hold onto the image of him that's starting to blur in front of me.

"Yes I will, bean. I will always be with you. Letting me go doesn't mean forgetting me. It means forgiving yourself. Don't bury me. Don't pretend like I didn't exist. Learn to live with what happened and find a way to be okay."

"Don't bury you," I say slowly, turning my eyes forward.

I suddenly realize that's exactly what I've been trying to do. I've been trying to bury his memory to ease my own guilt.

I ran away from North Carolina. I packed everything I had of his including his camera and his old Dodgers hat in a box and sealed it up tight so I wouldn't have to look at it every day. So I wouldn't have to face what I lost every single day.

"Your camera," I blurt, but when I look back to where Kam was sitting next to me just moments earlier, there's no one there. "Kam?" I look around, willing my mind to bring him back. "Kam?" I close my eyes hard, pleading, but when I open them I'm met with the truth I haven't wanted to see since the accident. Kam is gone and no matter how hard I wish and pray, he's not coming back.

I let the weight of that settle around me. Let myself feel it all the way into my bones. Let it seep through every pore until I have no choice but to face it.

"Don't bury me," I repeat his words, reaching out to lay my hand on the front of his headstone just as a hard wind whips around me.

I know it's probably wishful thinking but for some reason I feel meaning behind the wind. Like Kam really is here, telling me what to do, guiding me, and for the first time since he died, I close my eyes and let myself listen.

And suddenly it all becomes clear.

"I know what I have to do," I whisper. "I know what to do," I repeat, quickly shuffling to my feet.

"I've tried to forget. For months I've tried to forget what happened," I say, my face tilted down to his grave. "But you're right. I can't forget you. And I don't want to. I want to remember you. Every single thing about you. Because you were my best friend, Kamden Joseph Thaler. You were everything to me and you deserve so much more than to be stuffed into a box and forgotten. I know what I have to do now. I have to find a way to keep you alive forever; at least in my own way."

I smile down at him just as a tear slides down my cheek.

"Thank you, Kam." I kiss my fingers and lay them across the top of the cool stone. "Thank you." And with that I turn and take off through the cemetery. For the first time in a long time, I feel some of the weight I've carried with me for months start to lift.

Chapter Twenty-six
Elara

Three months later...

"Elara. Are you about ready?" Carol calls up the staircase that leads to my apartment over the garage.

"Yeah. Almost," I holler back, shoving papers in my bag, while praying to god I don't forget anything.

"Well come on already. You're going to miss your flight." I can hear her foot tap against one of the wooden steps.

"I'm coming. I'm coming," I say, snagging the Dodgers hat off my dresser before slipping it on my head.

Quickly pulling my ponytail through the back loop, I slide my duffel bag over my shoulder and exit my room, meeting Carol at the bottom of the stairs just moments later.

"You've got your ticket?" she asks.

"Yep." I nod, pulling it from my back pocket.

"And your pitch?"

"Folders are organized and ready to go." I tap the side pouch of my duffel.

"I can't believe you're actually doing this," she practically squeals in excitement.

"Me either," I admit, my eagerness and excitement a welcome emotion after the year I've had.

It's January now. A new year. A new chance to start fresh and leave the ghosts of the past behind me. Well, not all the ghosts.

I've spent the last three months cleansing myself of everything I've lost. I've cried. I've laughed. I've experienced days where I could barely get myself out of bed. But I pushed through and I completed what I set out to do.

After leaving the cemetery that day – after talking to Kam – everything became crystal clear. I went straight home, dug all of his belongings out of that box, and then I spent the next four hours staring at it before I finally got the courage to look at the pictures on his camera.

It wasn't easy. Hell, at one point I was crying so hard I felt like I'd never stop. But like everything else, I got through it and I came out on the other end better because of it.

Later that night, I opened my laptop and started writing. It didn't start out as anything other than words on paper at first, but as the days went on it started to become something so much more.

A story. A manuscript actually. One that told the story of a hazel eyed boy who stole my heart at fifteen. I didn't leave a thing out. I wrote moments I remember so clearly it was like they were happening in front of me as my fingers worked against the keyboard. I wrote the good, the bad, and the downright painful. I left no stone unturned. But then my story about my sweet hazel eyed boy started to take on a new meaning. Because it didn't just belong to him anymore.

So I kept writing. I wrote about Kane, about our time in Italy, about the baby we lost. And by the time I was done, by the time I was holding a full completed manuscript in my hand, it was no longer a story about loss. It was a story about love.

Kane did that for me. He gave me love in a story that was meant to be nothing more than heartbreak. Thinking about him was almost as hard as thinking about Kam but it did get easier. The further I got into the story the more I felt a renewed sense of hope that we would indeed find our way back to each other. Our road to this point hasn't been an easy one, but it was worth every single bump along the way. I'd do it all over again if I knew he would be waiting for me at the end.

I titled the manuscript *The Road to You.*

It took me five weeks to finish. I wrote nearly every waking moment for those five weeks and the night I finished was probably one of the most emotional nights of my life. But when I woke the next day I knew there was no way I could keep this story to myself. So, I started doing research and ended up sending my manuscript out to over twenty different agencies.

It was less than a month before I had two different companies interested in buying the rights. Less than four weeks. I couldn't believe it. And now here I am, getting ready to board a plane to Los Angeles to meet face to face with one of the biggest production companies in the industry.

It doesn't seem real. I've been pinching myself for the last couple of days since I got the call. Six months ago I thought my life was over. Now here I am, on an exciting new journey I never thought I'd ever get the chance to experience. And there are only two people I can thank for it.

"Now don't forget to call me the minute you land." Carol pulls me back into the conversation as I drop my bag in the backseat and climb into the driver's seat of my car.

"I won't forget," I promise.

"I really wish you would let me drive you," she says, leaning down into the open window.

"I'll be gone two days. I'd rather leave my car at the airport so you don't have to worry about picking me up."

"But I'd be happy to pick you up," she objects.

"I know. But I also know you're understaffed at the salon and business is picking back up. I'll be fine," I quickly add.

"I know you will." She smiles down at me, her face so much like my mother's it causes my eyes to well. "I'm so proud of you, Elara. You had a choice. To either let life beat you down or refuse to let it take you under. You've been through so much and for you to be able to turn it into something like you have – it's incredible. I just wish your mother could be here to see the amazing woman she raised."

"Me too." I force a smile.

"God, I'm sorry. Here I am getting all emotional on you when you need to be focused for your meeting." She makes a noise in the back of her throat and swipes at her eyes just as a tear falls from each one. "Knock 'em dead, sweetie."

"I will," I promise, firing the engine to life.

"I love you."

"Love you." I offer one last wave before backing out of the driveway.

****

"You did it?" Carol screams into the phone so loudly I have to pull the device away from my ear.

"I did it," I confirm, still not able to believe it myself.

Today I signed over the rights to *The Road to You* and while it was impossible to let it go, it also felt so liberating at the same time. Walking out of that office, knowing what I had accomplished, there's no way to describe that feeling. And yet it was surrounded by an air of sadness because the one person I wanted so desperately to share it with wasn't there.

269

I thought about calling him, several times in fact, but I made him a promise that day in the hospital and I had every intention of keeping it. He was right after all. We did need time. I was just too focused on being with him to see it in that moment. And while being away from him hasn't been easy, I know now it's what I needed.

"Oh my god! Oh my god! Oh my god!" I can picture Carol jumping up and down. "Did you call your dad?"

"Yep. I just got off the phone with him. He and Lynette are already planning on coming to town so we can all go out and celebrate."

"This is so incredible. I can't believe you did it. You actually did it, Elara. Do you feel different?"

"I feel like I'm in a bit of a dream state," I admit.

"I can imagine. I feel like I'm dreaming." Carol laughs and I can't help but smile at how excited she is for me.

She's been by my side through a lot. I'm so grateful I have her to share this with.

"And if your father thinks I'm waiting on him to take you out celebrating he's nuts," she quickly adds.

"We can just keep that to ourselves." I chuckle before quickly adding, "Listen, I'm at the airport so I'm going to let you go. I'll see you at the house later?"

"Sounds good, honey. Be safe and shoot me a text when you land."

"Will do."

We quickly say our goodbyes and I end the call before pushing my way inside the airport. For reasons I don't fully understand, I find myself pausing to look up at the flight schedule, freezing the instant I see a flight to Chicago leaving in less than two hours.

One minute I'm standing there staring at a screen flashing with cities and times, the next I'm at the counter purchasing a one way ticket to Chicago.

I don't think I fully processed what the hell it is I'm doing until I'm boarding the plane just over an hour later when the panic starts setting in.

Kane told me I had to come to him. He told me I had to be ready. He made me promise.

I am ready.

I think I've been ready for weeks but have been too scared to take the leap. Afraid that maybe he's changed his mind and doesn't want me anymore.

I push those doubts aside and quickly take my seat, knowing there is only one way to find out. I just have to jump and pray to God he'll be waiting to catch me when I reach the bottom.

****

I text Carol and my dad on the way to Kane's apartment and then silence my phone and slip it into my bag. I can't answer all the questions I'm sure they'll have, because honestly, I don't have the brain power right now.

The past two days have been an absolute whirlwind and now, knowing I'm here, minutes away from seeing Kane again has every inch of my body wound so tight I can physically feel the tension in my back as the cab slows to a stop on the curb outside of Kane's apartment building.

I look up at the building and then to the middle aged driver, feeling almost frozen in place.

"You okay, honey?" the driver asks, catching my gaze in the rear view mirror.

"Define okay?" I force a smile, reaching into my bag for my wallet before slipping him some cash. "Thank you," I quickly add before sliding out of the backseat.

Grabbing my bag, I hitch it onto my shoulder and stand on the sidewalk for another long moment, trying to gather the courage to enter the building. I'm seconds away from chickening out when I hear my name. The instant recognition of the voice washes over me like a bucket of ice water as I turn and meet the gaze of the man I've dreamed about seeing again for weeks.

"Elara," he repeats when I make no attempt to respond, my jaw slack, my feet rooted to the ground beneath me.

"Hi," I say after what feels like an eternity.

My eyes dart from his face, which is even more handsome than I remember, to his messy hair, to his blue t-shirt and dark jeans, to the grocery bags hanging from his hands.

"I'm sorry, I should have called," I start, realizing maybe this wasn't the best idea.

"I'm glad you're here," he cuts me off before I can say more. "You want to come inside?" He gestures to the building in front of us.

"Yeah, sure." I force a smile, taking a deep breath when he passes in front of me, his scent intoxicating all of my senses.

I follow him into the building, my stomach a mass of nerves, my hands trembling so bad you would think there was something medically wrong with me, and my heart hammering so violently against my ribs I swear I can hear it echo through the long hallway as he leads us to his apartment door.

He shifts the bags to one hand to dig his keys out of his front pocket before unlocking the door and letting us inside. If I thought my heart was beating fast before I was wrong because the minute the door closes behind us it starts hammering so rapidly it feels like it's seconds away from beating straight out of my chest.

Kane doesn't say a word as he crosses the space, depositing the bags on the kitchen island before turning back to where I'm still standing right inside the front door. My eyes dart around the space and I'm instantly transported to the last time I was here.

The baby. The memory hits me before I can stop it and my stomach twists. I know there's not a thing I could have done to save that child but that doesn't mean that thinking about it, remembering what happened, doesn't hurt like hell.

I shake it off and focus on Kane. On the way his dark eyes watch me as I slowly move across the space toward him.

I open my mouth to speak, to explain, to say *anything*, but instantly snap it closed when I catch sight of the thick stack of paper on the island next to Kane, bound together with string to look almost like a book.

My eyes blur before refocusing as I approach. My hand reaches out and touches the title page the moment I reach it. I can feel Kane's eyes on me, sense his closeness as I stand next to him, staring down at the manuscript on the counter. *My* manuscript.

"Carol sent it to me," Kane answers my question before I have the chance to ask.

"Carol," I repeat softly, my gaze still on the bound paper. "Did you read it?" I ask, almost afraid to look at him.

"I did." His answer sends my eyes straight to his face and I find him watching me hesitantly, like he's not sure how to proceed just yet. "It's incredible, Elara."

"I sold it," I blurt, not really sure what to say.

"I heard you were pitching to *Element Studios*. I take it all went well."

"It did," I confirm, nodding slowly. "Though I'm not sure I've really processed it all. It happened so quickly."

"It doesn't surprise me." He gestures to the manuscript. "This is probably one of the best things I've ever read. I had no idea how talented you are."

"I don't know if I'd go that far." I shrug, blowing out a slow breath.

"I would." He shifts so he's facing me, his dark eyes boring into mine as his hands come out to cup my face. "Did

273

you mean it?" he asks softly, his gaze going to my lips before finding my eyes again.

"What?" I breathe, my pulse pounding so hard there's no way he can't feel it.

"In the story, did you mean what you said about the other brother? The one who brought you back to life?"

"Every word," I admit.

"This wasn't just any story, was it, Elara? This was your truth."

"It was. It is," I stutter.

"And since you're here right now..." He trails off, his thumb skirting along my bottom lip.

"It means I'm ready," I push out past the knot in my throat.

"Thank God." That's all he says before his face dips and his lips meet mine.

My body remembers his touch perfectly. The way he starts soft, sliding his tongue along the seam of my mouth, asking, coaxing. The way one hand slides up the back of my shirt, his palm flattening against the bare skin on my lower back, while the other snakes around my neck holding me to him.

I don't know how long the kiss lasts. One minute. Five. Ten. All I know is that when he finally pulls back I've been reduced to nothing more than a puddle at his feet.

"Do you have any idea how hard it's been for me?" He drops his forehead to mine. "How many times I've wanted to come to you? How fucking miserable I've been without you?" He pulls me tighter against him. "I kept telling myself I was doing the right thing, but the more time that passed the more I regretted my choice to walk away from you."

He pauses, pulling his face back to look at me. "But then I got that." He nods toward the island behind me where the manuscript is sitting. "And I knew it was all worth it. Every day of missing you. Every day of wishing

I could hold you, kiss you, make love to you. It was all worth it because I knew reading your words that you had finally found the peace you needed to find."

"You gave me that," I tell him, tears forming behind my eyes.

"No, I simply pointed you in the right direction. You did all the work."

"I couldn't have done it without you," I say, keeping my face tilted up to hold his gaze. "I realized something while I was writing."

"What's that?" he asks when I don't elaborate.

"I realized that it's okay to love you both. For the longest time I felt guilty for loving you because loving you meant I loved him less. But I don't love him less, I just love you differently. You'll never replace Kam because you're not Kam, and I don't want you to be. I love you with every part of me, not just my heart. What you mean to me goes beyond friendship or connection or history. Kam was my best friend. Perhaps even my first love. But you, Kane Thaler, you are my everything. You are my heart. My lungs. My flesh. The very blood that flows through my veins. You are as much a part of me as I am myself. This *is* with you." I pull his hand from my neck and place it flat on my chest, directly over my heart. "I think it's been with you from the first moment our eyes met, I just didn't know it at the time."

"Are you really here?" he whispers, arm tightening around my back, eyes refusing to lose my gaze. "I've been dreaming of this moment for weeks and now that you're here, looking at me the way you are right now, saying the things you're saying, I feel like maybe I'm dreaming and any moment I'm going to wake up and you won't be here."

"Do you want to be with me?" I cut him off.

"You know I do." A slow smile forms on his lips.

"Then I'm not going anywhere," I reassure him, my hands reaching up to cup either side of his scruff covered jaw.

"I love you." He leans forward, murmuring against my lips.

"I love you," I repeat, deepening the kiss as I pull him impossibly close.

Kane works my body with expert precision. Knowing exactly where to touch me, kiss me, how to move just right so that I'm nothing more than putty in his hands. And that's exactly how I like it.

I used to be a girl who needed to control everything. Now I know that sometimes the best things happen when you just let go.

And as Kane lifts me into his arms and carries me toward his bedroom, I have only one thought in my mind. I'm exactly where I'm meant to be. After everything, I've finally found my place, my peace, my home, and I found it all in Kane Thaler.

Epilogue
Kane

"Hey, little brother." I slide down in front of Kam's headstone. "Sorry it's been so long since I've visited. It's been a crazy few months," I say, finding it hard to believe it's been nearly four years that he's been gone.

So much has happened since then. I've experienced heartbreak like I never thought possible but I've also experienced more happiness in the last three years than I thought I'd find in an entire lifetime. And while I'm eternally grateful for every moment of that happiness, a part of it will never feel fully complete because my brother is not here to share it with me.

"I have a lot to fill you in on. So much has happened since the last time I came to see you, though I'm sure you probably already know everything I'm going to tell you." I smile, knowing I've felt his presence in every major moment over the last three years.

Especially the day I married Elara. It was last April, over a year ago now. We had a small ceremony in Italy. Elara insisted we do it on a cliff overlooking the water and who was I to deny her. I'd have married her diving off that cliff had she asked me to, as long as I got to call her my wife at the end of the day.

Her dad and Lynette were there, as were my parents, and her Aunt Carol. It was one of those perfect days and I knew in that moment like I know right now, Kam was with me. I could feel his hand on my shoulder, hear his voice in my ear, sense the smile I knew he was wearing. And while I wish he could have been there in body, knowing he was there in spirit was enough for me and Elara.

"Elara sold her second manuscript last month. She's so amazingly talented, Kam. Though I know you know that already. You should have seen her. Belly out to here." I gesture with my hands in front of me. "Handling those pitch meetings like she owned the damn room." I smile. "She always did know how to command a room of men. We are living proof of that, brother." I chuckle.

"We sold the apartment in Italy. It killed Elara to do it but we need something bigger. We bought a place about thirty minutes outside of Milan. It's incredible, Kam. The view is unlike anything you've ever seen. The green space. The water. It's like something out of a movie. Every day when I wake up I walk out and find Elara sitting on the porch, rocking back and forth on the porch swing she insisted I hang, and every day I think to myself 'how did I ever get so lucky?' And then I think of you." I touch his headstone, hearing the soft footsteps approaching from behind.

"But that's not the reason I'm here, little brother. I thought." I turn, smiling up at Elara who looks like an angel standing over me, her blonde hair blowing in the breeze. "I thought you'd like to meet your nephew," I finish, taking my son from his mother's arms and cradling him against my chest.

Elara slides down onto the ground next to me and presses into my side, her hand curling around my bicep as her head goes to my shoulder.

"I'd like you to meet Kamden Samuel Thaler," I say, looking down at the dark haired sleeping boy in my arms. "You once told me that if I ever had a son I had to name him after you. While I'm pretty sure that conversation only happened in my mind, neither of us could imagine naming him anything else," I say, looking down at my teary eyed wife, to my sleeping newborn son, and then back up to my brother's headstone.

"Life was taken from you way too soon but you will live on every day in your nephew. In me."

"And in me," Elara speaks up, not lifting her head from my shoulder.

I smile down at her and my son, silently thanking my brother for the incredible life I've been given. Whether he realizes it or not, none of this would've been possible without him and though I'll never get to tell him any of this face to face, deep down I know he already knows.

Acknowledgments

First I want to say thank you. Thank you for reading *The Road to You*. Thank you for allowing these characters and their story to be a part of your lives. Just thank you.

As a high school student I started writing my first book. It was choppy and messy but I knew, hidden beneath all the plot holes and typos, there was a story worth telling. Fast forward nearly twenty years later and my vision has finally come to life. It was one hell of a ride and I truly hope you enjoyed it.

Of course none of this would have been possible without an amazing group of people standing behind me. To my husband and kids—You are my life. I love you more than words could ever say. To my friends and family— Thank you for your support and love. It means so much.

To my reader group Melissa's Mavens—You ladies rock so freaking hard! Thank you for everything you do. I love each and every one of you.

To my ARC and Beta readers—Thank you for taking the time out of your own lives to help me bring this book to life. It means more to me than I will ever be able to express with words.

To Angel—I can't thank you for just one thing because you do it all. You truly are a blessing and I will never be *able to thank you enough for everything you do for me. I am so honored to call you my friend.*

To Rose—Thank you for all your hard work on this project. Editing is never an easy task and I know this book wouldn't be what it is without you. Thank you for seeing my vision and helping make this book the best it could be. You truly are incredible.

Most importantly I want to thank my readers. Thank you for taking the time to read my work. Thank you for your continued support. You are the backbone, the most important part of this entire operation, and without you none of this is possible. From the bottom of my heart, thank you.

Remember, the road isn't always smooth but life has a way of taking us exactly where we need to go. Enjoy the journey.

XOXO

-Melissa

Stalk Me

www.mtoppen.com
www.facebook.com/mtoppenauthor
www.facebook.com/melissatoppen
www.goodreads.com/mtoppen
www.twitter.com/mtoppenauthor
www.instagram.com/melissa_toppen
www.pinterest.com/mtoppenauthor
www.amazon.com/author/melissatoppen
www.bookbub.com/authors/melissa-toppen